DEAD ON CUE

Sally Spencer

severn
House

This first world edition published in Great Britain 2001 by
SEVERN HOUSE PUBLISHERS LTD of
9–15 High Street, Sutton, Surrey SM1 1DF.
This first world edition published in the USA 2001 by
SEVERN HOUSE PUBLISHERS INC of
595 Madison Avenue, New York, N.Y. 10022.

British Library Cataloguing in Publication Data

Spencer, Sally 1949–
  Dead on cue
  1. Woodend, Chief Inspector (Fictitious character) – Fiction
  2. Police – England – Fiction
  3. Detective and mystery stories
  I. Title
  823.9'14 [F]

ISBN 0-7278-5706-1

Typeset by Palimpsest Book Production Ltd.,
Polmont, Stirlingshire, Scotland.
Printed and bound in Great Britain by
MPG Books Ltd., Bodmin, Cornwall.

For Ingerbrit

Monday Evening

One

There were three of them in the room when it was announced that Jack Taylor would shortly have to die. The announcement was made by the eldest of the trio, a man in his late forties with a shock of greying hair and a nose which wouldn't have looked out of place on the face of a Roman patrician. The other two men, who had both just begun to edge towards thirty, looked suitably shocked, as he'd expected they would. For perhaps fifteen seconds neither of them seemed able to find any words at all, then the one with the fluffy blond hair – which he carefully combed over his bald spot at least ten times a day – spoke.

'Are you sure that's a wise decision, Bill?' he asked. 'I mean to say, are you *absolutely, positively* sure?'

Bill Houseman nodded. 'Yes, I *am* absolutely, positively sure,' he said. 'Or at least I'm sure that *someone* has to die – and our research unit seems to believe that Jack Taylor is the best candidate.'

The third member of the group, a red-haired, ruddy-faced Irishman, had been focussing his eyes on the corner of the room, as if seeing in it somewhere he'd much rather be. Now he shifted his gaze to the table.

'Something wrong, Paddy?' Bill Houseman asked.

'I'm a writer,' the Irishman replied. 'I take a situation, and I develop it according to what I understand about the human condition. I don't like having that process interfered with by a so-called "research unit", which, in reality, is nothing more than a couple of girls with clipboards who ambush busy people as they cross St Peter's Square.'

Bill Houseman frowned, and rose to his feet. He would probably have liked to pace the conference room agitatedly, but the table took up most of the available space, and instead he had to content himself with walking over to the window and looking out at the concourse which ran down the centre of the studio. As he gazed on the busy scene outside, his body relaxed, and his confidence seemed to return.

He swung round to face the other two men again. 'That was a very nice little speech you just made, Paddy,' he said. 'And no doubt it was appropriate for a writer starving in his garret for his art's sake. But you're not that kind of writer any more, are you? You're a well-paid member of a team now – a team that *I* run. And if you ever find that that's too much for your integrity to stand, well, nobody's stopping you from going back to your garret, are they?'

Paddy Colligan felt a shudder run through him. Bill was right, he thought. He could leave the show any time he wanted to. The problem was that since he was neither the founding father of *Madro*, as Houseman was, nor a university gradate with other avenues open to him, like Ben Drabble, a future without his regular pay check looked decidedly bleak.

'So what's it to be?' Houseman demanded, sensing his weakness. 'Do you go along with my idea? Or should I start looking for a replacement?'

Paddy Colligan swallowed hard enough to get down the humble pie he was being forced to eat. 'Sorry, Bill,' he said. 'I know it's a team effort. Must just have got out of the wrong side of bed this morning.'

Houseman ran his left hand through his white hair, and smiled the smile of an emperor watching his gladiators making their ritual submission. 'Forget it,' he said graciously.

Was he actually feeling as superior as he was acting? Paddy Colligan wondered. Or was he using that smile to mask the worry and uncertainty which had plagued him for the previous few weeks?

Houseman took a deep breath and resumed his seat. 'Look at it this way,' he said to Paddy Colligan. 'Larry wants to leave the show in a few weeks anyway, so even if we didn't kill him off, we'd still have to write him out.'

'If we wrote him out, we'd always have the option of writing him in again if he decided to come back,' Paddy pointed out.

4

'And do you think it's likely that he will?' Bill Houseman asked.

'No, but . . .'

'Well now that's settled, let's get back to the matter in hand,' Houseman suggested. 'The question is not whether Jack Taylor *should* die, but *how* he dies.'

'We could have him run over by a corporation bus,' Ben Drabble suggested.

'It's a good idea, but I don't see how we could do it technically,' Paddy Colligan said, making an attempt to redeem himself in Houseman's eyes – and hating himself for it.

'Quite right,' Houseman agreed, giving him an encouraging nod, which showed he had already forgiven the earlier revolt. 'Now if we were talking about a show which was on the wireless, it would be an entirely different matter. The roar of the engine! The sudden screech of brakes! Perhaps a muted grunt from the Laughing Postman as a couple of tons of metal slam into him. All very effective. But as big as this place is, I don't think we're up to bringing a double-decker bus in here.'

'We could always use an outside location,' Ben Drabble said.

Bill Houseman shook his head. 'I don't think that would be a good idea at all. We have created a world which our audience feels comfortable in. Take them outside it – step beyond the genre – and we might start to lose some of our appeal.'

So we'll play it safe, like we always do, Paddy Colligan thought. We'll pretend we're presenting a picture of the real world, but it will actually be no more realistic than the children's puppet show Bill Houseman used to run.

He thought it – but this time he did not put his thoughts into words.

'Could we have an accident in the home?' Ben Drabble asked.

'Now you're thinking!' Houseman said enthusiastically.

'We could have Jack doing the ironing,' Ben Drabble continued. 'There's something wrong with the iron, and he gets a terrific electric shock. He squirms around for a while, then falls to the floor.'

5

'We roll the credits, leaving the viewers asking themselves whether he's survived or not,' Bill Houseman said. 'When they tune in for the next episode, they find out, of course, that he hasn't.'

Jack Taylor had largely been Paddy Colligan's creation, and now the Irishman felt another bubble of revolt bursting inside him.

'Jack would never even think of doing the ironing,' he said sullenly. 'He's simply not that kind of man. It would be like seeing Hopalong Cassidy doing the ironing.'

'He's not a cowboy, and he doesn't ride around on a white horse,' Bill Houseman said. 'I don't see the parallel at all.'

He doesn't get it, does he? Paddy Colligan asked himself. He's in charge of the whole thing, and he simply doesn't get it.

'Jack's like Hopalong Cassidy in as much as he travels around solving other people's problems,' he argued. 'He's something of a hero on Maddox Row. And you wouldn't expect a hero to be doing anything as domestic and commonplace as ironing. And Dot Taylor wouldn't like it, either,' he added, playing what he considered his trump card. 'The house is her domain. She'd think Jack had gone mad if he started helping her around the home.'

Bill Houseman sighed. 'We are going out of our way to make difficulties today, aren't we, Paddy?' he asked.

'No!' Colligan countered. 'I'm just pointing out that—'

'There's something in what both of you are saying,' Ben Drabble interrupted hurriedly. 'Couldn't we perhaps steer a middle course?'

'Like what?' Bill Houseman asked.

'The iron is broken,' Drabble said, improvising furiously. 'Dot . . . Dot wants to take it down to Wally Simpson's repair shop, but Jack says that's a waste of money and insists on fixing himself. That would be in character, wouldn't it, Paddy?'

'Yes,' Paddy Colligan agreed reluctantly. 'I suppose that would be in character.'

'He does fix it, but he makes a bad job of it. Still in character?'

'Still in character.'

6

'He decides to try it out. He would never, of course, think of doing the ironing himself – you're quite right about that, Paddy – but this is more in the nature of an experiment to see if he's really repaired it. It's while he's conducting this experiment that he's electrocuted.

'That would work,' Bill Houseman said. 'Don't you agree, Paddy?'

'It would work,' Colligan said grudging. 'But if we're really going to kill anybody off, then I think it should be—'

'That's settled then,' Houseman interrupted. 'Make sure that Jack Taylor has a prominent part in next Friday's episode, and then we'll give him the chop the following Monday.' He checked his watch. 'That about wraps it up. See you on the set just before we go on air.'

He stood up again and bustled importantly out of the room, leaving the two scriptwriters staring at each other. For a while, neither of them spoke, then Ben Drabble said, 'Well, it *was* his idea.'

Yes, Paddy agreed silently, it was his idea. *Maddox Row* had been Bill Houseman's baby right from the start – and getting on the air at a time when glamorous American shows like *Seventy-Seven Sunset Strip* were all the rage had been no easy task.

A series based on the lives of people who live in a street in a northern industrial town? the programme planners at NWTV had asked incredulously. *How could that possibly be of interest to anybody? And if it's such a good idea, why hasn't it been done before?*

But despite Houseman's relatively lowly position in the corporate hierarchy – he'd been known as 'Squeaky' Houseman in those days, after one of the three glove puppet mice who'd appeared in his children's show – the man had stuck to his guns and insisted that it *would* work. And he'd been proved right! Unquestionably right! *Maddox Row*, originally scheduled for one thirteen-week run, had been continuously on the air for over two years. It went out twice a week, and drew a regular audience of over twelve million devoted fans.

Ben Drabble picked up his pencil and made a couple of abstract doodles on the notepad in front of him.

7

'So what do you think we should do to draw particular attention to the Laughing Postman in his last appearance before we fry him?' he asked.

Paddy Colligan, giving into the inevitable – even if he *knew* it was wrong – sighed resignedly. 'I suppose we could make Jack have a stroke of good luck,' he suggested.

'Why, especially?'

'Because tragedy's always more poignant when it comes right on the heels of happiness.'

Drabble nodded. 'True,' he agreed. 'So what kind of luck did you have in mind? A win on the football pools?'

'Yes, that would do,' Colligan said wearily, wishing he could summon half the enthusiasm he'd once felt for the show.

'A big win?' Drabble asked.

'No, the viewers wouldn't like that. He wouldn't be ordinary – the kind of man you could bump into on the street – any more.'

'A modest win, then? Something he could buy a bigger house with?'

'Except that he'd never even think of buying a bigger house – because that would involve moving away from the Maddox Row he loves,' Colligan warned. 'He wouldn't give up his job, either – not for all the money in the world.'

'So he goes on just as normal,' Drabble said. 'And even though he could afford to buy a hundred new irons if he wanted to, he repairs the old one himself – and that's what kills him. Nice!'

The two scriptwriters spent another half hour sketching out the sequence of events which would lead to the Laughing Postman's death just before the final credits rolled. There was still more work to do, but by the time the following Monday night came around, they would have it timed down to the last second.

The victim would be seen to jump suddenly. There would probably be a close-up of the shock and agony on his face. But realism would not be taken *too* far. Though the make-up department was undoubtedly up to the job, the camera would not zoom in on a hand whose flesh had been burned away

8

to reveal the bones, because, at half-past seven on a Monday evening, such gruesome details were to be avoided. Thus, the scripted death was planned.

The *un*scripted death – the death that only one person in the entire studio knew was about to occur – would be an entirely different matter. The shock it would deliver to the cast and crew of *Madro* would be much sharper and much deeper than the shock that same cast and crew were planning to inflict on their twelve million viewers. And unlike the carefully sanitised death of the Laughing Postman, it would be a messy affair. In fact, there would be blood everywhere.

Two

There were four actors in the rehearsal room – two men and two women – that particular late Monday afternoon. The men were standing on their marks, already playing out their scene. The woman stood against the wall, fairly close to one another, but conspicuously *not* together.

The two men were roughly the same age – in their early forties – but one of them, George Adams, had adopted the stance of a much older man, and was leaning forward as if it required an effort for him to hear what the other man, Larry Coates, was saying.

'I heard about that row you had with your niece, Sam,' Coates said in a serious, almost mournful voice. 'It's not right that families should fall out like that, you know.'

'You're right,' Adams agreed gravely, 'but now it's happened, I don't know what to do about it.'

'I didn't think you would,' Coates told him. 'That's why I popped round an' had a word with her meself.'

'An' . . . an' what did you say to her?' Adams asked tremulously.

'I said you never meant to hurt her canary, an' she should know that as well as I do. I pointed out that when somebody gets to your age it's very easy to mistake birdseed for rat poison. An' I reminded her about all the things you've done for her in the past.'

'An' what did *she* say?'

'She agreed she should never have lost her temper like that, an' she's comin' round this afternoon to apologise. An' Sam . . .'

'Yes, Mr Taylor?'

'You could have been more careful when you were feedin'

that bird of hers, now couldn't you? So when she does come round, don't to be too hard on her.'

Adams nodded. 'I won't,' he promised. 'It'll be such a relief to have our Edith back again. I don't know how I'd have gone without her. Thank you for all you've done, Mr Taylor.'

Larry Coates shrugged, slightly uncomfortably. 'There's no need to thank me.'

'Indeed, there is. You're more than just our postman – you're a marvel. We'd all be lost on Maddox Row if you ever decided to move away.'

Larry Coates gave the infectious laugh which had become Jack Taylor's trademark. 'Don't go worryin' your head about that, Sam,' he said. 'I was born an' bred on Maddox Row, an' when I do finally leave, they'll have to carry me out.'

'That's perfect!' the young assistant director said. 'You'll have all the old biddies at home thinking of their own nieces and sobbing into their hankies. Let's move on to the last scene just before the commercials, shall we? Jack Taylor's gone off on his rounds, and Sam Fuller runs into Madge Thornycroft.'

Larry Coates, no longer the Laughing Postman, moved across to the edge of the room, and lit up a cigarette. George Adams, losing his old man's stiffness for a second, walked over to another set of chalk marks where Jennifer Brunton was waiting for him. Later, when the show went out, Jennifer would be wearing the hairnet and a steely expression of Madge Thornycroft, the Row's malicious gossip-monger, but at that moment she was elegant enough to be a guest speaker at a Women's Institute – a role she was not unfamiliar with.

'OK, let's take it from the top,' the assistant director said.

George Adams hunched over again and looked into Jennifer Brunton's eyes. 'Are you sure all them rumours you've been spreadin' about Liz Bowyer are true?' he demanded.

Jennifer stuck out her jaw, Madge-like. 'All I know is, I saw her leavin' Ted Doyle's house at well past midnight,' she said.

George/Sam looked suitably shocked. 'But what were you doin' out on the street at that time of night, Madge?' he asked.

'I wasn't out on the street. I got up to spend a penny an' I saw her through the window.'

'Even so . . . ?' George said dubiously.

'An' I know for a fact that Ted's wife has been workin' nights at the pie factory all this week.'

'Still, if Liz finds out what you've been sayin' about her, she's bound to blow her top.'

'I don't care *what* she does. When I see somebody doin' somethin' wrong, I don't keep it to myself.'

George Adams glanced stiffly to his left. 'She's comin' down the street now,' he whispered.

'Who is?'

'Liz Bowyer. An' she looks furious. You'd best go.'

'I'm stayin' where I am,' Jennifer/Madge said. 'It'd take a better woman than Liz Bowyer to make me turn tail an' run.'

'Nearly right,' the assistant director told them. 'Just a couple of seconds too fast. If you, George, could just count one more beat before you say, 'She's comin' now,' and you, Jennifer, could glare for a moment more before you say you're staying where you are, we should be right on target.'

As the two actors hit their marks again, the rehearsal-room door opened softly, and Ben Drabble entered. He looked around him, ran his hand over the hair covering his bald spot, then made his way on tiptoe to where Larry Coates was standing.

'I just thought you'd like to know that the decision's finally been made about when you leave the show,' the scriptwriter whispered. 'Jack Taylor's due to be killed off next Monday.'

Coates grinned. 'Killed off, is he? How does he die?'

'He gets electrocuted when he's testing the iron he's just repaired for Dot.'

'Electrocuted! That's a bit boring isn't it? It would have been more dramatic if he'd been run over by a bus or something.' Larry Coates paused for a second. 'I bet Paddy wasn't too chuffed about the idea, was he?'

'No, he wasn't,' Ben Drabble agreed. 'Jack Taylor was pretty much his creation, you know, and he always hoped you might come back eventually.'

'No chance of that,' Larry Coates said with feeling. 'Still, I'm going to miss the Laughing Postman – in a way. I like to tell myself I got the new role on my own merit, but even an egotistical actor like me has to admit that it helped that I'd been playing such a strong character. And I owe that to Paddy.'

The rehearsal-room door swung open again, much more noisily than it had when Ben Drabble had opened it – so noisily, in fact, that it knocked the actors completely off their stroke.

The assistant director swung around, ready to scream at whoever had dared to upset the atmosphere he'd been working so hard to create. Then he saw who was standing there.

'Can I . . . can I help you, Mrs Houseman?' he asked the platinum blonde in the suede jacket and tight, leopardskin pants.

'I'm looking for my husband,' Diana Houseman said. 'Do you have any idea where he might be?'

The assistant director shrugged. 'When we're only a few hours from going on the air, he's usually got a lot on his plate,' he said.

'Is that just another way of saying I should bugger off and leave him in peace?' Diana Houseman demanded.

The young assistant director blushed. 'No, of course not, Mrs Houseman. That wasn't what I meant at all.'

'Because if it is, Bill will be hearing about it.'

'I only meant—'

'As it happens – not that it's any of *your* business – there's something I need to talk to him about urgently.'

'I'll . . . if you like, I can put a call through to the switchboard and see if they know where he is,' the flustered assistant director suggested.

'Don't bother, I'll find him myself,' the producer's wife said contemptuously, before turning and slamming the door behind her.

The assistant director waited until he was sure she really had gone, then said in a loud voice, 'The woman thinks she owns the bloody place.'

'She owns Bill Houseman – and that's the next best thing,' George Adams said softly to Jennifer Brunton.

The assistant director took a handkerchief out of his pocket, and wiped his brow. 'Yes, well, now that bit of unpleasantness is over, let's get back to work, shall we?' he suggested shakily. 'We'll start with the last line from Jennifer before Val makes her appearance.'

'It'd take a better woman than Liz Bowyer to make me turn tail an' run,' Jennifer Brunton said.

It was Valerie Farnsworth's cue. Hips swinging exaggeratedly, she made her way between the two chalk lines which represented the edges of the pavement on each side of Maddox Row.

'I want a word with you, Madge Thornycroft,' she said.

Jennifer put her hand on her own hip. 'Oh aye, you do, do you?' she said. 'An' what might that word be about?'

'Have you been spreadin' more of your tales about me, you evil-minded old bat?'

'I've been tellin' people what I've seen with my own two eyes, if that's what you mean.'

Valerie Farnsworth squared up in front of Jennifer Brunton. 'Well, it's got to stop,' she said.

'It'll stop when you learn to start behavin' yourself properly,' Jennifer countered.

'Oh no, it won't! It'll stop now!'

'An' if it doesn't?'

'Then you're goin' to be very sorry you've let that malicious tongue of yours flap so much.'

Jennifer turned to George Adams. 'You heard her,' she said. 'She's threatenin' me.'

'I'll do more than threaten you,' Valerie Farnsworth said. 'When I've finished with you, you won't know what's hit you.'

'And we go into the break, leaving the audience holding its breath and hoping to see a resolution in the second half,' the assistant director said. 'Yet sadly that's not about to happen – so they'll just have to tune in for the next episode if they want to know how it all turns out, won't they?' He turned to Ben Drabble. 'Do we already know how Liz is going to get her revenge on Madge?'

The scriptwriter nodded. 'Yes, the whole thing's been mapped out.'

The assistant director returned the nod. 'Good! Excellent!

I think we'll just run through the last scene one more time, shall we?'

Valerie Farnsworth snorted. 'You can if you like,' she said, 'but as far as I'm concerned it's as good as it's ever going to be – and I need some time on my own before the show.'

'Now look here, Val—' the assistant director said, trying to keep his rising anger under control.

'No, *you* look here,' Valerie Farnsworth interrupted. 'I know you like standing there playing the boss, but when all's said and done, you're only one step up from the tea boy. And if you've think I'm going to tire myself out before the show, just so you can feel important, then you've got another think coming.'

She turned, and flounced towards the door.

'Talk about your prima donnas,' Jennifer Brunton said in a quiet aside to George Adams.

'Yes, she can be pretty bloody when she wants to be,' Adams agreed.

'And it's not just that poor lad she's treating like dirt. She's the same with everybody – even her fellow actors. It's all about Liz – and bugger everybody else! She doesn't only want to be in all the best scenes, but she wants the best *lines* in them as well. Who do *you* think will come out best in this row between Liz Bowyer and Madge Thornycroft?'

Adams smiled cynically. 'If I had to put money on it, I'd bet it would be Liz,' he said.

'You're damn right it will be Liz Bowyer! Val's probably already had a word with the scriptwriters about it. And if they won't do what she wants, she'll go whining and complaining to Bill Houseman. Of course, I could do the same thing myself. But I won't. I've got far too much self-respect for that.'

'Besides, it probably wouldn't get you anywhere,' George Adams said.

'She thinks that just because she gets more fan mail than anybody else, she's the queen bee round here,' Jennifer Brunton railed. 'But she bloody well isn't! There's a lot more to *Maddox Row*'s success than just Valerie high-and-mighty Farnsworth. Madge Thornycroft's an important part of the show, too.'

'And even Sam Fuller gets the occasional fan letter,' George Adams said sourly.

'Of course you do, George,' Jennifer Brunton said hastily. 'You're important, too. We all are. And it's about time Val learned that. In fact, if you ask me, it's more than time that somebody taught her a lesson she won't forget in a hurry.'

Three

The first episode of *Maddox Row* had been broadcast on the same day as Fidel Castro had nationalised all private businesses in Cuba, but for the executives of NWTV there was soon little doubt about which of the two events would turn out to be more world-shattering. Even in its first few weeks it had become apparent that *Madro* was a television phenomenon, and that the cramped NWTV studios were placing too much of a limit on its potential. And so the company's top executives had decided, over one of their long expense-account lunches, that a new home had to be found for the programme.

The old Calcutta Mill on the outskirts of a village near Bolton had immediately suggested itself as the ideal choice. Not only was it large, but – since no one else was interested in buying it – it was also going cheap. There had been the inevitable objections to the change of usage, of course, most notably from the Lancashire Industrial Archaeological Society, which claimed the mill had great historic interest and should be retained for educational purposes. But since the members of the society were known to be cranks of no consequence, and since the local authority was tired of being responsible for a relic of a bygone age, the objections were brushed aside. Thus it was that, as the Society's members were writing impassioned letters to the local newspapers and even thinking about getting around to organising some kind of protest, a team of bricklayers was hard at work in the mill's weaving shed, transforming the vast, open space into a number of smaller, more manageable units. The past was dead. From now on, the mill would be dedicated to creating an image of a present reality which was already starting to slip away.

*   *   *

17

Bill Houseman wandered – apparently aimlessly – through the studio which had been constructed at the far end of the old mill. All around him there were signs of activity: the lighting technicians were carrying out last-minute adjustments to their lamps; the grips moving equipment and laying fresh cables; the set dressers stood in the middle of the interior sets, adjusting an ornament here and a picture frame there.

It was Bill Houseman's fancy – and as the man with overall control of the programme he was entitled to whatever fancy he cared to indulge – to see the team which worked inside the mill as one living entity, a single huge creature with its own pulse, heartbeat and moods.

'And it's very much a creature of habit,' he said softly to himself.

At nine o'clock in the morning it was still only half-awake, yet looking forward to the day with some optimism. By one o'clock in the afternoon, having gone through countless repetitions of same routines – but also having endured periods when nothing much seemed to happening at all – the beast was ready for some food, even if that food was only the soggy sandwiches and lukewarm soup which the catering company provided. Most of the afternoon was conducted on autopilot – the beast accepting that certain things had be done, and stoically getting on with them. Then the big hand of the studio clock touched twelve, the small hand scraped against six – and the whole atmosphere changed.

Now, at five minutes past six, the beast was as alert as any hunter, knowing that its performance in the next two hours would determine whether or not it went home satisfied – or with a gnawing ache in its stomach.

It was always Houseman's favourite time of day, and no more so than when he needed a shot in the arm, as he did at that moment. For the last half-hour he'd been suffering the effects of the emotional battering he'd received at the hands of his wife, but now he was starting to feel like a god again. And not just *any* god. Not the petty god of some low-budget children's programme which centred on the moronic activities of glove puppets, but the mighty god of a roaring, runaway success of a peak-time drama.

'A mighty god!' he repeated to himself.

And why shouldn't he feel like that? He was, when all was said and done, the creator of all he saw before him. Without him – without his inspiration – none of these people would be there, and something entirely different would be filling the six or seven million flickering television screens in an hour and twenty-five minutes time.

He was relieved to find that this feeling of divinity had finally returned with all its former force. For the previous few weeks, even as he'd watched the world from the top of his Olympian mountain, he had been hearing the low, menacing thunder of the viewing figures in the distance. The show had been losing some of its audience – not a significant portion, but enough to cause concern – and he had been living in fear that he would soon be cast out of his paradise by a younger, more virile god. But that fear had passed now. For a god to remain strong, he had to sustain himself on the sacrifice of human blood, and that process – thank Himself! – was already under way.

He glanced up at the central control room – the eyes of the beast he had created. There were two people in it at that moment. One of them was a man in his late thirties with foppish brown hair who, whatever the weather, always wore a short silk scarf around his neck. Jeremy Wilcox had been the show's director for only a few months, but already he was acting as if it were *his* show – as if any success it had came from his basic ability to order the right camera to be pointed in the right direction at roughly the right time. And Wilcox's ambitions didn't stop with directing, Houseman suspected. The fop in the scarf was already starting to see the words 'executive producer' after his name.

The other occupant of the control room was a woman – or perhaps, more accurately, a girl. Lucy Smythe had blonde hair pulled tightly to her skull and heavy-framed glasses which she probably didn't even need. She had joined the series at the same time as the director, and followed at his heel like a too-eager-to-please puppy. Wilcox, for his part, took great pains to show that he took her for granted, in the hope that this would create the impression that he was used to such dogged devotion from his subordinates. Houseman wondered whether this devotion would be sustained once Wilcox was back to directing trailers for other people's creative work, which – once the human sacrifice had made him strong again – would not be long in coming.

The cast dressing rooms were at the other end of the weaving shed to the *Maddox Row* studio. From the outside, they looked like nothing more than low brick boxes constructed under the mill's tall roof. Inside, however, they were cosy little retreats where the actors could enjoy relaxing during their free time.

Most of the boxes were designed to be shared between two or three members of the cast. But there were some actors – the fortunate chosen few – who had a dressing room entirely to themselves, and Valerie Farnsworth was one of them.

At the moment, less than an hour and a quarter before the show was due to go out, Valerie was sitting at her dressing table and examining her reflection in the mirror. It was a slightly rounded face which gazed back at her, with full lips and big, dark eyes. An attractive enough face – certainly one which turned a few heads whenever she entered a pub – but not one which she had ever thought would be her fortune.

Yet that was just how things had turned out! After nearly twenty years on the stage, first in the music halls and then in provincial repertory theatre, she had finally made a name for herself. And what a name! She was Liz Bowyer, Maddox Row's resident divorcee – a bit of a trollop, if truth be told, but only in a sanitised, peak viewing hours sort of way, of course. She had risen from obscurity and was now an opener of village fêtes, bingo halls and self-service shops. At just a shade under forty she had become, if she believed the papers – and she did! – a national sex symbol.

The success of *Maddox Row* was due to many things, but no small part of it was due to her, and from the way she was treated by the people she worked with, it was obvious that they were as aware of that as she was herself.

She heard a soft noise behind her as her dressing-room door clicked open, and, moving her head slightly, she could see the reflection of the person who had entered the room.

20

'Don't you ever knock?' she asked, not even trying to keep the irritation out of her voice.

'I'm . . . I'm sorry,' her unexpected visitor said. 'I thought you might be asleep, and if you were, I didn't want to disturb you.'

'If I'd been taking a nap, I'd have locked the door – and you know that as well as I do,' Valerie said sharply. 'Shall I tell you the real reason that you didn't knock?'

'I—'

'It was because if you had done, I'd have asked who it was, you'd have had to answer, and I'd have told you to go away. You probably worked out that by not knocking I'd get a chance to see just how pathetic you look, and might start to feel sorry for you.'

'You can be very hard,' the visitor said sadly.

'I'm as soft as anything,' Valerie replied. 'But there has to come a point when even I've got to be firm. If I could make you happy just by snapping my fingers, I'd do it in a second. But what you're asking is really too much.'

'Valerie . . . Val . . .'

'Don't try using that wounded tone with me again, because it just won't wash. It's time you learned how to stand on your own two feet, like I've had to learn to stand on mine.'

'If you'd only—'

'Just go away!' Valerie said. 'Go away and give me a bit of peace. I need my rest. I've got some big scenes to play tonight.'

She dropped her eyes so she was once again looking at her own reflection instead of her visitor's. She heard the door click closed, and automatically assumed that she was alone again.

It was only a second later that the soft footfalls behind her told her she'd been mistaken – but by then it was too late to do anything about it. It was even almost too late to scream.

21

Four

Detective Chief Inspector Charlie Woodend was sitting on the sofa in the living room of his recently acquired handloom weaver's stone cottage, a large mug of tea in one hand and a Capstan Full Strength cigarette dangling in the other. His eyes were on his new seventeen-inch television set, but his ears were listening to the sound of his wife, Joan, washing up the tea plates in the kitchen.

'Do you want any help, lass?' he asked.

'Now there's a worryin' question,' Joan called back cheerfully.

'Worryin'? What's worryin' about it?'

'When you offer to come into the kitchen, it always starts me thinkin' there must be somethin' wrong with you. You haven't got a fever, have you, Charlie? You're not feelin' delirious?'

Woodend grinned. 'I'm fine. I just thought that if I gave you a hand, you'd be finished with the washin'-up by the time *Maddox Row* came on.'

'I *might* be finished by the time the programme starts – but not if you help me,' Joan said tartly. 'With you as my assistant, we'll still be doin' the dishes when the last show's finished, an' all there is to watch is that bubble in the centre of the screen.'

Woodend's grin widened. Joan might occasionally complain about having to do so much around the house herself, but she didn't *really* want him in her kitchen. She was typical of the northern women of her generation – like Dot Taylor on *Maddox Row* – and she wasn't about to stand for any interference in her preserve. As far as she was concerned, men brought home wages, lagged the cockloft and whitewashed the coalhouse – and they had absolutely no business sticking their big noses into anything else.

He heard the key scraping in the lock and then the sound of the front door opening.

'Is that you, Annie?' he called out – though who else could it be but his darling daughter, the apple of his eye?

Annie didn't reply, though he could hear the rustle of cloth as she took off her coat.

'I said, is that you?' he repeated.

'Yes, it's me.'

She sounded sullen, he thought. Sullen – and perhaps a little resentful. He balanced his cup carefully on the arm of the sofa, stood up and walked into the hallway. Annie had already hung up her coat, and was heading for the stairs.

'Are you all right?' he asked.

'I'm fine,' Annie replied, not looking at him. 'I'm going up to my room.'

'Aren't you goin' to eat anythin'? Your mam's been keepin' your supper warm in the oven.'

'I'm not hungry.'

'You should eat a bit of somethin'.'

'I've told you – I'm not hungry!' Annie said – almost *shouted* – and then she took the stairs two at a time.

'Don't you think you should . . . ?' Woodend began, but Annie had already turned the bend, and disappeared from sight.

He was worried about her – had *been* worried since the family had moved back up North, which had meant her leaving her school and her friends behind. For a while he'd thought she'd made the transition easily enough, but plainly, he'd been wrong.

He was on the point of following his daughter upstairs when he felt his wife's hand on his elbow.

'Leave it, Charlie,' Joan said.

'But she seems upset.'

'Then this is just about the worst time to talk to her, isn't it? You'd be far better off waitin' until she's calmed down a bit.'

'I suppose you're right,' Woodend said, not totally convinced.

23

'I *am* right,' Joan said firmly. 'Give it an hour, then go up an' see her. An' in the meantime, sit down and watch your show.'

He allowed himself to be led back into the living room, and lowered himself carefully on to the sofa, so as not to upset his mug of tea. He'd been aware of his concern about Annie ever since he got the 'gypsy's warning' during his investigation on Blackpool's Golden Mile. But he was sure he'd been unconsciously worrying about her for much longer than that – probably since the moment he'd been given the choice between being kicked off the force or moving back to Lancashire.

'I can feel you frettin' even from in here,' Joan called from the kitchen. 'There's no point in talkin' to her while you're all wound up yourself. Try to relax a bit.'

His wife was talking good sense – like she always did – he thought. He pushed Annie temporarily to the back of his mind and focussed his eyes on the television screen. He really *did* need to calm down a little, he told himself.

An advertisement for a toothpaste, which promised to banish the yellow from your teeth forever, came to a close. North West Television's logo appeared on the screen, and then disappeared again to be replaced by a picture of endless rows of terraced roofs. To the accompaniment of brass band music, the credits began to roll for *Maddox Row*.

Woodend remembered what a sensation *Maddox Row* had created when it had first appeared on the box a couple of years earlier. And rightly so, in his opinion! Before then, all the characters in television dramas had lived in awfully nice houses on awfully nice estates and spoken the sort of awfully nice Standard English which hardly any normal people actually used. The only hint of a regional accent in those programmes had come from the minor players who appeared briefly to deliver the milk or read the gas meter. The people of *Maddox Row*, on the other hand, lived in terraced houses in urban backstreets, dropped the Gs from the ends of their words, mended punctured bike inner-tubes in their front rooms and worried about the kinds of things that the ordinary

24

folk he knew worried about. Aye, it was a real change to see a genuine slice of life on the telly.

'It's on!' Woodend shouted.

'Stop your blinkin' mitherin'! I've told you I'll be there in a minute,' Joan replied.

The real difference between men and women wasn't what they'd got between their legs, Woodend thought. What made them breeds apart was that while a man would willingly postpone washing up the last few cups until the end of a programme, women were simply incapable of leaving the kitchen until everything was perfect.

By the time Joan finally sat down on the sofa beside her husband, Jack Taylor, the Laughing Postman, had already assured Sam Fuller, the old-age pensioner, that despite his poisoning his niece's canary, she would soon be coming round to see him, and now Sam was standing on the street talking to the hair-netted Madge Thornycroft.

Jeremy Wilcox shifted his gaze from the preview monitors – which showed what all the cameras in the studio were seeing – to the master monitor which contained only the image being beamed into seven million homes. George Adams stood in the centre of the screen, a look of uncertainty crossing his face.

Perfect, Wilcox thought. Absolutely perfect! There wasn't a viewer in the land who wouldn't feel for poor old Sam Fuller as he grappled with the problem of how to tackle Madge Thornycroft. And the reason they would feel for Fuller was not because Adams was such a good actor – though he wasn't half bad – but because he was being directed by a man who really knew what he was doing.

He turned his attention back to the preview monitors. Camera Two was focussed on Madge Thornycroft; Camera Three was already in position to focus on Liz Bowyer when she walked down the street. This was the moment in the week that Wilcox lived for. *His* moment of divinity. The point in the process at which he – and *only* he – could see what all the cameras in the studio were seeing.

'Are you sure all them rumours you've been spreadin' about

Liz Bowyer are true?' Sam Fuller demanded, from the speaker on the wall.

'Shot Twenty-Eight, cut to Camera Two,' said Lucy Smythe to the vision mixer who was sitting next to her.

The image changed – Madge Thornycroft, her jaw stuck out defiantly.

'I saw her leavin' Ted Doyle's house at well past midnight,' she said.

'Shot Twenty-Nine, cut to Camera One,' Lucy Smythe instructed.

Sam Fuller, looking shocked, filled the screen again.

'But whatever were you doin' out on the street at that time of night?' he asked.

'Shot Thirty, cut to Camera Two.'

'I wasn't out on the street. I got up to spend a penny an' I saw her through the window.'

'Shot Thirty-One, cut to Camera One.'

'Even so . . .'

'Shot Thirty-Two, cut to Camera Two.'

'An' I know for a fact that Ted's wife has been workin' nights at the pie factory all this week.'

'Shot Thirty-Three, cut to Camera One.'

'Still, if she finds out what you've been sayin' about her, she's bound to blow her top.'

'Shot Thirty-Four, cut to Camera Two.'

'I don't care what she does. When I see somebody doin' somethin' wrong, I don't keep it to myself.'

Woodend took a sip of his tea, and chuckled.

'There was a woman just like that Madge Thornycroft who lived on our street when I was growin' up,' he told his wife. 'An' there was a Liz Bowyer type who lived just around the corner.'

'There was a Madge Thornycroft and Liz Bowyer on *everybody's* street,' his wife replied.

On the screen, Sam Fuller had turned away from Madge Thornycroft, and was looking up the street. 'She's comin' now,' he whispered.

'Who is?'

'Liz Bowyer. An' she looks furious. You'd best go.'

'I'm stayin' where I am,' Madge said. 'It'd take a better woman than Liz Bowyer to make me turn tail an' run.'

'Shot Thirty-Nine, cut to Camera Three,' Lucy Smythe said.

Jeremy Wilcox turned his eyes towards the central monitor. Camera Three was pointing down the set of the exterior of Maddox Row, just as it was supposed to be – but it was revealing nothing more than empty street.

'She's missed her bloody cue,' Jeremy Wilcox said furiously. 'The bitch has missed her bloody cue!'

Why didn't these actors ever seem to realise that every second counted – that beyond their own little world there was a whole apparatus which depended on split-second timing? They weren't on the stage, where it didn't matter whether the production lasted a minute or two longer than it was intended to. They were on bloody live television!

There was still no sign of Valerie Farnsworth on the central monitor.

'I'll have the stupid cow for this!' Jeremy Wilcox exploded. 'I'll make her pay for it if it's the last thing I do!'

The picture had changed again. Now the camera was no longer focussing on the empty street but on the Row's old age pensioner and resident gossip. Both of them looked distinctly uncomfortable.

'She . . . she won't be long now,' Sam Fuller said nervously. 'I expect the reason she's takin' so long to get here is that she's in such a temper.'

Woodend, from the comfort of his sofa, remembered going to Saturday matinees at his local cinema. Whenever the villain had appeared on the screen and starting creeping up on the hero, he and his mates had screamed at the hero to look behind him, even though they'd really known the hero couldn't hear them. And he felt like that now – felt like shouting to Sam Fuller that it wasn't that Liz Bowyer was walking slowly, it was that she wasn't there *at all*.

The camera angle shifted hopefully back up the street, but there was still no sign of Liz Bowyer.

'Maybe she . . . maybe she slipped into somebody's house while we weren't lookin',' Sam Fuller suggested off-camera, the panic evident in his voice.

'An' maybe it's better we don't have an argument right now,' Madge Thornycroft said shakily. 'Maybe it'd be better if I just went home.'

For a moment, the television screen went completely blank and then a black and white notice appeared, promising that normal service would be resumed as soon as possible. Another second passed, and the commercials began.

'There's been a real bloody cock-up somewhere or other,' Woodend said to his wife.

Jeremy Wilcox hit the intercom button angrily with his index finger. 'What the hell is going on, Roger?' he demanded.

'Val . . . Val missed her cue,' the floor manager replied.

'I know she missed her cue,' Wilcox snapped, staring up at the bank of monitors. 'But is she there now?'

'No. There's no sign of her.'

Wilcox slammed his fist down hard on his desk. 'Here's what we do,' he said. 'As soon as we come out of commercials we go straight into the scene where the two kids try their hand at the thieving from the corner shop. Got that?'

'Yes, but—' the floor manager began.

'But nothing!' Wilcox interrupted him. 'We'll have to make some changes later on, but I can't tell you what they are as yet, for the simple reason that I don't bloody know myself.'

He flicked the switch back, and turned to Lucy Smythe. His personal assistant was gazing down at her shooting script in horror, and looked as if she were about to burst into tears.

'What are we going to do?' she moaned. 'We can't just leave it hanging in the air like that. It'll be too jerky.'

'We *will* have the argument,' Wilcox said. 'It just won't come in this episode, that's all.'

'But . . . but without the argument, we've got over two minutes of air time unfilled,' Lucy Smythe said.

True, Wilcox thought. All too bloody true!

'Give me the script,' he said. 'I'll call the camera shots for the rest of the show.'

'What will I . . . what do you want me to—?'

'I want you to find those useless bastards Drabble and Colligan. Tell them I want a short link scene to explain away Liz Bowyer's non-appearance. We'll slot it in after Harry Sugden's told a breathless world how worried he is about his whippets.'

'You . . . you can't expect them to write a new scene in five minutes,' Lucy Smythe protested.

'Yes, I bloody can. They're supposed to be professionals – it's about time they earned their money.'

'And even if they can come up with the lines, how are the cast going to have time to learn them?'

Wilcox sighed with exasperation. Why did he have to do all the thinking? he asked himself. Why was everybody else totally incapable of using even the tiniest particle of initiative?

'I only want a couple of extra lines,' he said. 'They don't have to be smooth – just plausible. And those idiots we fondly call the cast don't have to learn them – all they have to do is read them off a bloody cue card, which even they should be able to manage.' He glanced down at the script. 'And when you've talked to the writers, find Val Farnsworth. She's got a couple more lines towards the end of the show, and she'd better be there to deliver them.'

'Maybe . . . maybe she's not feeling well,' Lucy Smythe said tentatively.

'I don't care if she's bloody dying – I want her on the set mouthing her lines,' Wilcox said harshly. 'Now stop raising objections to everything I say and shift your arse!'

Lucy Smythe rushed to the door as if she were being pursued by a pack of ravenous wolves.

Hopeless! Wilcox thought. She was bloody hopeless!

And she was by no means alone in that. There was enough dead wood in the studio to build a replica of the *Titanic*. And he included the producer in that. Would the almighty Bill Houseman have coped with this emergency as well as he was doing? Not a chance!

The sound of the floor manager conducting the countdown came through the intercom. Wilcox turned his attention back to the monitors. On Camera One, the two child actors – brought in for this single episode – were about to try their hands at shop-lifting chocolate bars from the corner store. If God had decided to finally give him the break he so richly deserved, Wilcox told himself, the snotty brats should manage to get through their two minutes of fame without completely fluffing their lines.

On the screen, Harry Sugden was bending over his whippets' pen and looking worried. But he didn't look half as worried as Madge Thornycroft and Sam Fuller had looked just before the commercial break, Woodend thought, taking a drag on his Capstan Full Strength.

'What do you think went wrong earlier?' the chief inspector said to his wife. 'Somethin' technical?'

'What's point in askin' me?' Joan replied. 'How d'you expect me to know anythin' about anythin', when I spend all my time cookin' an' cleanin' up after you?'

Woodend chuckled. 'Don't come that "little woman stuck in the kitchen" line with me,' he said. 'You've got twice the brain power I have, an' you know it, don't you?'

'Well of course I know it,' Joan replied. 'How could it be any other way, when I'm a woman an' you're nothin' but a mere man?'

Woodend chuckled again. 'Quite right,' he agreed, and turned his attention back to the screen.

Sam Fuller had appeared at Harry Sugden's back gate. 'Have you heard about Liz Bowyer?' he asked, looking straight ahead of him as if he were reading the words off a card.

'No! What's happened to her?' Harry Sugden asked, his own eyes focussed on the middle distance.

'She's had a funny turn.'

'Is it serious?'

'I don't think so. I shouldn't be surprised if she's already back on her feet.'

Woodend laughed.

'What's so funny?' Joan asked.

'They're actin' so woodenly at the moment that they sound like bent bobbies givin' evidence in the witness box. "An' then, m'lud, the prisoner said that he'd done it, it was a fair cop, an' I should put the bracelets on him."'

'I sometimes worry about that sense of humour of yours,' Joan told him.

Lucy Smythe sprinted down the mill's central concourse towards the dressing rooms, and tried to calculate how long she'd got left. It was true that Val Farnsworth wasn't due to appear again until just before the closing credits, but even so it was going to be a push to get her in the studio on time, even assuming she *was* in her dressing room. And if she *wasn't* in her dressing room? She had to be – there was nowhere else *for* her to be.

Without slackening her pace, she turned left and dashed down the alley which ran along the side of the dressing room block. Nearly there, she told herself.

She took a right at the end of the block, and saw one of the trainees standing uncertainly in front of Valerie Farnsworth's door.

'She missed her cue, didn't she?' the boy asked worriedly.

'Bloody right she missed her cue,' Lucy panted. 'And it was your job to see that she didn't. Mr Wilcox will have your head for this.'

'It's not my fault,' the boy whined. 'I gave her a knock forty-five minutes ago, just as I was supposed to do. An' then I gave her the last call ten minutes before she was due to go on.'

'Did she seem all right to you?'

'I don't know.'

'You don't *know*?'

'She didn't answer either of my knocks. I tried the door – but it was locked. I thought she must already have gone to the set.'

'You're not paid to think,' Lucy Smythe said. 'You're paid to make sure.' She hammered on the door. 'Val? Val? Can you hear me? What in God's name do you think you're doing in there?'

'Shall I . . . shall I open it?' the boy asked tremulously.

'What!' Lucy exploded. 'You mean to say you had the bloody key on you all along?'

'Yes . . . I . . .'

'Then why didn't you go in there when you got no answer?'

'Miss Farnsworth doesn't like . . . she doesn't like . . .'

'Open the bloody door!' Lucy said furiously.

The boy took out his set of keys with trembling hands, and slid one into the lock. Lucy pushed him to one side, and flung the door open.

The first thing she saw was that Valerie Farnsworth was still in the room – and was slumped over her dressing table. The second thing she noticed was the blood. It had stained the back of her dress. It had trickled down her arm. And it had formed glistening puddles on the floor.

Lucy fought back the scream that was building up in the back of her throat, and clutched the doorjamb for support.

This couldn't really be happening, she told herself. It had to be one of those practical jokes that members of the crew were always playing on her – jokes which she had never dared to report because she knew it would only make her look foolish.

But all those jokes had been played during rehearsals, when it didn't matter. Surely nobody would pull such a stunt when they were on air – when Valerie should actually have been appearing before millions of people.

Yet it had to be a joke, she told herself desperately. It just *had* to be!

Then she saw the electrical screwdriver, lying on the floor next to the pool of blood. It was a long, sturdy, professional tool, and at least half of its twelve-inch shaft was stained red.

No joke then. No joke at all.

Lucy Smythe closed her eyes and tried to decide what she should do next. She was still working on the problem when her brain shut down, her legs crumpled beneath her, and she fell to the floor.

Five

It was just after eight fifteen that Detective Chief Superintendent Richard Ainsworth of the Central Lancashire Constabulary answered the telephone in his lounge and found himself talking to John Dinnage, his chief constable.

'Were you watching *Maddox Row* tonight, Dick?' Dinnage asked.

'Maddox Rowe?' Ainsworth repeated, mystified. 'Who's Maddox Rowe, and why should I have been watching him?'

The chief constable sighed. 'It's a television series,' he explained. 'It comes on every Monday and Friday at half past seven.'

'Oh that!' Ainsworth said.

He sounded dismissive – and he was. He came originally from the garden county of Kent, and felt he got more than enough 'gritty realism' from just *living* in the North, without adding to it by watching it on the telly.

On the other end of the line, the chief constable let out a sudden gasp.

'Something the matter, sir?' Ainsworth asked.

'Indigestion,' Dinnage told him. 'It's been playing me up all day.'

Pity! I was hoping it would be a heart attack, Ainsworth thought. But aloud he said, 'I'm really sorry to hear that, sir.'

'Goes with the job, I suppose,' Dinnage replied, through clenched teeth. 'I'm surprised I don't have a peptic ulcer as well. But to get back to the point of this call, am I to take it from your tone you didn't see the programme tonight?'

'No, I didn't. Why, did I miss anything?'

'You missed one of the characters not appearing on cue because she'd just been murdered.'

'Nasty,' Ainsworth said.

More than nasty. In all probability, he thought, it would turn out to be one of those celebrity murder cases where the police couldn't conduct a proper investigation because they were knee-deep in reporters watching them like hawks and just waiting for them to make a wrong move. It was like playing 'pass the parcel' with live hand-grenades – you never knew when the whole thing was going to blow up in your face. Which was why he was delighted that this particular mess wasn't about to fall in his lap.

'I expect the Manchester police aren't exactly over the moon at getting something like that dropped on them,' he said cheerfully, having long ago reached the conclusion that the best way to fully appreciate your own good fortune was by contemplating the *misfortunes* of others.

'It hasn't been dropped on them,' the chief constable said heavily. 'It's been dropped on us.'

'I beg your pardon, sir?'

'NWTV's main studios are in Manchester . . .'

'That's what I thought.'

'But they broadcast *Maddox Row* from an old cotton mill which is a couple of hundred yards outside Manchester's jurisdiction – and a couple of hundred yards inside ours.'

'Still, I don't expect the Manchester force will be too fussy about a couple of hundred yards,' Ainsworth said hopefully.

'They're being *very* fussy. In fact, they're insisting that the case belongs to us.'

Which is just what I'd have done if I'd been in their situation, Ainsworth thought.

'That's not very friendly of them, is it, sir?' he asked. 'I would have thought that in the best interests of cross-jurisdictional relations—'

'They've promised to co-operate with us, if and when the need should arise – which is another way of saying "Don't call us, we'll call you",' the chief constable said. 'Face it, Dick, whether we like it or not, we're stuck with the case. So you'd better alert your lads.'

Who should he assign to the investigation? Ainsworth

wondered. Who on his team was best equipped to sail through choppy waters without making any waves himself?

'I'll put DCI Whittle on the case, right away, sir,' he said.

'The only difference between Whittle and an undertaker is that while they're both oily, an undertaker at least knows one end of a shovel from the other,' the chief constable said contemptuously.

'Whittle knows how to handle—'

'You'll put Charlie Woodend in charge of the team.'

'Woodend!' Ainsworth exclaimed.

'Woodend!' Dinnage repeated firmly.

Ainsworth gripped the phone tighter. He did not like Woodend. He didn't like the way the man dressed, deliberately kitting himself out in hairy sports jackets and cavalry twill trousers instead of wearing smart lounge suits like everyone else of his rank. He didn't like the way Woodend conducted his cases – abandoning the office from which he should be directing his team in order to wander around the scene of the crime himself. He didn't like—

'Are you still there?' the chief constable asked.

'Yes, sir, but I think I may have misheard you. You didn't actually say I should put Chief Inspector Woodend in charge, did you?'

'Indeed I did.'

Ainsworth shook his head to the empty room. 'Look, I know Woodend's an old friend of yours, sir,' he said, remembering that it was Dinnage who had brought the bloody man up to Lancashire when Scotland Yard had kicked him out, 'but even so, given the circumstances—'

'You think that Charlie goes about things like an angry bull rampaging through a china shop?' the chief constable said. 'You think that when he's pursuing a particular line of inquiry, he'll steamroller anybody who gets in his way, and that that might not be the best approach in a case like this?'

'Exactly, sir,' Ainsworth agreed.

'You've never really given Cloggin'-it Charlie his due . . .'

'I like to think I give all the officers serving under me their due.'

'However, in this case, I happen to agree with you,' the

35

chief constable continued, ignoring Ainsworth's obviously insincere comment. 'Woodend really doesn't react well to outside interference.'

'That's putting it mildly.'

'But . . .'

'But what?'

'A few years ago, when he was still working for the Yard, he investigated a fishmonger's murder up in Accrington. It was quite a famous case at the time, and the man who was mayor of the town during that investigation was Horace Throgmorton.'

'So?'

'So he's gone up in the world since then. Now he's *Lord* Throgmorton, and, among other things, he's the chairman of NWTV.'

'I still don't see where you're going with this.'

'Horace Throgmorton was very impressed with the way Charlie handled himself in Accrington, and he's put in a personal request that Woodend investigates this case.'

'And can't you tell him to get stuffed?'

'Would you be prepared tell one of the richest and most powerful men in the North West to get stuffed?'

'I suppose not,' Ainsworth conceded.

'And neither am I. So set Cloggin'-it Charlie loose on it.'

'If that's what you want, sir.'

'It's not what I want, necessarily, but it's certainly what we're going to do.'

As soon as he'd hung up, Ainsworth walked over to his cocktail cabinet and poured himself a very stiff whisky. He took a gulp, and suddenly began to see things from a more rosy perspective.

He had been *ordered* to put Woodend on the case, he reminded himself. Which meant that when the chief inspector rode roughshod over any obstacle which stood in his way – as he undoubtedly would – no blame could be attached to his commanding officer. Which, in turn, meant that all the blame would fall on the man himself.

Ainsworth walked over to the window. It wasn't *just* that he disliked Woodend, he thought. The man worried him – and with good reason.

Any man in Woodend's position should be able to see police work as a delicate balancing act. Crime had to be dealt with, of course – that was what the law was there for. The public expected murderers to be arrested, so it could walk the streets without fear. It wanted burglars locked up, so it could feel secure about its property.

But not everything was so black and white. For example, a respectable businessman might, after a hard day working for the good of the community, have a few drinks too many and cause a road accident. That was unfortunate, but most responsible police officers would probably recognise the fact that the man's own conscience would provide punishment enough, and there would be little point in putting him through the indignity of being dragged through the courts.

Of course, the businessman would not escape the consequences of his actions completely. There would, no doubt, come a time when the lenient policeman would require a professional – or personal – favour in return, and the businessman would have no choice but to smile and pay up. There was nothing wrong with that. It was the way things worked in the real world. In order to ensure progress, wheels had to be greased and backs scratched.

But Woodend, with his holier-than-thou attitude, refused to see things in that light, and Ainsworth's main fear, ever since the chief inspector had been posted to Whitebridge, was that Woodend would come across some of his own particular back-scratching and blow it up out of all proportion.

Now – although he had not recognised it as such at first – he was being handed the opportunity to do what he'd wanted to do all along. To put Cloggin'-it Charlie in a situation through which he would ensure his own destruction.

Ainsworth took another generous slug of his whisky. Murder was a terrible thing – as he had often pointed out in public – but this particular murder might turn out to be a real stroke of luck.

Six

It was shortly after the final credits for *Maddox Row* had appeared on the screen that the first policeman – Detective Inspector Hebden – arrived at the studio. He was quickly followed by several more detectives in unmarked cars and a dozen uniformed constables in a Black Maria. Under Hebden's guidance, the policemen swarmed all over the old mill like busy worker ants. A specialist team examined Valerie Farnsworth's dressing room, taking measurements and dusting for fingerprints. Other officers made lists of names and took down the details of what would, hopefully, prove to be alibis. At half past eight, the police doctor arrived and examined the body. By nine o'clock, both the corpse and the murder weapon had been removed.

'So what happens now?' Hebden's sergeant asked him at a quarter past nine.

'Not a lot,' the inspector replied. 'We've done about as much as we can ourselves. The rest will be up to the Big Cheese that headquarters sends down in the morning. Post a few lads at key points around the studio to make sure that nothin's disturbed, and send everybody else home.'

'What about the television people?'

'They can go as well.'

'But one of them might be the murderer.'

'One of them probably *is* the murderer, but if he's not done a runner already, it's unlikely he'll go missing now.'

Hebden positioned himself by the main exit, and watched the cast and crew troop out. Reactions to Valerie Farnsworth's death were as varied as the people themselves, he noted. Some had eyes which blazed with the kind of wild excitement you always saw in the eyes of crowds gathered near the scene

38

of a crime. Others left the building almost like zombies, as if they still found it hard to accept that violent death could ever impinge on their secure little lives. As he had told his sergeant, one of these people had probably killed that night, but watching them, Hebden found himself totally unable to point the finger.

'Is that it?' the inspector asked, after the initial flood had become a trickle, and then even the trickle had dried up. 'Is the building empty now?'

'Not quite,' his sergeant said. 'The producer and a few of his team asked if they could stay on. There's no harm in that, is there, sir?'

'No harm at all,' Hebden replied. 'But why should they *want* to stay on? I'd have thought they'd have had enough for one night.'

'It seems they have a problem,' the sergeant told him.

'*They* have a problem!' Hebden repeated, incredulously.

There were five of them in the conference room. Bill House-man sat at the head of the table, Jeremy Wilcox at the other end. Paddy Colligan and Ben Drabble, as befitted their status as mere writers, sat together along the left-hand side, and a secretary, her eyes red with tears, was positioned at Houseman's right.

'This has been a terrible shock for all of us,' the producer said sombrely, 'but even in the face of tragedy and loss, life still has to go on. And as distressed as we are by Val's death, we still have to face the fact that several of the plot lines we've developed for future episodes will have to be abandoned.'

Yes, they will, won't they, Paddy Colligan thought. And why? Because every time Val asked for more lines, you gave in without a fight, until *Maddox Row* had become less of a portrait of a Northern working-class street and more a personal showcase for Valerie Farnsworth. He thought it – but, wisely, he said nothing.

'What we need is something light and humorous,' House-man continued. 'Something that will leave the viewers with a smile on their faces.' He turned to the writers. 'That shouldn't be any problem, should it?'

None at all, Paddy Colligan thought. At least, not for you. You're the producer – the man who can demand results. *You* don't have sit staring at a blank sheet of typing paper until your eyes start to bleed.

'It's going to be rather tricky coming up with several new incidents at such short notice—' Ben Drabble said.

'But it can be done?' the producer interrupted.

'Probably. If we don't hit any snags.'

'Then *don't* hit any,' Houseman said. 'So that's the medium term dealt with. Now let's get on to the short term – Friday's episode. How do we deal with Valerie's – or should I say, Liz Bowyer's – demise?'

'We could simply ignore it,' Paddy Colligan suggested.

'Ignore it!' Jeremy Wilcox repeated. 'How, in God's name, can we possibly bloody ignore it?'

Paddy Colligan shrugged. 'It's what people do in real life,' he said. 'You know how it goes. You meet somebody for the first time since they've lost a relative, and you say how sorry you are for their loss. But after that, everybody goes out of their way never to mention the deceased again.'

'That may *well* happen in real life,' Bill Houseman said, 'but for some of our viewers the characters in *Madro* are *more* real than real life.'

That was true, Paddy Colligan thought. When they had plotted a pregnancy for Tilly Woods the previous year, the television studio had been deluged with toddlers' clothes that eager viewers had knitted for the expected baby. There were people out there in television-land – a large number of them – who seemed unable to grasp the idea that what they saw on their screens was no more than a story. There were people out there for whom Liz Bowyer seemed to have more reality than their own next-door neighbours.

'So what do you propose, Bill?' Ben Drabble asked.

'We kill Liz off on Friday's show,' Houseman said.

'But she's already dead!'

Houseman sighed exasperatedly. 'For goodness' sake, don't go making the same mistake as the people you're writing for.

Valerie's dead. We know that. But Liz *isn't*. Yet! She isn't dead until we say she is.'

'What have you got in mind?' Paddy Colligan asked. 'A conversation in the corner shop between Sam Fuller and Madge Thornycroft, in which Madge says something like, "Terrible thing Liz having that unexpected heart attack, isn't it, Sam?" And Sam answering, "Yes, she mustn't have been feeling too well the other day. That's probably why she turned back instead of havin' a row with you, Madge."?'

'Is that the best you can come up with?' Houseman demanded.

'Well, it's a bit crude at the moment,' Paddy Colligan admitted, 'but once we've polished up the lines—'

'You could polish them all you liked, and it still wouldn't do.'

'Why not?'

'If you'd just take the trouble to stop to think about it for a few seconds, you'd be able to work it out for yourself,' Houseman said cuttingly. 'The story of what's *really* happened will be splashed over the front pages of all the papers tomorrow. Correct?'

'I suppose so.'

'And after exposure like that, do you really think we kill Liz off with mere words?'

'So what *do* you want?'

'I want to see her die on screen. And so will the punters!'

Paddy Colligan wondered for a second if he was dreaming, and then decided that even his fertile imagination couldn't come up with a dream as bizarre as this.

'It's a good idea, but the problem is, she's already dead,' he said. 'Now if she'd thought to inform us last week that she was about to be murdered, we could already have had something in the can, but since she decided to spring it on us unexpectedly like this . . .'

Houseman glared at his scriptwriter. 'I think you're showing very poor taste to make a remark like that,' he said.

I'm showing poor taste! Colligan thought. What the bloody hell have *you* been showing ever since we sat down?

'I think you're still one step ahead of us on this, Bill,' Ben

Drabble said. 'If you could just spell it out a little more clearly . . .'

'Why not?' Houseman asked. 'And then I'll go and do the cleaner's job for her, shall I?'

'I think I'm starting to get the picture now,' Paddy Colligan said, knowing he was making a mistake, and not giving a damn. 'You want us to find a medium who can summon up Val's ghost at precisely half past seven on Friday night.'

Houseman slammed the palm of his hand down hard on the tabletop. 'I've just about had enough of this,' he said. 'I really bloody have! If all you can do is sit there and make snide comments, Colligan, you can just piss off right now – and I'll hire a monkey to do your job.'

'Paddy didn't mean it,' Ben Drabble said. 'He's just a bit tense. We all are. If you'd just explain what you've got in mind . . .'

'I suppose that would save time,' Houseman said wearily. 'Look, we've been doing this show for two years now, haven't we? We must have thousands of feet of film in the archive. Look through it. Find something we can use.'

'Use?' Ben Drabble repeated, mystified.

'Something we can incorporate into the death scene.' Houseman clicked his fingers, as if he'd had a sudden inspiration. 'Ironing!' he exclaimed.

'Ironing?'

'We've always gone out of our way to show our characters doing the same mundane household tasks as the viewers themselves. Surely we can find a few shots of Valerie doing the ironing.'

'Probably,' Drabble agreed. 'But what good would that—?'

'We show the old footage first: close-ups of Val doing the ironing. Then we cut to a live shot: a back view of a woman with the same build as Val – and wearing the same frock as she is in the clip – standing over the ironing board. She starts to writhe, and then, without turning her face to the camera, she falls on to the floor. And there we have it – the part of our audience which is so thick that it believes in Liz Bowyer as a real person will actually see her die.' He turned to Jeremy Wilcox. 'That's all technically possible, isn't it?'

'Yes,' Wilcox agreed. 'It's technically possible.'

'But sick!' Paddy Colligan said.

'Sick?' Houseman demanded. 'What's sick about it? Valerie's dead, isn't she? There's nothing we can do to hurt her now. And we have a responsibility to keep the show running as smoothly as possible. We owe it to our viewers. We owe it to our mortgages.'

'But we've already got one death at the ironing board scripted,' Ben Drabble protested. 'We can't have two in a matter of a couple of weeks.'

Bill Houseman sighed again, and wondered how he'd ever come to be lumbered with a pair of incompetents like Drabble and Colligan.

'Of course we can't have two characters die in the same way in just a couple of weeks,' he said. 'We can't have two characters die in *different* ways in a couple of weeks. So Jack Taylor, the Laughing Postman, will just have to stay in the show for a while, won't he?'

'Yes, I suppose he will,' Drabble agreed.

Houseman glanced down at his watch. 'Right,' he said, 'you all know what you've got to do before Friday afternoon. Get on with it.'

'Will you be attending the script conferences yourself, Mr Houseman?' Ben Drabble asked.

'No, I won't,' Houseman told him. 'I've decided to give up keeping a dog and barking myself. Besides, I'll have quite enough on my hands looking after the PC Plods who'll be tramping all over the bloody studio trying to find out who killed Valerie.'

'How long do you think they'll be here?' Jeremy Wilcox asked. He paused, as if he wished he'd never asked the question. 'I mean . . . they're going to be in the way, aren't they?'

'Undoubtedly they'll be in the way,' Houseman agreed. 'As to *how long* they'll be in the way, I really couldn't say. My confidence in the boys in blue's ability to do their job isn't exactly overpowering at the best of times, and in a case like this, when they'll be faced with more suspects than their befuddled little brains can handle, well, they could be here for the duration.'

43

Suspects! Paddy Colligan turned the word over in his mind. He hadn't really thought about it in those terms before, but now he came to consider it, he supposed that that was what they all were – Suspects, with a capital S!

'Why . . . why should you think they'll have a lot of suspects?' Ben Drabble asked uncertainly.

'Isn't that obvious?' Houseman countered. 'They'll be looking for people who might have wanted Valerie dead – and there are enough of them around, aren't there?' He stood up. 'Fancy a quick one before we call it a day, Jeremy?' he asked the director.

Wilcox nodded, but without much enthusiasm, and the two men left the room. The secretary closed her notebook, dropped it and her pencil in her handbag, and followed them, leaving the scriptwriters alone.

For a few moments Colligan and Drabble sat in silence, then Drabble said, 'You should watch your step, you know.'

'Watch my step?'

'With Bill Houseman. A couple of times back there I thought he was on the point of hitting you.'

'If he had have done, he'd have got back as good as he gave.'

'He's the boss,' Drabble said. 'He's the one who pays our wages.'

'Bugger him!' Paddy Colligan said. 'And bugger his bloody money, too!'

'That's stupid talk,' Drabble said. 'You're tired and upset. We all are. Things will look different in the morning.'

'Maybe you're right,' Paddy Colligan agreed.

'Of course I'm right. And whatever your opinion of Bill Houseman, you have to admit he thinks quickly, don't you?'

'What are you talking about?'

'That idea he came up with about finding some footage of Val ironing and then matching it up with shots of another actress.'

'Yes, it was quick thinking,' Paddy Colligan said. 'Perhaps just a little too quick.'

'What do you mean?'

'It's only a couple of hours since they found Val's body.

I hadn't even got around to thinking that we might all be suspects. But he had. And he'd gone beyond that. He'd found time to think about what impact her death was going to have on the show.'

'That's his job,' Ben Drabble said.

'You don't think there's a chance that the reason he came up with a solution so quickly was because he'd had more time to work on it than we have?'

'What are you saying? That he's thought through the possibility that some key members of the cast might suddenly drop out of the series for one reason or another? That he's gone on from that to work out what he'd do if such an eventuality did occur? I'm sure he's done precisely that. He'd have been a fool *not* to.' Drabble frowned. 'That was what you meant, wasn't it, Paddy?'

'I suppose so,' Paddy Colligan said grudgingly.

'Because if it wasn't – if you're suggesting he knew something more specific – then you're treading on very dangerous ground indeed. Nobody likes having the finger of suspicion pointed at them. And you've no reason to point it. So Houseman thought fast! That's the kind of work he's in. Producers aren't like writers, pondering over every word. They thrive on making quick decisions. It's the same with directors. Five seconds after it became obvious that Val wasn't going to appear on the set, Jeremy Wilcox had already worked out what to do about it. It's just the nature of the beast.'

'He didn't seem very fast on his feet in the meeting just now, though, did he?' Paddy Colligan asked. 'He hardly said a word all the time he was sitting there. And that's not like him at all. Usually, if Houseman says "black", he'll say "white" as a matter of principle. Yet tonight all he did was agree that what Houseman wanted done *could* be done. That – and ask how long the police were likely to be here.'

'So he was unusually quiet. That could easily be because of delayed shock or something.'

'Yes,' Paddy Colligan agreed. 'Or *something*.'

Seven

It was half past nine in the evening when the two men and one woman entered the public bar of the Drum and Monkey, an unassuming little pub on the outskirts of Whitebridge where – if your face became known – it was possible to order a drink long after the more legally-minded establishments had put the towels over the pumps. Under the watchful eye of the landlord, the trio looked quickly around the room, and then selected a table in the corner, as far away from the rest of the customers as possible.

Once they were seated, the younger of the two men stood up again. He was obviously intending to go to the bar and order drinks, but the landlord caught his eye and waved him to sit down again.

'Serve that table in the corner, will you, Phil,' the landlord told his waiter. 'Pint of best bitter, half a bitter an' a double vodka.'

'I didn't know there *was* waiter service in the public bar,' replied the other man, who was new to the job.

'There isn't usually,' the landlord conceded. 'But them three are bobbies, so, as far as I'm concerned, the normal rules don't apply.'

The waiter took the drinks across to the table. The pint was for the large man in a hairy sports jacket. The half of bitter was for a much younger man who was wearing a smart suit and could easily have been a dynamic young businessman – but wasn't. The double vodka was destined for the short-haired blonde woman who was pretty enough in her own way, though that way was not *quite* English.

Woodend picked up his pint and took a slurp that lowered the level by a good two inches.

'There are cases I'd almost kill to get my hands on, an' there are cases I wouldn't give to my worst enemy as a Christmas present,' he said. 'This is, without doubt, one of the latter.'

'Why's that?' Monika Paniatowski asked.

'You mean, aside from the fact we'll have the press breathin' down our necks every inch of the way, just waitin' for us to make a cock-up?'

Paniatowski smiled. 'Yes, apart from that.'

'Well, for a start, it involves actors.'

'So?'

'I don't know much about them as a breed, but from what little I *have* seen I'd have to say that I've found them a pretty odd bunch who I'd rather keep away from if I had the choice. But I *don't* have the choice, do I? Mr Ainsworth's made sure of that. He's better than anybody else I know at recognisin' a hot potato when he sees it – an' at passin' it on again before it has a chance to burn him.'

'Do we know much about this particular hot potato yet, sir?' Bob Rutter asked in his usual businesslike manner.

Woodend shook his head in mock despair. 'I sometimes think I'm wastin' my breath talkin' to you, lad,' he said. 'How many times do I have to tell you that until we get to the scene of the crime, we know bugger all!'

There'd been a time – not so very long ago – when such a dour comment from his boss would have intimidated Bob Rutter. Now that he knew Woodend better, it merely brought a grin to his face.

'So you're saying we have no details at all, are you, sir?' he asked.

'If you're lookin' for bare bones to chew on, I suppose I could throw you a couple,' Woodend admitted reluctantly. 'I don't imagine, bein' as how you're a bloody Southerner – an' a grammar-school lad at that – that you've ever actually watched *Maddox Row*, have you?'

'As a matter of fact, I have,' Rutter countered. 'I'm using it as a learning aid to help me come to grips with the strange traditions and customs of the Northern tribes I find myself living in the midst of.'

Woodend chuckled, but noticed that Paniatowski did not seem in the least amused.

'I know you only made that smart-arse remark to score points off me, lad,' he told his inspector, 'but there's an element of truth in what you've just said. If you want to learn about the North, you could do a lot worse than watch *Maddox Row*. I'm not sayin' it's anythin' like as accurate as one of them documentary programmes would be, but as a reflection of Northern workin'-class life, it's not at all bad. Any road, if you've been watchin' it, you'll know that Liz Bowyer is one of the central characters. Or, at any rate, she was until tonight, when the actress who was playin' her . . .' He looked questioningly at Paniatowski.

'Valerie Farnsworth,' the sergeant supplied.

'. . . Valerie Farnsworth, went an' got herself stabbed to death. Now, from my own limited experience, it seems to me she couldn't have been killed at a more inconvenient time – at least from our point of view.'

'What makes you say that?' Rutter asked.

'When we were livin' down in London, my Joan was involved in the local amateur dramatic societies, an' one year she talked me into takin' part in the production.'

'You, sir?' Rutter asked, unable to hide a smile as he pictured his boss standing self-consciously on the stage.

'Aye, well, I wouldn't normally have agreed to do it – but it was Dickens they were puttin' on, an' I couldn't very well turn down a chance to speak the Great Man's lines, now could I?' Woodend said.

Rutter gave a stage groan. On almost every case they were involved in, Woodend managed to drag Dickens in somehow. If he had his way, the complete works would probably be required reading for the sergeants' exam.

'You can groan, but there's a lot you can learn from Dickens,' Woodend said, for perhaps the hundredth time.

'I know I'm going to hate myself for asking this, but which book was it?' Rutter said.

'You should be able to work that out for yourself,' Woodend told him. 'When do most amateur dramatic societies put on their plays?'

'Christmas and the summer?'

'This one was at Christmas. So it would be . . . ?'

'*A Christmas Carol*?'

'We'll make a half-way decent detective out of you yet,' Woodend said.

'And who did you play, sir? Scrooge?'

'No, I didn't, you cheeky young bugger. I played the ghost of Jacob Marley – complete with chains and loud wailin' voice.'

'Can we get on, sir?' Paniatowski asked.

She doesn't like being left out of things, Woodend thought. She doesn't like it all.

'The point I was about to make, before Inspector Rutter saw the opportunity to take the piss out of me, was that in putting on a theatrical performance there's always plenty of scope for confusion,' he said. 'When we were on stage, everythin' went as smooth as clockwork, because we all knew exactly what we should be doin'. But before the performance, it was an entirely different matter. All kinds of things went wrong. One of the cast got stuck in a traffic jam on the way to the theatre. Another one ripped her costume on the head of a nail. There was a bit of the scenery which kept refusin' to stay upright. Now, I'm well aware that there's a big difference between an amateur production and a professional one, but even so, given that they're doin' a new show every single time, I should think there's a fair amount of pandemonium before they . . . what's the term, Monika?'

'Before they go on air.'

'Aye, before they go on air. That's why it would have been better for us if she'd been killed durin' the broadcast – because then it would have been noticed if anybody hadn't been where they should have been.'

'At least we know it was an in-house murder,' Rutter said.

'An' what do you mean by that fancy-soundin' term?'

'It couldn't have been an outsider who killed her. A stranger in the studio would have been spotted – and anyway, a stranger probably wouldn't have known where to find Valerie Farnsworth.'

'Unless he'd been to the studio before – as a guest,'

Woodend said. 'Or unless he had worked on *Maddox Row* in some capacity in the past. Still, your idea's worth thinkin' about,' he conceded. 'Make a note of it, Monika.'

DS Paniatowski scribbled a few words on the pad in front of her – but nowhere near as willingly as she would have done if the suggestion had come from herself or her boss, rather than from Bob Rutter.

Rutter and Paniatowski were like two cats who found themselves stuffed into the same sack, Woodend thought – all claws and teeth. Which was a pity because, in their own distinctive ways, they were both excellent bobbies.

'How are we going to approach this case, sir?' Rutter asked.

'I plan to go to the studio first thing in the mornin',' Woodend told him.

'Alone?' Paniatowski asked.

'Aye, that's right. I'll probably spend most of the day just nosin' around – seein' if I spot anythin' unusual. Though, like I said before, when you're dealing with show-business folk, the only thing that *is* likely to strike you as unusual is somethin' that'd be completely normal anywhere else.'

'And what will we be doing?' Paniatowski asked.

She hadn't quite said she'd rather swim through shark-infested water than work with Rutter, Woodend thought, but the meaning was clear enough. In a way, he supposed the tension between them was his own fault. If he'd run the tightly structured kind of team DCS Ainsworth would have liked him to, there would have been no scope for such tension. But then he would have been working with zombies – and zombies weren't very good at solving complex crimes.

Anyway, he told himself, they should take a share of the blame, too. Bob had still not quite got used to the idea that he was no longer Woodend's bagman. He didn't like it when Monika had the facts at her fingertips – as a good bagman should – while he himself had to be briefed. And as for Monika, her problem was that she was not the least intimidated by her relatively lowly status, and often acted – as a younger Charlie Woodend had once done – as if she were a law unto herself. Together, they made a combination which

50

was not always easy to deal with – but at least it made life interesting.

'So you want to know what you'll be doin', do you, Sergeant?' he asked Paniatowski.

Monika Paniatowski smiled. 'It might help,' she said.

'Well, while I'm poncin' about like some kind of poor man's Hercules Poirot, Bob – Inspector Rutter, I should say – will be in charge of the real police work. You know the sort of thing I'm talkin' about – collectin' witness statements, cross-referencin' them for inconsistencies, trackin' down any leads that are thrown up by the forensic evidence.'

'And I'll be assisting him, will I, sir?' Paniatowski said, doing her best not to bridle.

'No, I've got an entirely different job in mind for you. Do you know anythin' about the way television works, Monika?'

'Not a thing'

'Well, apparently television directors have somebody to help them – a sort of civilian bagman.'

'Yes?'

'The director of *Maddox Row* is a feller called Jeremy Wilcox. His bagman's a lass who goes by the name of Lucy Smythe, which I suppose means she's too posh to be called just plain "Smith". She was the one who actually found Valerie Farnsworth's body.'

Paniatowski nodded, though it was clear she had no idea where Woodend was going.

'This Miss Smythe doesn't appear to have as strong a stomach as you do, Sergeant,' the chief inspector continued. 'She saw all that blood an' gore, an' right away she had an attack of the vapours. The doctor who examined her when she came round again is of the opinion that it might be better if she stayed away from work for a couple of days.'

Rutter and Paniatowski were both still looking puzzled – and Woodend was starting to enjoy himself.

'I know one of the top fellers in North West Television vaguely,' he said. 'I met him on a case a few years back, while the pair of you were still crawlin' around in nappies. Horace Throgmorton, his name is. I was talkin' to him on

51

the phone, not half an hour ago. I put my idea to him, an' he thought it was a right good one.'

'What idea?' Rutter asked exasperatedly, beating Paniatowski to it by a fraction of a second.

'It should be obvious,' Woodend told him. 'This director feller needs a new bagman, an' I need to have one of my people movin' around the studio without attractin' too much attention to themselves.'

'You're saying you want me to pretend to be a director's personal assistant?' Paniatowski asked.

Woodend chuckled. 'On that case in Blackpool, you pretended to be interested in curtain design,' he pointed out, 'an' I know for a fact that if it hadn't been useful to the investigation, you'd never even have noticed there *were* curtains over the windows.'

'But I've already told you I know nothing at all about how television works!' Paniatowski protested.

Woodend chuckled. 'You're a smart lass – you'll soon pick it up.'

'So I'm supposed to learn a new set of skills *and* do police work at the same time, am I, sir?'

Woodend nodded. 'Like I said, you're a smart lass.'

'And no one at the studio will know I'm a bobby?'

'Not a single one of them. The only people who'll have been told the truth about you will be a couple of clerks in the personnel department back in Manchester.'

Paniatowski thought about it for a second, then grinned. 'Could be an interesting challenge, sir,' she said.

'Oh, it'll be that, all right,' Woodend agreed. 'What with us blunderin' around in a world we know nothin' about, an' the press screamin' at us to come up with a quick result because – after all – it's not every day that a big television star gets herself topped, it could turn out to be far too bloody interestin'.'

It was a quarter past ten when Woodend turned off the asphalted road and headed down the rutted track which led to his handloom weaver's cottage.

He didn't like arriving at the scene of a crime with any preconceptions, so, as usual, he was trying not to think about

52

the murder. But that was not proving as easy as it normally did, because this was not like a normal case. He had never met Valerie Farnsworth – and now he never would – but having watched her on his television screen twice a week, he felt as if he already knew her.

He shook his head in annoyance at himself. He *didn't* know her, of course – he only knew the character she'd played in *Maddox Row*. Yet he couldn't cast off the feeling that though she'd only been acting the role, she must have put a part of herself into Liz Bowyer – that he must have at least glimpsed a little of her individual essence even though she had only spoken someone else's lines.

And it was not just true of her. Jack Taylor, the laughing postman; Sam Fuller, the cranky old-age pensioner; Madge Thornycroft, the Row's gossip – he felt he knew a little about the actors who played all of them.

Yet how much do we really know about *anybody*? he wondered.

How much did he even know about his daughter – his own flesh and blood? He was sure it must have been hard for her to leave all her friends behind in London. But *how* hard? Was the semi-tantrum she'd thrown merely a sign that she was fighting her way through the painful process of adolescence? Or was there a more fundamental problem behind it? He'd meant to have a talk to her earlier in the evening, when she'd calmed down – but then he'd had to go out to meet Rutter and Paniatowski.

If she was still up, he'd talk to her before he turned in for the night, he promised himself. And it would be a *real* talk in which he'd let her speak frankly without him interrupting – a real talk during which he would hide his own feelings and concentrate on her needs.

He turned the corner and glanced up at Annie's window. The curtains were drawn closed, and the room was in darkness.

Tuesday

Eight

'Slow down,' Woodend said, as Bob Rutter drove him across the moorland road which ran between Whitebridge and Bolton.

'Slow down?' Rutter repeated.

'Aye. The murder's not goin' to go away, you know, an' it's far too nice a day to rush.'

It *was* a nice day. There was a crispness to the air that morning which served as a sharp reminder that the warm hazy days of summer were now long gone and shimmering ground frosts were already on the way, but the sun was shining and showing off the moors in all their untamed beauty.

From his side window, Woodend watched the red admiral butterflies alighting on the clumps of purple heather, then spreading their wings to savour whatever warmth was being offered by the autumn sun. Most of the delicate, flittering creatures would not survive the winter, but that was nature's way. You'd had your time, and so you died – and only a fool would bother to complain.

Murder was not like that, he thought. Murder was a *disruption* of that natural order – an attempt by mere fallible human beings to play God – which probably explained why it often made him so angry.

They had left the moors behind, and were approaching the old industrial village which had once depended for its livelihood on the mill that had become the home of *Maddox Row*. Time to turn their minds to work. Woodend sighed, and began to flick through the sheaf of morning newspapers he held on his lap.

'Valerie Farnsworth's murder may have been badly timed as far as our investigation goes, but it was bloody convenient for the press,' the chief inspector growled. He held up one of the newspapers. 'Look at this!'

'I'm driving, sir,' the ever-cautious Bob Rutter reminded him.

'Aye, so you are,' Woodend agreed. 'All right, I'll read it out to you. "Death of a Modern-day Siren". That's from the *Daily Express*. "Television Glamour Girl's Tragic End", the *Daily Mirror* calls it. Even the stuffy old *Times* has got in on the act, though, to be fair to it, it at least calls a spade a spade, an' refers to Valerie Farnsworth as a "sex symbol".'

'And was she?' Rutter asked, sounding slightly mystified.

'Why do you need to ask that? I thought you told me you'd seen *Maddox Row*.'

Rutter frowned. 'I have, but—'

'But what?'

'Did *you* find her sexy?'

'Aye,' Woodend said, surprised. 'Didn't you?'

'She was nearly *forty*,' Rutter answered.

'So?'

'My mother's not much more than that.'

'Do you know, lad, sometimes you make me feel very, very old,' Woodend said, thinking that perhaps it was not only red admiral butterflies which had almost had their day.

They had reached the edge of the village, and the old mill loomed up massively and impressively in front of them. It had been built to last, Woodend thought – constructed at a time when people had assumed that the mills would keep on churning out cotton fabric for a hungry British Empire forever. But things changed. Life moved on. Smoke had not belched out of the mill's tall chimney for years, and now the stack served as no more than a pillar on which to display the bright, shining NWTV logo.

There was a car park directly in front of the old mill, and in addition to the vehicles which would normally have been parked there, Woodend noticed two large television outside-broadcast vans and a number of cars with their owners standing beside them.

'The gentlemen of the press seem to be out in force today,' he groaned. 'That's just what we needed. Drive the car as close to the main entrance to the buildin' as you can, lad. With a little bit of luck, it should be possible to slip in unnoticed.'

It proved to be a groundless hope. The moment he had stepped out of the Humber, Woodend heard someone call out, 'It's Cloggin'-it Charlie,' and within seconds he was surrounded by a bunch of men in trench coats, baying as loudly as any pack of hounds which has the scent of the fox in its nostrils.

'Do you have any leads to go on yet, Chief Inspector Woodend?' one of the journalists shouted out.

'Was the murderer a member of the cast?' demanded another. 'Can you tell us if it's anybody our readers might have heard of?'

'Will you be making an arrest soon?' bawled a third.

Woodend faced the pack, and held his hands up for silence.

'I'm know some of you lads from my time at the Yard, an' there's a few more of you I've met since I've been workin' up here in Lancashire,' he said. 'So quite a lot of us are old friends, in a manner of speakin' – but *only* in a manner of speakin'.' He paused for a moment, to allow the journalists he'd had dealings with before to chuckle. 'There's a lot of new faces here as well,' he continued. 'People who don't know me from Adam yet.'

He surveyed the crowd, and felt his heart sink just a little as he noticed for the first time that among the male reporters, there was one woman. She was standing at the edge of the pack, as if she didn't really want to intrude – but Woodend was not fooled for a moment. Their paths had crossed before – or perhaps it would be more accurate to say they'd crossed *swords* before – and despite the fact that she'd been a blonde then and now her hair was jet black, he had no difficulty recognising her face.

Elizabeth bloody Driver! Just what he needed!

'I've got a bit of advice for you newcomers,' he said, focussing his eyes on the dark-haired woman. 'An' it's this. Talk to the old hands who've covered my investigations in the past. They'll tell you that I never rush into a case – that I like to get a feelin' for the scene before I start to draw any conclusions. So don't go expectin' any sudden dramatic statements in the next few hours, because you'll only be disappointed. An' don't start thinkin' that I've got a few pet reporters who I'll brief ahead of the rest of you. When I've got somethin' I want to say, you'll all hear it at exactly the same time.' He paused again, to light up a Capstan Full Strength. 'That's about all for the moment. You can hang about if you like, but you'll only be wastin' your time. It's a lovely mornin', an' if I was in your shoes I'd take advantage of it an' go for a walk on the moors.'

A couple of the reporters laughed, as if he'd made a joke. And it probably was a joke to them, he thought. Most of the reporters he knew considered their trek from the car park to the lounge of the pub as more than enough exercise for any man.

One of the journalists standing close to Elizabeth Driver turned around, and cannoned into her. The woman was knocked slightly off balance, and her notepad flew out of her hand. The reporter mouthed an apology, then – despite his considerable middle-aged spread – bent down with alacrity and picked up the pad. As he handed it back to her, she gave him a warm – almost promising – smile.

Nicely done, Woodend thought. Very nicely done indeed. To most people, it would have seemed like a complete accident, but even if he hadn't seen Elizabeth Driver manoeuvering herself into a position which made such a collision inevitable, he'd have known better. The woman collected men the way other women collected money-saving offers from magazines – not because she wanted them at that moment, but because a time might come when it would be to her advantage to cash them in.

The two detectives turned their backs on the journalists, and headed for the studio's main entrance.

'That was a very diplomatic little speech, sir,' Bob Rutter said. 'Especially considering that it came from you.'

'Aye, well, maybe I'm gettin' a bit mellower as I slip gently, but inexorably, into the autumn of my years,' Woodend replied.

Rutter laughed. 'The autumn of your years? I wouldn't have used quite that term myself, sir.'

'Wouldn't you?' Woodend asked. 'Why not? After all, I am older than your mother!'

The studio was entered through two large plate-glass doors, just beyond which sat a commissionaire in an ornate uniform the colour of the moorland heather they had seen earlier. As Bob Rutter pushed one of the glass doors open, the commissionaire rose smartly to his feet.

'Are you the press, gentlemen?' he asked, with an edge of polite contempt in his voice.

'Do we look like experts in fiddlin' expense accounts?' Woodend asked.

'I—' the commissionaire began.

'We're bobbies,' Woodend said. 'Show him your warrant card, Bob.'

Rutter took his card from his pocket, and handed it over. Most doormen would have given the card no more than a cursory glance, but this one examined it carefully before returning it.

'That seems to be in order, sir,' he said. 'Now if you'd just like to take a seat while I call—'

'There's no need to call anybody,' Woodend told him. 'We'll find our own way around.'

The commissionaire looked dubious. 'The studio's a lot more complicated than it looks at first, sir,' he cautioned. 'You might get lost.'

'We probably *will* get lost,' Woodend replied. 'In fact, I rather hope we do. You'd be surprised just how many interestin' things you can find when you're not really lookin' for them.'

The commissionaire studied Woodend's face to see if he was joking, decided he wasn't, and shrugged his broad shoulders.

'Well, you're the bobbies, so I suppose you know what you're doin',' he said philosophically.

'An' you used to be a bobby yourself, if I'm not very much mistaken,' Woodend said.

The commissionaire beamed with obvious pleasure. 'I most certainly was, sir,' he said.

'Desk sergeant by the time you retired?' Woodend guessed.

'Spot on, sir.'

Woodend nodded. 'Well, it's nice to know the security in this place is in a safe pair of hands,' he said.

He stepped clear of the door, turned his gaze on the interior of the mill, and tried to imagine it as it must have been in the old days.

'You'll not have had places like this in the South, will you?' he asked Rutter.

'Not that I know about,' the inspector agreed.

'This weavin' shed was once one vast room that housed hundreds of workers,' Woodend said. 'But it was more than just bricks and mortar. It stood as a cathedral to the religion of industrial might – a vast, stark, utilitarian monument which, despite its ugliness – or maybe because of it – attained some kind of terrifyin' majesty.'

'That's a bit deep for this time of the morning, isn't it?' Bob Rutter asked jovially.

But Woodend was talking more to himself than to his inspector. 'Life was hard back then,' he continued, 'but there was a comfortin' certainty about it, too. The mill was part of the community – and the community was a livin', breathin' thing. We were all involved in the same struggle, you see. Neighbours helped neighbours. An' when you talked about your family, you didn't just mean your wife an' kids – you were talkin' about all your aunties and uncles an' second cousins as well.'

He ran his eyes over what the NWTV builders had done to the mill. At the far end, a brick wall had been built right up to the high ceiling, and it was behind that, presumably, that the actual studio itself was located. An open concourse ran though the centre of the building, all the way from the far wall to the main doors. On either side of the concourse, low brick buildings had been erected, each with a flat roof – as if the high ceiling above them were really open sky.

'Fragmented,' Woodend said softly.

'What was that?' Rutter asked.

'The place has been fragmented – just like society itself. It's been broken down into smaller, more manageable units – the sort of units the modern mind can comprehend.'

'You sound as if you wish time had stood still,' Rutter said.

'Do I?' Woodend asked, surprised. 'I didn't mean to. Only

an idiot thinks the good old days were really that good. Still, there *were* some good things – an' now they've gone for ever.'

The chief inspector reached into his pocket for his packet of Capstan Full Strengths, and turned his attention back to the central concourse. Though it was still early in the morning, the business of the television studio was already well under way, and quite a number of people were scurrying from one place to another. Woodend watched them for a while – the executives in smart suits; the workmen in overalls and khaki half-length coats; the young women in skirts and jumpers; the young men in suede jackets – and as he watched, a smile came to his lips.

'You seem to have cheered up all of a sudden,' Bob Rutter said.

'Oh, I have,' Woodend agreed. 'I was a bit concerned for a while back there about how I'd manage in the world of television, but I'm not any more.'

'So what's changed your mind?'

'Just look at this place,' Woodend said. 'What does it remind you of?'

Rutter studied the central concourse, just as his boss had done. 'In a way, it's a bit like a village,' he said.

'Aye, it is,' Woodend agreed. 'Maybe it's not got the same sense of community as the one I grew up in, but it's a village, right enough. An' if there's one place I feel at home in, it's villages.'

Nine

O stensibly, Jeremy Wilcox was studying the shooting script which lay on his desk in front of him. In practice, his thoughts had ranged far beyond the mundane technical details of the next episode. He was wondering, specifically, how best to let the people who mattered in NWTV know that it was he – and he alone – who had saved the previous evening's show from disaster. He could tell them directly, of course. Or he could let it accidentally slip out in a conversation over drinks. But there had to be subtler ways to do it – ways that would somehow also give the impression that he was too involved in being creative to ever think of indulging in office politics.

There was a knock on the door.

'Answer that, Lucy,' he said, without looking up. 'And tell whoever it is that I'm far too busy to see anyone right now.'

He turned his mind back to the problem of getting credit where credit was due. Who had access to the people who mattered? And how could he prevail upon them to work on his behalf?

Whoever was outside on the concourse knocked again.

'Have you gone deaf all of a sudden, Lucy?' Wilcox asked irritably, turning his head to glare at his assistant.

He found his glare was being wasted on a vacant desk, and remembered that Lucy had used the fact she'd been the one who'd discovered Valerie Farnsworth's body as a justification for taking the day off.

There was a third knock on the door.

'Come!' Wilcox shouted irritably.

He'd been quite prepared to give whoever had chosen to disturb him an absolute rocket, but when he saw the tasty blonde woman standing in the doorway, he changed his mind.

'Can I help you?' he asked.

The tasty blonde giggled. 'Actually, I'm here to help you,' she said. She advanced across the room, and held out her hand to me. 'Monika Peignton. That's Monika with a K. I'm your new, temporary assistant.'

Wilcox frowned. 'I wasn't told about this.'

'Apparently, your regular assistant is going to be away for several days, and Personnel in Manchester thought you'd need me,' Paniatowski said, not quite simpering.

'I still should have been told,' Wilcox said.

But, in fact, he was not feeling as sulky as he was sounding. It was good Personnel should have taken such prompt action. It showed Manchester was really starting to take him seriously. And the girl *was* a little cracker.

'Sit down, Monika with a K,' he said genially, indicating the chair directly in front of his desk.

As Paniatowski sat, she crossed her legs. It was not a gesture that Wilcox missed. Nor had she intended that he should.

'So, since Personnel sent you, I assume you have extensive experience in acting as a director's PA,' Wilcox said.

'Not really,' Monika replied, letting her skirt slip a little further up her thigh. 'Not at all, actually. But I'm very willing to learn.'

I'll bet you are, Wilcox thought, running his tongue quickly over his lips.

'So if you have no experience, how did you get the job?' he asked. 'Family influence?'

Paniatowski shrugged awkwardly, causing her breasts to jiggle a little. 'I wouldn't put it quite like that,' she said. 'Although it is true that my Uncle Desmond occasionally plays a round of golf with Horry Throgmorton . . . Lord Throgmorton, I *should* say.'

Typical! Wilcox thought angrily. Bloody typical! And then he realised how he might be able to turn things to his advantage.

The girl's uncle played golf with the boss of NWTV. She seemed to know Throgmorton herself. If she went away with the impression that it was Jeremy Wilcox who was holding *Maddox Row* together, there was every chance that her opinion would eventually reach the right ear.

'Well, experience doesn't count for everything,' he said magnanimously. 'If you work hard, I expect you'll soon learn what you need to know. Would you like me spell out your job for you?'

'I'd really appreciate it if you could do that, Mr Wilcox,' Paniatowski told him.

'The director is central to the process of putting on a television programme,' Wilcox said. 'To put it in its simplest terms, without him, there is no show. Your job – again to put it in its simplest terms – is to make sure that nothing happens which might prevent me from doing my work. Whenever I want any sort of errand running, you're to be there to run it for me. If I need to be alone, you're to make sure that no one disturbs me. A good director's PA should learn to anticipate the director's needs even before he realises that he has them himself. Is all that clear?'

'Very clear,' Monika said, sounding both sweet and earnest.

Wilcox nodded sagely. 'Good,' he said. 'Now before we get started, are there any questions you would like to ask me?'

What kind of question would Charlie Woodend ask at this point? Monika wondered. Probably one which would knock Wilcox off-balance – one which would make him reveal more of himself than he'd ever intended to.

'Well, there is just one little thing that puzzles me,' she said, with a show of reluctance.

'And what is it?'

'It's silly. I don't suppose it matters really.'

Wilcox chuckled. 'If we're going to work together, then we've got to learn to say what's on our minds – even if it does turn out to be silly,' he said. 'So come on – out with it.'

Monika feigned further hesitation for a second. 'It's just that Daddy was in the army – a major general, actually,' she said.

'Yes?'

'And he always says that what's really vital when you're

working somewhere is to get a clear picture of the chain of command.'

'I'm not sure what your point is.'

'Well, I know you're tremendously important to *Maddox Row* – and it's a privilege to be working for you, it really is – but aren't you sort of like the colonel to the producer's general? I mean, I'm sorry if I've got it wrong, but that's how it seems to me – that it's the producer who actually—'

'Let me tell you about the so-called producer!' Wilcox interrupted. 'The man had an idea – *one* idea, mark you, an idea which someone else would have been bound to come up with sooner or later – and because of that he's come to believe he's the only one who really counts. Well, I can assure you—'

He'd gone too far, he realised, coming to a sudden halt. The tales he wanted Monika to carry home were of a dedicated, superbly efficient director – not a director riven with jealousy.

'You can assure me . . . ?' Monika prompted.

'Of course, the producer is important,' Wilcox said. 'Everyone involved in *Maddox Row* is important in their own way. It's a team effort. But that's not to say that some of us don't have a bigger contribution to make than others.'

'Oh, I can quite see that,' Monika said dutifully.

Ten

Woodend took to Inspector Hebden immediately. The other man was in his mid-thirties, he guessed. He had an intelligent face and sharp blue eyes which probably missed very little. All in all, the chief inspector thought as he, Rutter and Hebden sat around the table in the small conference room Hebden had been using as his temporary office, the local man was just the sort of feller that senior officers always hoped would be put in charge of babysitting an investigation until they could reach the scene themselves.

'Let's start at the beginnin',' Woodend suggested. 'When were you first aware that somethin' had gone seriously wrong up here?'

'We got the call at the station at nine minutes to eight last night,' Hebden replied.

'Who made it?'

'The producer's assistant, a woman called Jane Todd.'

'An' you came here straight away?'

'As soon as we'd rung the studio back to make sure it wasn't a hoax call, yes.'

'How long did it take you?'

'The station's only two miles from the studio. I arrived here at two minutes to eight. My back-up teams all arrived within five minutes after that.'

'Had anybody been allowed to leave in the meantime?'

Hebden shook his head. 'No, definitely not.'

'How can you be so sure of that?'

'I talked to the commissionaire – the same one who's on duty now. His name's Teddy Kendrick. He's an ex-bobby. I've worked with him myself, and he's a good man. If he said nobody left, then nobody did.'

'Somebody could have slipped out while he was on the bog.'

Hebden grinned. 'They used to call Teddy "Iron-bladder" when he worked at the station as desk sergeant. He could do a whole shift and never leave his post. Besides, if he does have to answer the call of nature he's got strict instructions that he's to alert the chief security officer so a replacement can be sent to cover the desk. And Teddy's not the kind of man who ignores strict instructions.'

'So the murderer didn't leave *after* the body had been discovered,' Woodend mused. 'But there's nothing to have stopped him making his escape between the time he killed Val Farnsworth and the time you arrived, now is there?'

'Yes, there is. The doctor estimated Miss Farnsworth met her death not more than three-quarters of an hour before she was found. That was at least an hour after anybody had left the studio.'

'Again, are you sure?'

'Positive. Teddy Kendrick keeps a ledger in which he logs people in and out. The last entry was at just after six o'clock.'

'Isn't it possible that our killer could have slipped out through one of the other exits?' Woodend asked.

'No, sir, it isn't. All the other exits are fire doors, and they're wired up to the central alarm system. Nobody could have gone through one of them without setting that alarm off.'

'An' you've checked that the alarm systems on the fire doors haven't been tampered with?'

'Not me personally, but it's one of the first things I got one of my team to do.'

Woodend nodded. 'You seem to have been very thorough,' he said. 'So at least we know that the murderer – whoever he or she is – was still in the building when you arrived. So how many suspects does that leave us with?'

'In round figures?'

'That'll do for a start.'

Hebden grinned awkwardly. 'With all the actors, technicians, make-up artists, camera and sound men, costume people and management, I'm afraid it comes to more or less seventy-five,' he said. 'And if it had happened earlier, before the clerical staff went home for the night, it would have been even higher.'

'Seventy-five,' Woodend repeated to himself. He turned to Rutter. 'How do you feel about those numbers, Bob?'

Rutter shrugged. 'We've had more suspects than that to deal with in our time.'

'Aye, we have,' Woodend agreed. 'When we were investigatin' that case in Liverpool, we had a whole bloody city as suspects.' He turned back to Hebden. 'I take it you've got the names an' addresses of everybody who was here, haven't you?' he asked. 'Only I expect my keen young inspector is just itchin' to run his highly-trained eye over them.'

'Yes, sir. I've got the names and addresses,' Hebden confirmed. 'I've also got accounts of everybody's movements for the hour before the victim was discovered.'

'But from the tone of your voice, you don't sound as if you think they'll be particularly useful,' Woodend said.

'The accounts will eliminate some of the possible suspects.'

'But not that many?'

'I haven't have time to study the results thoroughly,' Hebden admitted, 'but as far as I can tell from a cursory glance, there are very few people who have an alibi for the whole of that period.'

'Fragmentation,' Woodend said.

'Pardon, sir?'

'I was sayin' to Bob earlier that what goes on here isn't all part of one process – as it was when the place was a mill. It's a lot of different processes which occasionally mesh together. For the rest of the time, everybody's concerned with doin' their own little job – so it's not surprisin' they don't have alibis.' He lit up a Capstan Full Strength. 'What about forensics? Have the boffins been able to come up with anythin' useful?'

'The victim was stabbed several times with a heavy-duty electrician's screwdriver,' Inspector Hebden said. 'It's been positively identified as belonging to the studio's maintenance department. It should, by rights, have been in the storeroom.'

'An' who has a key to that storeroom?'

'Quite a number of people – but you'll probably get nowhere with that particular line of inquiry, since the store wasn't locked.'

'Of course it wasn't,' Woodend said, almost fatalistically. 'So does the murder weapon offer us any other clues?'

'It had been wiped clean of prints.'

'Aye, it would have been,' Woodend said. 'That's the problem with murderers these days. They watch far too many cop shows on the television, an' learn just what mistakes not to make. Were there any prints in Valerie Farnsworth's dressin' room?'

'Obviously there were the dead woman's – but there were also dozens of others we haven't even begun to check on yet.'

'Probably won't do any good, anyway,' Woodend said. 'If the killer remembered to wipe off the screwdriver, he's not likely to have left his dabs anywhere else, now is he – at least, not on that particular visit.'

'No, it doesn't seem likely he will have,' Hebden said. 'Anything else I can do for you, sir?'

'Aye. Get together all them statements an' reports you've been collectin', an' hand them over to Inspector Rutter here. He'll be takin' them back to Whitebridge with him.'

'I'll be *what*?!' Bob Rutter exclaimed.

Woodend looked first at Rutter, and then at Hebden. 'Why don't you nip down to the studio canteen, an' get yourself a cup of tea?' he suggested to the local inspector.

Hebden took the hint, and rose to his feet. 'Yes, I'll do that.'

Woodend waited until Hebden had left the room, then said, 'An' what was that little almost-outburst about?'

'You're sending me back to Whitebridge?' Rutter demanded.

'What else did you expect?'

'I *imagined* that my team would be given space here in the studio.'

'If it was left up to me, that's probably what would happen,' Woodend admitted.

'And *isn't* it left up to you? You are the boss?'

Woodend sighed. 'That's the kind of comment I'd expect

71

from a young constable with bum fluff still on his chin,' he said. 'You're an inspector now, an' you should be able to see further than that. You should know that all I am is your *immediate* superior.'

'So whose tune are we *both* dancing to?' Rutter asked. 'DCS Richard Ainsworth's?'

'Dick Ainsworth's sold on this daft idea of a "crime centre" based in a police station,' Woodend said. 'It gives him somethin' to show the press – somethin' he can brag about when he gets together with all the other DCSs. But he can't brag about it if it's just an empty room, can he? He needs bodies to fill it. So we'll give him some, if that's what it takes to keep him happy.'

'And that's what I am?' Rutter asked. 'A body? One of the extras hired to fill in the background?'

'Just because this case involves television people, there's no need for you to start talkin' like one of them,' Woodend said, a little sharply. 'Of course you're not just a body. Them witness statements need lookin' into. You know that yourself. It's a slow, painful process, but it's got to be done – an' there's no reason why it can't be done as well in Whitebridge as it could be done here. Besides, the closer Maria gets to givin' birth, the more she'll want to see you—'

He came to an abrupt halt, a look of distress crossing his face. Maria Rutter wouldn't be seeing *anybody* – ever again – he reminded himself. Ever since she'd been injured at the Belgrave Square demonstration, she'd been totally blind.

There was a short, awkward pause, then Woodend said, 'Well, you know what I mean. She'll want you *around*. An' it'll be a lot easier for you to be around if you're workin' out of Whitebridge.'

'Meanwhile, you'll be here with the trusty Sergeant Paniatowski, actually solving the crime.'

'There's no sayin' the murder *will* be solved here in the studio,' Woodend said. 'The big break in this case could come just as easily through some inconsistency in the statements.'

'Whatever aspect of the case I'm working on, I'd still rather do it from here,' Rutter said stubbornly.

Woodend shook his head. 'That's not possible. If you'd been

a blonde with bosoms like WDS Paniatowski, I might have given you the job of snuggling up to Jeremy Wilcox instead of her,' he said. 'But you're not, an' I couldn't.'

'You've changed,' Rutter said bitterly. 'All this talk about keeping Ainsworth happy! There was a time – not so long ago – when you wouldn't have given a damn what your boss wanted.'

'I've never had a boss who was close enough to breathe right down my neck before – that was one of the advantages of workin' for the Yard,' Woodend said. 'But maybe you're right, an' I have changed,' he conceded. 'People do, you know. An' so do situations. That's what's happened to our partnership – it's changed.'

'Because of Paniatowski!'

'Sergeant Paniatowski has nothing to do with it.'

'Doesn't she?'

'No, she bloody doesn't,' Woodend said. 'Listen, Bob, for the first couple of days on that case in Blackpool, I really missed havin' you with me. I felt half-naked without you by my side. Then I realised somethin'. Do you know what it was?'

'I'm sure you're about to tell me, whether I want to know or not.'

'I realised I wasn't missin' *you* at all. The person I was missin' was *Sergeant* Rutter. Well, you're not him any longer – nor ever can be again.'

'Meaning?'

'Meanin' you've outgrown the job of bein' my sidekick, an' it's about time you accepted the fact. So however much we both might regret it – an' *I* do, for one – you can't be my Tonto any longer, an' it's time you started learnin' to be your *own* Lone Ranger.'

Rutter stood up. 'Thank you for that little speech, sir,' he said. 'I'll bear that in mind when I'm back in Whitebridge, up to my neck in paperwork.'

'You do that,' Woodend agreed.

Bob Rutter walked over to the door, opened it, then turned round to face Woodend again.

'Hi ho, Silver, away!' he said, before stepping into the corridor and disappearing from sight.

The chief inspector sat perfectly still for a few seconds, then reached for his packet of Capstan Full Strengths.

'Oh dear,' he said regretfully, as he lit up one of his cigarettes. 'Oh dear, oh dear, oh dear.'

Eleven

Bill Houseman's office was a very far cry from the homely living rooms which were inhabited by the fictional characters of *Maddox Row*. The desk was made of flawless teak. The sofa covered in a soft white leather. Theatre posters in expensive metal frames hung complacently from the pastel-blue walls, and each of the exotic scatter rugs on the polished wooden floor had probably taken some poor bloody Bedouin tribeswoman months to produce.

It was an office which had been designed to impress any visitor with its occupant's importance, Woodend decided, and though he'd seen plenty of other offices which had had much the same aim, it did seem to him that in this case the occupant had tried just a little *too* hard.

Houseman waved Woodend to a chair, and sat down himself behind his opulent desk.

'We're both very busy men,' the producer said briskly, 'so why don't we get straight down to business?'

'Aye, why don't we,' Woodend agreed.

Houseman picked up an elaborate paper knife from his desk in his right hand, and ran the point softly along the length of the index finger on his left.

'I fully appreciate the fact that you have a job to do, Mr Woodend, but I hope you realise that you're not unique in that,' he said.

'You mean, all I've got to do is catch a murderer, whereas you have an important television show to produce?' Woodend asked mildly.

'Is that some kind of joke?' Houseman said sharply.

'More of a comment than a joke,' Woodend replied. 'I must say, Mr Houseman, it doesn't seem to me as if you're takin'' the murder of Valerie Farnsworth very seriously.'

A look which might almost have passed as an apology crossed the producer's face, and he laid the paper knife down on the desk again.

'You're quite right, of course,' he admitted. 'I probably haven't taken it seriously enough. But the fact of the matter is, I haven't had the time to stop and consider it properly yet.'

'Haven't had *time* to consider the murder of one of your cast?' Woodend asked sceptically.

'You have to understand my situation, Chief Inspector. I'm totally wrapped up in the world of *Maddox Row*. I have to be – it dominates every hour of my day – and for me, at this particular moment, the death of Liz Bowyer is both more immediate and more tragic than the death of the woman who played her. I expect that when I can finally step off the roller-coaster ride which this job has become for a few hours, the implications of what has happened will really start to hit me, and I will begin my grieving. But for the moment, the show must go on.'

Nobody should be *that* obsessed with his job, Woodend thought. And then, just before he put the thought into words, he pulled himself up short.

Wasn't he just as bad as Houseman? he asked himself. When he was working on a case, didn't he develop tunnel vision, so that while he might notice the slightest nuance in something one of his suspects said, he was totally oblivious to anything which did not help him to solve the murder?

Joan had told him as much, in her gentle way, and Annie had been far more outspoken on the matter. His bosses, too, constantly complained that he ran a one-man show to the exclusion of the wider concerns of policing – and for the first time he began to wonder if they might be right.

He would try to be a better husband, father and member of the police team, he resolved – but first he had to find out who'd killed Valerie Farnsworth.

'Can you think of anybody who might have wanted to see Miss Farnsworth dead?' he asked.

'No,' Houseman replied – far too quickly.

'No one at all?' Woodend persisted. 'You've never heard

anybody threaten her? Anybody say they wished she was dead?'

Houseman sighed. 'Of course I have.'

'Who?'

'Everybody in the cast, at one time or another. But you have to understand that what we're dealing with here is actors.'

'Would you mind explainin' that?' Woodend asked.

'I'll do my best,' Houseman agreed. 'Actors live in a very strange world. At nine o'clock in the evening, they're strutting around the stage with the eyes of the entire audience on them. They can bring forth from that audience both tears of joy and shudders of fear. It gives them a tremendous feeling of power.'

'It must do,' Woodend agreed.

'Then the performance is over, and by eleven o'clock they're sitting on the last bus home, worrying about where they're going to find the money to pay the rent for the crummy little bed-sits they live in. Do that for a while, and it's bound to have some effect on you, isn't it?'

'Could you be more specific?'

'Since drama is so much more rewarding than real life, they infuse real life *with* drama. So when they threaten to kill someone, they really believe that they mean it. But only for that moment. Then the scene changes, they're in a different play, and the former object of their hate becomes their dearest love.'

'You're talkin' about strugglin' actors here, aren't you?' Woodend asked. 'Actors whose only reward is the audience's applause. I would have thought your cast had other compensations. Aren't they quite well-paid?'

'They're *very* well-paid,' Houseman said. 'But they *have* all struggled in the past, and it's not a mantle they can easily shrug off easily.'

It's not a mantle you can shrug off easily, either, if I'm readin' you right, Woodend thought.

'Val Farnsworth never even considered the possibility that she would end up a star,' Houseman continued. 'She had the wrong accent, for a start. And then, suddenly, a star was what she was. But that doesn't mean she felt secure. None of them do, because part of their mind is always back in that tatty bed-sit.'

An' I bet you could describe yours in great detail, even now, Woodend thought.

'So Val was never happy with what she had,' Houseman said. 'She always wanted more. More lines, better lines. And she wanted the very faults and weaknesses which had made her character so popular written out of the script. If she'd had it all her own way, Liz Bowyer would have become a perfect being – and incredibly boring. But Val wasn't the only person suffering from actors'-disease. Every member of the cast, from the stars right down to the humblest walk-on, feel exactly the same way.'

'But they don't all have the power to turn their wishes into reality,' Woodend said thoughtfully. 'I imagine Val Farnsworth was popular enough with the audience to make things go pretty much the way she wanted them to.'

Houseman laughed, but without much evidence of genuine amusement. 'If I may say so, you've completely misunderstood the situation. Actors are rather like children. Or perhaps dogs. Of course, they'd rather have things going entirely their own way, but I can't allow that. I treat them firmly, but kindly, and eventually they end up doing what *I* want them to do.'

'So you're sayin' you had Val Farnsworth under control?'

'I have everyone who's concerned with *Maddox Row* under control. That's my job.'

'You don't seem to have had the murderer under control,' Woodend pointed out.

Houseman winced. 'That was a little below the belt, wasn't it, Chief Inspector?' he asked.

'Killers don't normally play by the Queensberry Rules – so I can't afford to, either,' Woodend replied. 'There is one thing that's been puzzlin' me, Mr Houseman.'

'And what might that be?'

'I started out, if you remember, by askin' you if you knew of anybody who might have wished to see Val Farnsworth dead.'

'And I thought I'd pretty much answered the question.'

'That's just where you're wrong. You haven't at all. Because you immediately started talkin' about the *actors* in the series.'

'I thought that's what you wanted me to—'

'An' there were more people than just actors in this buildin' when Val Farnsworth was killed. A lot more. In fact, I'd guess that the majority of folk who work on *Maddox Row* aren't actors to all.'

'You'd be right in your assumption.'

'So why did you confine your answer to the actors?'

Houseman gave him a puzzled frown. 'I suppose it was because, in drama, if a noble lord is killed, it's normally by one of his own kind, rather than by a member of the peasantry,' he said finally.

'So you're comparin' the actors to aristocrats, an' everybody else involved to serfs?'

'Essentially, I suppose I am.'

'Do you see yourself as a serf?'

'Of course not!'

'An' the director?'

'He might be an oaf, but he's certainly not a serf.' Houseman paused. 'You're surely not suggesting that I could have killed Val, are you?' he demanded.

'I'm not suggestin' that anybody in particular killed her at the moment, sir,' Woodend said. 'I don't have anythin' like enough information to make that kind of judgement.'

'But you're not ruling me out?'

'I think we're gettin' a bit ahead of ourselves here, sir,' Woodend said, side-stepping the question. 'If my investigation's goin' to make any progress at all, I need to get a better mental picture of the studio, an' how it works. An' that means I need to do some wanderin' around. I imagine that on my first wander you'd prefer it if I was accompanied by one of your staff.'

'I'd prefer it if you were *always* accompanied by one of my staff,' Houseman said.

'That's not the way I work.'

'A television studio is a very complex and finely balanced set of structures,' Houseman said. 'You wouldn't allow a layman to blunder around the scene of a crime, because of the damage he might inadvertently do. And I'm afraid I can't allow you to blunder around the studio for exactly the same reason.'

'You seem to be missin' the point,' Woodend said. 'This is both a television studio *an'* the scene of a crime. And as far as I'm concerned, it's the scene of a crime *first*.'

'Naturally, when you're looking at it from your perspective—' Bill Houseman began.

'My perspective's the only one that matters at the moment,' Woodend interrupted him. 'There's somethin' else you should get clear, an' all. I wasn't askin' your permission for what I intend to do – I don't need it. What I was proposin' when I mentioned a guide was a compromise between what you want, an' what I want. If you knew me better, you'd realise compromisin's not somethin' I do very often – so if I was you I'd grab the chance while it's there.'

'I don't think we're going to get along, Chief Inspector,' Houseman said coldly.

'I don't give a bugger whether we do or not,' Woodend told him. 'Are you goin' to give me a guide? Or should I just find my own way around?'

'I'll give you a guide,' Houseman said, through gritted teeth. 'But I shall also be writing to your superiors to complain about your attitude.'

'Aye, well that'll be nothin' fresh for them,' Woodend said.

He leant back in his chair and lit up a Capstan Full Strength. So much for the new, improved Charlie Woodend, the policeman-diplomat, he thought.

Twelve

The central concourse was not as busy as it had been earlier, but Woodend suspected it was no more than a temporary lull, and that by one thirty, when he was given his tour of the studio, it would be as hectic as it had been when he first arrived.

He was to be shown round by Jane Todd, Bill Houseman's personal assistant – the woman who had contacted the local police after Val Farnsworth's body had been discovered. In his mind, Woodend was already starting to build up a picture of her. She was the producer's gatekeeper, which probably meant that she was as hard as nails and as unyielding as an iron bar – the sort of woman who can make a slavering Dobermann seem like a cuddly toy.

The chief inspector checked his watch. He had over an hour to kill before he met Houseman's gorgon, which was more than enough time to give his brain cells their necessary infusion of best bitter.

He reached the end of the concourse, nodded to the vigilant commissionaire, and stepped cautiously into the car park. But caution was not necessary. The reporters' cars had all disappeared, and though the two outside-broadcast vans were still there, they looked empty and forlorn.

Woodend grinned. He should have known it would be like this. He might run on bitter, but journalists ran on whisky and soda, and it was already well past their filling up time.

Bob Rutter had left him the Humber, and Woodend climbed behind the wheel. There was a pub on the edge of the village, he remembered from the drive in that morning, but as it was the closest watering-hole to the studio, it would undoubtedly be the one the journalists had chosen themselves.

If he wanted a bit of peace and quiet, he would be wise to go further afield.

He drove for four miles before he came a pub called the Green Man. He parked the Humber, headed straight for the bar and ordered himself a pint. It was only as the barman was pulling it that he noticed the woman with the jet-black hair sitting on a tall bar stool at the other end of the counter.

'Hell an' damnation!' he said softly to himself.

'I'll pay for that drink,' the woman called out to the barman as she reached into her purse.

The barman looked questioningly at Woodend, and when the chief inspector firmly shook his head, he said, 'If it's all the same to you, madam, the gentleman would prefer to buy his own drink.'

The woman slid off her stool and edged up the bar so she was standing next to Woodend. The chief inspector sorted out some change, and slid it across the counter as if she wasn't there.

'I wasn't trying to pick you up,' she said.

'I didn't think you were,' Woodend replied, before taking a slow sip of his beer.

'You don't remember me, do you?'

Woodend sighed. 'Don't I?'

'It's probably because my hair's a different colour from the last time you saw me. My name's Eliz—'

'It'd take more than a change of colour that's come out of a bottle to make me forget a pain in the backside like you,' Woodend interrupted her. 'Your name's Elizabeth Driver, an' the last time we talked you were a junior reporter on the *Maltham Guardian*.'

'I don't work there any more,' Elizabeth Driver said, with an edge of reproach to her voice.

'I'm not in the least surprised.'

'No, you wouldn't be. After all the fuss you made to my editor, he really had no choice but to sack me.'

'You brought it on yourself,' Woodend said indifferently. 'An' I'll tell you somethin' else, Miss Driver – you were lucky just to lose your job. After the way you deliberately buggered about with my investigation at Westbury Park, you could have ended up in jail.'

'You'd never have made the charges stick,' Elizabeth Driver said with a complete absence of remorse. 'Anyway, I wasn't unemployed for long. I told you at the time I'd soon get another job. You remember that, don't you?'

'Aye, I remember.'

'And only three days after I'd picked up my cards from that tired little rag in Maltham, I was offered the plum post of northern crime correspondent for the *Daily Globe*.'

'I'm sure you an' the paper are well suited to one another,' Woodend told her.

'And just what do you mean by that?'

'Given the choice, the *Globe* has always preferred makin' up the news to reportin' it. Well, that's a lot less effort, isn't it?'

'The *Globe* is a serious national newspaper,' Elizabeth Driver said tightly.

'No, it isn't. It's a sensationalisin' scandal sheet of the worst kind,' Woodend corrected her. 'Always has been. Anyway, I take it that this meetin' isn't purely by chance.'

'Very few things I do are by chance,' Elizabeth Driver said complacently. 'I knew you'd want a pint, and I calculated you'd think that this pub was just far enough away from the studio to ensure you'd be safe from reporters.'

'You always were a smart lass,' Woodend told her. 'That's why it's such a pity to see you squanderin' your talents on a rag like the *Globe*.'

'It's not just my job situation which has changed since the last time we met – yours has as well,' Elizabeth Driver pointed out, with a cutting edge to her tone. 'You were a hot-shot from Scotland Yard back then. Now you're nothing but a country policeman.'

Woodend laughed with genuine amusement. 'You've got it all wrong,' he said. 'I've never been a hot-shot *anythin*', lass. I'm just a simple bobby whose job it is to catch criminals – when he can.'

'You don't *have to* stay out in the sticks for ever,' Elizabeth Driver told him. 'Scandal sheet or not, the *Globe* could do you a lot of good.'

'Could it?'

'Of course it could.'

'But you'd want somethin' in return?'

'Naturally I would.'

'An' what might that somethin' be?'

'If you were to make sure that I was told of new develop-
ments in the case a few hours before any of the other reporters,
I could build you up into some kind of national hero.'

'An' what if I don't want to be a national hero?'

'*Everybody* wants fame,' Elizabeth Driver said dismissively.
'Especially when you consider the alternative.'

'Which is?'

'Instead of portraying you as a hero, I could paint you as
a complete buffoon – the sort of music-hall comic policeman
who can't even find his own way home without a trained police
dog to show him the way. Imagine six million people picking
up the *Globe* and reading that!'

'Aye,' Woodend said. 'Just imagine it.'

'So what's it to be?' Elizabeth Driver demanded impatiently.
'Hero or buffoon? The choice is yours. Either of them will sell
papers.'

'I'll tell you the way I see it,' Woodend said softly.

Elizabeth Driver favoured him with a smile which was not
yet *quite* triumphant. 'Yes?' she said.

'I think you should do your job in the way you see fit, an'
I'll do the same thing with mine.'

'If that's a "no", you'll live to regret it,' Elizabeth Driver
cautioned him.

'Not as much as I'd regret it if I allowed myself to slip down
to your level,' Woodend replied.

'You'll never learn, will you?' Elizabeth Driver demanded
angrily. 'You've already lost one job through refusing to play
the game like everyone else – and if you're not careful, you'll
soon be losing another.'

Thirteen

When the phone rang on the desk he shared with Ben Drabble, Paddy Colligan made a dive for it, and once it was in his hand, he clamped the receiver tight against the side of his head.

'Colligan,' he said. 'Yes, I . . . No, it really isn't very convenient.'

Sitting opposite him, Ben Drabble wondered why Colligan seemed so concerned that even a hint of his caller's voice should not be allowed to seep out into the room.

'Yes, I was expecting you to ring just like you said you would,' Colligan mumbled. 'And of course I still . . . It's not that easy . . . There are a lot of things going on here right now.'

Drabble recognised the tone in his partner's voice as just like the one he himself used when he was talking to his bookmaker. But Paddy didn't gamble. As far as he knew, Paddy had no vices at all.

'I can't now,' Colligan said, '. . . because I just can't, that's why . . . you must understand the pressures.' He listened to his caller for perhaps thirty seconds without interruption, then sighed heavily. 'All right!' he said resignedly. 'Fifteen minutes – but no longer than that.'

Colligan slammed the phone back on its cradle. 'I have to go out,' he told his partner.

'Now?'

'Now! I won't be long. I told . . . I said I couldn't be away for more than fifteen minutes.'

'So it's somebody in the studio you have to meet?'

'I don't think that's really any of your business, is it, Ben?' Colligan asked coldly.

'Isn't it?' Drabble countered. 'We're working to a deadline here. You do realise we're still missing seven and a half minutes dialogue from Friday's show, don't you?'

'We'll probably work better after a short break,' Colligan said defensively. 'Anyway,' he continued, suddenly shifting into attack mode, 'I don't complain about all the time you spend on the phone placing bets on the horses, so what right have you got to start bitching when I want to slip out for a few minutes?'

It was not a good time to have an argument, Ben Drabble realised – not with seven and a half minutes of script still left to write.

'Sorry, I didn't mean to poke my nose in your affairs,' he said.

For some reason, the words seemed to make Paddy Colligan wince, then the Irishman forced a smile to his face and said, 'Don't worry about it. These things happen. With all the pressure we're under, it's actually a bit of miracle we haven't killed each other.'

Bad choice of words, given the circumstances, Drabble thought – but he knew what his partner meant.

Paddy Colligan had been gone from the office for less than five minutes when the phone rang again.

Ben Drabble, wrestling with the script, tried to ignore it, but the bloody thing kept on ringing. Finally, when it was plain it was not going to go away, he snatched up the receiver.

'Yes?' he said irritably.

The man on the other end of the line chuckled. 'Is that any way to talk to the person who's going to make your fortune for you?'

'Sorry, Vince,' Drabble said. 'Things are pretty tense in the office at the moment.'

'I imagine they are – for most people,' his agent said. 'But they shouldn't be for you. Hell, you should be cracking open a bottle of champagne after the stroke of luck you've had.'

'Stroke of luck?' Drabble repeated, mystified. 'What stroke of luck?'

'The murder! It couldn't have come at a better time, could it?'

'Couldn't it?'

'I'll say it couldn't,' his agent said cheerfully. 'Is that life imitating art – or what?'

'You're talking about my manuscript,' Drabble said, finally catching his agent's drift.

'Of course I'm talking about your manuscript. I've got *The Shooting Script* on my desk in front of me, right now. I was going to start submitting it last week – but am I glad I waited?! The murder should at least triple the advance we can expect to be paid. And as for sales – they'll go through the roof! When the publishers reveal that the writer of a book about a murder in a television studio was actually working in a *real* television studio where a *real* murder was committed, the public will be queuing up to buy copies.'

A vision of sudden wealth swam before Ben Drabble's eyes – but unlike many other people's visions in similar circumstances, it did not centre on what he could buy. Or perhaps, in a way, it did. The money would buy him peace of mind. The money would help him to escape from the fear which periodically gnawed at his innards. There would be no more menacing late-night phone calls. He would be able to walk down a dark alley without wondering whether there were two large men at the end of it, waiting to break his legs. He could pay off all his gambling debts. He would be free to start life again.

'Well, aren't you going to say anything?' his agent asked.

Words seemed inadequate to describe the feeling of well-being which had swept over him, Drabble thought.

'I suppose you're right,' he said weakly.

'You *suppose*!' his agent repeated, incredulously. 'Don't try to tell me that you haven't been worrying about your book sinking without trace – just like so many others do.'

'I—'

'And don't try to tell me you haven't already worked out for yourself that this murder is the best possible publicity you could have got.'

'I may have thought about it in vague terms,' Drabble confessed, 'but I certainly wouldn't have put it as strongly as you have. And if I can make a suggestion, Vince?'

'Yes?'

'When you start negotiating with the publishers, it might be a good idea if you didn't sound quite so enthusiastic about the fact that Valerie Farnsworth has been murdered.'

'Oh sure, I get it,' the agent said – and Drabble could almost see him giving a broad wink.

'Anyway, thanks for calling,' the scriptwriter said, eager to put the phone down and revel in his new-found freedom in private.

'Hang on a minute. I haven't quite finished what I rang up to say to you,' his agent told him.

There was a new edge to the man's tone – a wheedling, yet commanding edge – which made Drabble's stomach suddenly turn over.

'Go on,' he said cautiously.

'The thing is, I know that all you writers are a mite touchy about changing anything once you've actually written it down . . .'

'Touchy?' Drabble repeated.

'Sure. And I can understand it. You think you've finished the job, and you'd rather go out and have a good time than plough through the same material all over again.'

'What are you suggesting?' Drabble demanded angrily. 'That our unwillingness to change things is no more than laziness?'

'Hey, kid, don't get so tense,' the agent said.

'We don't *just* write it down, you know,' Drabble said passionately. 'We agonise over every word. We sweat blood. And when we do finally manage to come up with the exact expression we've been searching so hard for—'

'Yeah, I know you work very hard,' the agent said, trying not to sound indifferent. 'And it's because I know it's such hard work that I don't want to see it all go to waste. That's why – just to make *absolutely* sure we've got a rip-roaring success on our hands – I'd like you to make just a few adjustments to the plot.'

'Writing's not like painting a wall!' Drabble protested. 'When you've finished, you can't just step back and look at the finished result, then touch up the odd spot here and the odd spot there. A book is an organic whole in which everything relates to everything else.'

'Well, *I* know that,' the agent said. 'Of course I do. But the changes I want you to make are very minor.'

'How minor?' Drabble asked suspiciously.

'This is only a suggestion. Right?'

'Right.'

'I think the book would have a lot more punch – publicity-wise – if you changed the victim?'

'If I *what*?'

'Changed the victim. See, in the light of the murder, *The Shooting Script* would make more of an impact if the person who got killed was one of the actresses, rather than the show's producer.'

Fourteen

M aria Rutter heard the front door of her new detached home click open and she shifted her weight as a preliminary manoeuvre in the complicated process of getting out of her armchair.

She would be glad when her pregnancy finally came to full term, she thought, because however difficult it might turn out to be for a blind woman to look after her baby, it would be nothing less than a blessed relief after all this backache and general discomfort.

There were heavy male footsteps in the hallway.

'Is that you, Bob?' Maria asked.

'It's me,' Rutter answered – and from the sound of his voice she could tell that something or other was not quite right with his world.

'I didn't really expect you to be coming home for lunch, sweetheart,' Maria said.

'I didn't expect to be home myself,' Rutter replied, almost gruffly.

Maria waited for him to expand on the comment, but when it became plain that he wasn't about to, she said, 'I thought you were working somewhere near Bolton.'

'Not me. Just Cloggin'-it Charlie and Paniatowski. It turned out I wasn't really necessary.'

Maria frowned. In the previous few months, as she had grown accustomed to her blindness, she had become much better at imagining people's expressions from the sound of their voices – but she still wished that she could see her husband's face.

'I'll make you some food,' she said.

There was an awkward pause, then Bob said, 'Actually,

I'm in a bit of a hurry, so I'll fix it myself.'

She had to get quicker at doing things, she told herself. She had to learn to perform tasks around the house almost as well as if she could see.

Rutter walked into the kitchen, and Maria forced herself out of her chair and followed him. She heard the sound of a cupboard door being opened, and the noise of several tins being banged together.

'Baked beans on toast?' she guessed.

'That's right,' Rutter agreed.

For the first time since he had entered the house, she could detect a smile in his voice. Well, whatever had happened that morning, at least he could still summon up the energy to smile!

She reached out with her hand, and was pleased to discover the back of the kitchen chair was exactly where she'd thought it would be. She pulled the chair out and lowered herself carefully into it.

'Are you going to tell me what it's all about?' she asked.

'What what's all about?' Rutter said brusquely, as he clamped the tin-opener over the can and began to turn.

'I may be blind, but I'm not stupid,' Maria said angrily.

The tin-opener stopped turning. Rutter walked over to her and began softly stroking her hair.

'I know you're not stupid,' he said apologetically. 'And I'm so sorry for taking my mood out on you.'

'Why are you in the mood in the first place?'

'The boss has sent me back to Whitebridge because he thinks that he and Paniatowski can handle the investigation in the studio by themselves,' Rutter told her, bitterly.

'I'm sure Charlie Woodend would never have phrased it quite like that,' Maria said.

'No, he didn't,' Rutter admitted. 'What he actually said was that I could be most useful supervising the team which was checking the statements for inconsistencies, and that if I did it from headquarters rather than from the studio, it would help to keep DCS Ainsworth – or Dick the Prick, as he's affectionately known – happy.'

'Well, then? What's your problem?'

Rutter sighed. 'Well, it's just sugaring the pill, isn't it? What he really means is that he'd rather work with Paniatowski.'

Maria shook her head. 'How can you even think that?' she asked. 'You know as well as I do that the reason Charlie stuck his neck out to get you an early promotion was because he didn't want to leave you behind in London – because he didn't want to break up the team.'

'That was then,' Rutter said. 'That was before he started working with the wonderful Sergeant Paniatowski.'

'This has nothing to do with Monika,' Maria said quietly.

'Doesn't it?'

'No.'

'Then what has it got to do with?'

'With Charlie finally coming to realise that things have to change – and your refusal to see it yourself.'

'You sound as if you always knew that this kind of thing was going to happen,' Rutter said.

'Well, of course I knew. It was practically *bound* to happen.'

'Would you care to explain why?'

'Because you're what Charlie Woodend would call "a very bright lad". You're an inspector now, and in a few years' time, you'll be a chief inspector – his equal.'

'Unless he's been promoted to superintendent by then.'

Maria laughed. 'The way Charlie goes about conducting his cases, he'll *never* be promoted,' she said. 'I'm not sure that he even wants to be. But that's not the point.'

'So what is?'

'Sooner or later, you've got to stop acting like his bagman – and it might as well be sooner.'

'That's pretty much what he said to me himself,' Rutter admitted.

'And he was spot-on. Look, Bob, if inspectors didn't have a role to play in their own right, the job wouldn't exist. So what you should do is find out exactly what that role involves – and get on with it.'

Rutter gently pulled her head to his chest. 'You're a complete marvel,' he told her.

'Yes, I do have my uses,' Maria said complacently. She

paused for a second. 'There is one other thing you can do.'

'Yes?'

'It's something that Charlie's been doing for everyone who's worked under him for years – but which he'd never ask anybody else to do for him.'

'And what's that?'

'You know what he's like when he's working on a case. Nothing else exists for him. Other men of his rank spend half their time plotting and scheming – Charlie just gets on with the job.'

'That's true enough,' Rutter agreed. 'I suppose that's what makes him such a bloody good bobby.'

'But he does need somebody watching his back,' Maria said, 'and since he won't do it himself, I think that "someone" should be you.'

Fifteen

It would not have been quite accurate to describe the *Maddox Row* studio canteen as a 'room', Monika Paniatowski decided. It was really no more than a large alcove off the central concourse. Its walls were made of bare breeze-blocks, and its floor covered with heavy chocolate-brown industrial linoleum. Strip lighting hung overhead, filling the whole area with an antiseptic glare. It was not the kind of place she would choose to spend much time in, she thought as she paid for her cup of tea and digestive biscuits at the counter – but then perhaps the whole purpose of its design had been to discourage unnecessary lingering.

The sergeant looked quickly around the room. Several of the cheap Formica tables were unoccupied, but she was not tempted to go to one of them, because she would learn absolutely nothing sitting alone. Instead, her gaze settled on a table which was occupied by three women. They were all in their early twenties and all respectably – if not expensively – dressed. And, as if they'd been drawn together by the need to create a contrast, one was a heavy blonde, one a skinny brunette and the third a curvaceous redhead.

Perfect! Monika thought.

She carried her tray over to women's table, hovered uncertainly for a moment, then said, 'Do you mind if I join you?'

The women looked up.

'You what?' the heavy blonde asked.

'I was wondering if I could join you,' the detective sergeant repeated meekly. 'You see, it's my first day here, and I don't know a soul in the place. Then I saw you, and I thought to myself: Come on, Monika, don't be a wallflower all your life – force yourself to start talking to somebody.'

94

The three women exchanged questioning, almost tribal looks, then the redhead smiled and said, 'Well, I suppose that now you've made the effort, you'd better sit down.'

Monika returned the smile with an artfully shy and grateful one of her own, and slid into the spare seat.

'You chose a rum day to start working here – what with there bein' a murder an' us havin' bobbies runnin' all over the place,' the blonde said.

'I wouldn't have been working here *at all* if it hadn't been for the murder,' Monika said.

'How's that?'

'I'm only a temp. I'm replacing the girl who actually found the body. Apparently she's in too much of a state to come into work herself.'

The announcement caused the temperature around the table to drop by several degrees.

'So you're working for Jeremy Wilcox, are you?' the heavy blonde girl asked warily, after several seconds had passed.

'That's right,' Monika agreed.

'Ooh!' the skinny brunette said, in what could only be called mock awe. 'So you're practically management, then!'

Which automatically makes me an enemy, Monika thought.

She laughed, self-deprecatingly. 'Not really management. Not at all, in fact. Like I said, I'm only here for a few days, until the regular girl feels better – then it's back to the typing pool in head office for me.'

'We're from the typing pool here in the studio,' said the blonde.

Well, of course you are. What else could you be? Monika thought. But she kept the remark to herself.

'So what do you think of our Mr Wilcox?' the brunette asked.

It was not so much as casual question as a test, Monika realised. If she gave the right answer, they would be on her side. If she gave the wrong one, they would freeze her out again.

'Mr Wilcox? I suppose he's much the same as every other boss I've ever worked for,' she said carefully.

'The same in what way?' the brunette asked sceptically.

'Oh, you know!'

'I'm not sure we do. Why don't you explain it to us?'

Monika shrugged. 'Well, he seems very full of himself, if you want to know the truth. And he seems quite happy to just sit back and let other people do most of the work, while he's the one who pulls in the big wage.'

The vigorous nods from the blonde and the redhead – and the grudging one from the skinny brunette – told her she'd said exactly the right thing.

'You want to watch him,' the brunette advised.

'Who?'

'Mr Wandering-hands Jeremy Wilcox, that's who. If he ever asks you to stay behind and do a bit of overtime for him, make sure he never gets between you and the door.'

'Like that, is he?'

'He's tried it on with every girl in the place,' the skinny brunette said. 'Of course,' she continued, glaring at the redhead, 'there's some who are more willing to give into him than others.'

'It was the Christmas party, and he caught me under the mistletoe,' the redhead protested. 'What was I supposed to do?'

'I know what I'd have done!'

'If he'd ever given you the chance!'

'Who do you think killed Val Farnsworth?' Paniatowski said, stepping into the middle of the developing catfight before any blood was actually drawn.

The three typists fell instantly silent, but Paniatowski did not miss the rapid glances they gave each other.

'Doesn't any of you have any idea?' the sergeant asked. 'I know if I'd been working here, I'd have been bursting with theories.'

There was more eye contact between the three women, then the blonde said, 'Well, when you think about it, it could have been anybody, couldn't it? I mean, for all we know, it might even have been a passin' tramp.'

'Come on, don't be so stuffy. We're only playing a game here,' Paniatowski cajoled. 'After all, it's not as if any of us know a bobby, is it?'

'If you must know, we think it was one of the cast,' the brunette said, almost in a whisper.

'One of the—!' Paniatowski exclaimed. Then she, too, lowered her voice. 'You think it was one of the cast? In heaven's name, why?'

'Because, as far as they were concerned, Val Farnsworth was getting far too big for her boots,' the brunette said. 'She hadn't quite gone as far as suggesting that they change the name of the show to *The Liz Bowyer Half-Hour*, but she would have done in the end. And the other actors didn't like it.'

'Did they tell you that themselves?' Paniatowski probed.

'Of course they didn't tell us!' the brunette said contemptuously. 'They're far too important, these days, to lower themselves to talk to anybody from the typing pool.'

'Then how do you—?'

'There are other ways we can get to know things. You'd be surprised how many scripts we've had to re-type because Valerie Farnsworth didn't like this line here, or wanted another line adding there. The woman was like a little tin god.' A horrified look came to the brunette's face, as if she were hearing her own words as others might hear them. 'Not that I want to speak ill of the dead,' she added hastily.

'Still, at least they won't have to kill anybody else off in the script, now,' the heavy blonde said.

'What do you mean?' Paniatowski asked.

'The show's been losing viewers recently – I know, because I was the one who typed up the reports.'

'The management think we're nothing but robots,' the brunette said. 'They think we just sit there hitting the keys on our machines, and we don't have a clue what it is we're typing. Well, they're dead wrong. We have more of an idea what's going on round here than most people do. Certainly more than the bloody actors – who can't see anything beyond their own lines.'

'Somebody at head office made the suggestion that the company should quit while it was ahead – take the show off the air when it was still quite popular,' the redhead whispered conspiratorially. 'I don't think it would have come quite to that, but even if they'd just cut it back to one episode a week – which was one of the other plans – things would have been bad enough. You don't need anything like as many people when you're filling half an hour of airtime a week, instead of an hour. Actors, technicians, caterers – they'd all have suffered. The typing pool wouldn't have got away unscathed, either.'

'I still don't see . . .' Paniatowski said.

'Have you ever listened to *The Archers* on the wireless?' the redhead asked her.

'Now and again.'

'It's a bit like *Maddox Row* in a way – except that it's set in the country rather than the town, and there's no pictures, but only voices.'

'True,' Paniatowski agreed, mystified.

'It's a very popular series, is *The Archers*, but the BBC were really worried that independent television might take a big chunk of its audience away from it. So do you know what they did?'

'No. As I said, I'm not a regular listener.'

'On the night of ITV's first broadcast, there was a fire in *The Archers*. A serious one. So serious that Grace Archer, who was one of the main characters, was burned to death. That was over five years ago, but I can remember it as clearly as it was yesterday.'

'So can I,' agreed the blonde. 'The next morning, everybody at work was still in a state of shock. Nobody mentioned the new television station. All they wanted to talk about was poor Grace's death.'

'Do you see what we're saying?' the brunette asked.

'I'm not quite sure,' Paniatowski said – although she thought that she had a pretty fair idea.

'When the last lot of viewing figures for *Maddox Row* came in, there were memos flying all over the place,' the brunette said. 'The management was going spare. Talk about your headless chickens! There was a lot of talk about what they should do get the figures up again, and in the end it was decided the best way was to kill one of the most popular characters off. The one they finally decided on was Jack Taylor, the postman. I expect that was because the actor who plays him – Larry Coates – is planning to leave the series soon anyway.'

'He was supposed to die in next Monday's episode,' the blonde said. 'The idea was that people would keep tuning in to see how the other characters would take his death for at least a week, and by then they'd have been hooked on another plot-line.'

'Would it have worked?' Paniatowski asked the redhead.

The other woman laughed. 'How am I supposed to know? I'm just a copy typist, not a highly paid executive like your new boss.'

'You seem like a bright girl, and you've been in this business for a while,' Paniatowski coaxed. 'You must have some thoughts about whether it would have been a good idea or not.'

'I think it *was* a good idea,' the redhead said, obviously flattered that her opinion carried so much weight with the new girl. 'Nobody would have given a monkey's if Andy Sutcliffe, the Row's layabout, had got himself topped, but Jack Taylor's a very popular character, and people would have felt as if they'd lost one of their own family. I know I would have watched, and I'd have already known what was going to happen. Still, there'll be no need for Jack to meet with an unfortunate accident now, will there?'

'Won't there?' Paniatowski asked.

'Of course there won't. After all the publicity we got in the papers this morning, we'll have the highest viewing figures we've ever had on Friday night – however they decide to explain away Liz Bowyer's disappearance.'

'And nobody will be in any danger of losing their jobs,' Paniatowski said sombrely.

'You don't think . . . ?' the blonde woman began.

'I don't think what?'

'You don't think that somebody killed Valerie Farnsworth just to make sure they kept getting a pay packet every Friday?'

'No, that never even occurred to me,' Paniatowski said.

But she had come across less compelling motives for murder in the past.

Sixteen

J ane Todd didn't look the least as Woodend had pictured she would. There was no evidence at all of a hard shell coating about her, nor did she have the young, sleek, sophisticated look which would have blended in well with Houseman's office décor. Instead, she turned out to be a plump, middle-aged woman with amused eyes and a no-nonsense air about her.

'Now where shall I take you first?' she asked, when Houseman had first grudgingly performed the introductions, and then beat a hasty retreat. 'The studio would be as good a place as any to start. But be prepared to be disappointed.'

'Disappointed?' Woodend repeated, puzzled.

'You are a fan of the show, aren't you?' Jane Todd asked. 'I can usually spot them.'

'Yes, I'm a fan,' Woodend admitted.

'Then I would say disappointment's pretty much inevitable.'

Woodend began to understand what she'd meant the moment they entered the studio and he saw the set for the house exteriors. The street looked so convincing on television, but close up it was revealed to be a shoddy plywood structure on which the slightly crumbled brickwork was merely painted, and the brass doorknockers were obviously made out of plastic. It looked narrower and shorter than it did on the screen, too.

'Clever camera angles – that's how they do it,' said Jane Todd, reading his mind.

The familiar *Maddox Row* living rooms were even more disillusioning. If he'd thought about it, Woodend would have realised that, for practical reasons, they would only have three walls – but he *hadn't* thought about it, and it came as something of a shock. And even the walls that *were* there ended at a point

100

which must have been only inches above the top of the taller characters' heads.

'What's the reason for that?' Woodend asked, touching the top of the wall gingerly with his fingertips. 'Do they build them so low to save money?'

'No, it's more to do with lighting,' Jane Todd told him. 'The higher the overhead lights have to be, the steeper the angle and the coarser the portraiture which results.'

'I see,' Woodend said unconvincingly.

More disappointments lay in store for him. The door at the back of Madge Thornycroft's living room led not a kitchen, but out on to the studio floor, only a few steps from Sam Fuller's living room – even though their houses were located at opposite ends of the Row. Dot Taylor had been standing on these stairs when she'd fallen down and broken her leg, but there seemed to have been no point in her being on them at all, since they didn't lead anywhere.

'Is this all there is?' Woodend asked, when they'd finished their tour.

'What makes you ask that?' Jane Todd wondered.

'I don't remember seein' Tilly Woods' livin' room,' Woodend explained.

'Even in a studio this size, there's not room to have all the sets erected,' Jane Todd said. 'The Tinker's Bucket and the corner shop are permanent fixtures, because they're in nearly every episode, but the rest of the sets are kept in storage when they're not being used.'

'I see,' Woodend said.

Jane Todd laughed.

'What's so funny?' Woodend asked.

'You are,' Jane said, with a complete lack of inhibition.
'Me?'

'Oh, not *just* you, but everybody we ever show around the studio. I told you you'd be disappointed, didn't I? You all know before you come in here that *Maddox Row* is nothing but make-believe, yet you still end up looking like kids who've just been told there's no such thing as Santa Claus.'

Woodend grinned ruefully. 'You're right. That's just how I feel.'

'Well, now you've had all your illusions well and truly shattered, shall I take you to see the rest of the place?' Jane suggested.

'Aye, we might as well have the full two-bob tour while we're about it,' Woodend agreed, following her to the studio door.

The world on the other side of the dividing wall was very different to the one they were leaving. If he'd chosen to glance upwards, Woodend would have seen the high mill ceiling, but looking straight ahead he once again had the feeling that he was in the open air, walking through a village.

'We just had dividing walls between the various departments at first,' Jane Todd said, following his gaze, 'but it didn't take us long to discover that that simply wouldn't work.'

'Why not?'

'The noise, mostly. We couldn't hear ourselves think, what with the carpenters banging away from one end of the building and the typists pounding away on their machines from the other. The actors didn't like it either – said they couldn't "compose" themselves before the show with all that racket going on. So Mr Houseman had the flat roofs put on, and now I can sit in his office and hardly hear any of the work going on around me.'

'He seems like a thoughtful man, your Mr Houseman,' Woodend said.

'Does he?' Jane Todd said enigmatically. 'That's the office block on your right. You've already been in there, haven't you?'

'That's right, I have,' Woodend agreed. 'Who else works in that particular block, apart from Houseman?'

'Well, it's where Mr Wilcox has his office, then there's the conference rooms, the typing pool, the finance and ordering department, the public relations office and the entertainment suite. It takes quite a lot of people who never have anything to do with lights and cameras to put on a television show, you know.'

'Aye, that's the picture I was already beginnin' to build up,' Woodend said.

'On the other side of the central concourse, we have the various technical departments,' Jane Todd continued, pointing out several more buildings-within-a-building. 'That's the scenery workshop, where the chippies build and maintain all the sets, and next to it is the scenery store. Beyond that is where we keep the technical equipment we're not actually using in the studio, and there's a repair shop attached to it. The last part of the technical department is the . . .' – her voice cracked a little – '. . . is the . . .'

'Is the tool store that the murderer got the screwdriver from,' Woodend supplied, noticing the police seal on the door.

'That's right,' Jane Todd agreed. 'It was a horrible way to be killed, wasn't it?'

'There aren't that many nice ways to be violently murdered,' Woodend pointed out.

They passed the café alcove, and Woodend averted his gaze from the blonde sergeant who appeared to be deep in conversation with three young women who were probably from the typing pool.

'Refectory and kitchen,' Jane Todd said, unnecessarily. 'And on the other side are the various departments with the responsibility for getting the actors ready to appear.'

'Like what?' Woodend asked.

'The props department – walking sticks, spectacles, anything the actors might need for a particular scene. Next to that is the costume department – which is pretty self-explanatory. Finally, there's the make-up department. A lot of their work is done on the set, of course, but if they have a particularly challenging job on their hands, they like to do it in there.'

'You seem to know a lot about everythin' that's goin' on in the studio,' Woodend said.

Jane Todd smiled. 'I work for Mr Houseman, and Mr Houseman likes to keep a finger in every pie. More often than not, that finger is me.'

From their table in the cafeteria, George Adams and Jennifer Brunton watched Jane Todd and the man in the hairy sports jacket walk past.

'He doesn't look much like a hot-shot policeman, does he?' George Adams asked.

'You can't judge a book by its cover,' Jennifer Brunton replied. 'And you should know that better than most people.'

That was true enough, Adams agreed silently. Whenever he opened a village fête – forty pounds in used notes in his back pocket, and no questions asked – he met dozens of people who seemed to feel almost cheated that instead of meeting the shuffling pensioner, Sam Fuller, from *Maddox Row*, they ended up talking to the vigorous actor who played him.

'Yes, to look at you now, nobody would ever guess you once had to get up at seven o'clock in the morning to slop out,' Jennifer Brunton continued.

So that was it! George Adams thought. She wasn't talking about him as an *actor* at all – she was talking about him as a man with a past. What a bitch she could be when she put her mind to it – and sometimes even when she didn't!

'Well, your fairy godmother must certainly have been working overtime for you yesterday,' he said casually, beginning his counter-attack.

'What exactly do you mean by that?'

Adams shrugged. 'Nothing much – just that you got your wish.'

Jennifer Brunton frowned. 'I don't know what you're talking about. What wish?'

'Don't you remember?' Adams asked, feigning surprise. 'We were all in rehearsal, and Val threw a tantrum. You called her – I think I've got the words right – "a bloody prima donna", and said it was about time somebody taught her a lesson she wouldn't forget in a hurry. Well, somebody *did* teach her a lesson, though she's never going to have the chance to learn from it now, is she?'

'I . . . I never meant I wanted to see her dead!' Jennifer Brunton protested. 'How can you even suggest such a thing?'

'I didn't actually *suggest* it,' George Adams countered. 'But you must admit that you're not exactly heartbroken now that she is, are you?'

'I'm very, very sorry that—'

'You're very, very sorry that the murderer didn't wait

until after Larry Coates had left the show before he did the dirty deed.'

'I don't know what you're talking about.'

'Oh yes, you do. Somebody has to step into the spotlight now that Val's gone, and if Larry hadn't been available, it would probably have been you.'

'Or you,' Jennifer Brunton said hotly. 'Neither of us can say for certain who Bill Houseman would have decided to make the big star if Larry hadn't been around. But I do know *one thing* for certain.'

'And what's that?'

'As much as I'd like to take Val's place, I don't care about it half as much as you do, George. You want to be the star so badly, you'd kill for it.'

Even without seeing the look which her remarks brought to George Adams' face, she would have realised she'd made a mistake the moment the words were out of her mouth.

'I was . . . er . . . only speaking metaphorically,' she added lamely.

'Perhaps you were, but you should still choose your words more carefully,' George Adams said. 'After all, an old friend like me isn't going to misinterpret what you said, but there are others who might – and that could be as dangerous for you as it would be for me – because neither of us are above suspicion.'

'Are you saying that *I'm* a suspect?' Jennifer Brunton demanded.

'You know you are. Both of us will benefit from Val's death, even if all it amounts to is a few extra lines each episode – and it won't do either of us any good to go pointing the finger at the other.'

He was right, Jennifer Brunton thought, and though she was loath to abandon the exchange when he was so far ahead on points, it was probably the wisest thing to do in the circumstances. She looked around her for some distraction, and found it in the shape of a platinum blonde who was just walking past the cafeteria.

'I wonder what's made the Queen Consort favour us with her presence again,' she said sourly, watching the blonde's buttocks roll in leopardskin trousers like two dwarfs fighting in a sack.

'Could be our revered leader is taking her out to dinner somewhere once his day of creative genius is done,' George Adams suggested.

'Perhaps he is,' Jennifer Brunton agreed. 'But I'd be willing to bet that before she sits down at the table with her husband, she'll be *lying* down with someone else entirely.' She paused. 'Do you think Bill *knows* that his wife's got a fancy man?'

'I can't make up my mind about that,' Adams replied. 'On the one hand, if he did know, you'd expect him to blow his top. But on the other, if he knew but thought that *we* didn't know, he might have decided his best course of action was just to keep quiet about the whole thing.'

'I don't think Bill *does* know,' Jennifer Brunton said. 'If he did, then surely he'd get rid of the bugger. I mean, it's not as if Diana's bit-on-the-side is anybody important, is it? Bill could find a replacement for him before he'd even had time to leave the building.'

'That's true,' George Adams said. 'It'd be easy enough to replace most of the people involved with the show. One electrician's pretty much like another. You never really notice when a new scriptwriter takes over. Any fool can tell the cameramen which direction to point their cameras in. And as for actresses, well, how hard is it play a one-dimensional character like the *Maddox Row* battleaxe, when you come to think about it?' He clapped his hand over his mouth in mock horror, then quickly removed it again. 'I'm sorry about that, Jennifer. I didn't mean to say it, but it just slipped out. Habit, I suppose.'

A dangerous gleam appeared in Jennifer Brunton's eyes as she abandoned their temporary truce.

'A very *bad* habit,' she said stonily. 'Like your habit of drinking with the hacks from the scandal sheets until all hours of the night. Of course, that particular habit shouldn't be too hard to break, now.'

'What do you mean – now?'

'There's more than one way to skin a cat,' Jennifer Brunton said reflectively. 'If the journalists had been prepared to print all those libellous stories you were feeding them about Val's sex life, she'd probably have lost her job. But they weren't prepared to print them, were they? Your little plan didn't work out. And now it doesn't need to.'

Seventeen

The building-within-a-building that Woodend and Jane Todd were standing in front of was quite unlike any of the ones the chief inspector had seen thus far. It was built in an L shape. The shorter arm of the L was at right angles to the main concourse, the longer one some distance away from it, much closer to the side wall of the mill. There were no doors in the long arm, but there were windows which looked out on to an area containing a number of shrubs and potted plants and park benches. The whole complex reminded Woodend of the chalets at a holiday camp where he'd once investigated a particularly macabre murder.

'Mr Houseman calls that "the Actors' Garden",' Jane Todd said, pointing to the shrubs. 'He says that it's somewhere the cast can go when they want to get away from it all.'

'He seems a very thoughtful man,' Woodend commented, once again.

'He can be,' Jane Todd said noncommittally.

'An' what's that supposed to mean?'

'Bill can be very kind and understanding, and totally unreasonable and dictatorial, almost in the same breath. What I think he is most of all is frightened.'

'Frightened?'

'Some achieve greatness, and some have greatness thrust upon them. In Bill's case, it was a combination of the two. He fought hard to get the show on the air, but he never imagined what a great success it was going to be. And the sad fact is you need to be totally ruthless to handle a great success properly, and Bill isn't. Oh, he tries – and sometimes he puts on a fairly good show – but it takes an effort. I think there are times when he almost wishes *Maddox Row* had never happened.'

'He could always give it up,' Woodend suggested. 'Go back to producin' puppet shows.'

Jane Todd shook her head. 'No, he couldn't. The show may not make him as happy as he might once have thought it would, but the prospect of losing it is enough to drive him to despair. He's like a drug addict who has to have his fix, even if he knows it's a very bad idea.'

'Must be difficult workin' for him sometimes,' Woodend said sympathetically.

'It is,' Jane Todd agreed, 'but it's worth it. I like being the producer's assistant. The job pays well, and it's a lot more interesting than most secretarial work. And if you're wondering why he employs me when he could hire some young tottie with legs all the way up to her neck . . .'

'I wasn't.'

'. . . it's because I'm the best damn PA this side of London.'

'Aye, I can well believe you are,' Woodend said. He shifted his gaze back to the shrubbery. 'Since this is the Actors' Garden, I assume the buildin' that runs around two sides of it is the actors' dressing rooms.'

'That's right.' Jane pointed to a window in the long arm of the L. 'That's Valerie's dressing room . . . *was* Valerie's dressing room, I should say.'

'An' how did she get into it? Climb through the window?'

Jane Todd shook her head. 'The doors to the dressing rooms are all around the back. That was one of Mr Houseman's ideas as well. It gives the cast a real sense of privacy, you see.'

Yes, and it also makes it very convenient for murderers who don't want to run too much of a risk of being spotted, Woodend thought.

They turned left, and walked down the alley which ran between the make-up department and the short arm of the dressing-room wing. It was as they rounded the corner that they came across the young uniformed constable. He was standing in front of the door to Valerie Farnsworth's dressing room, smoking a Woodbine. When he saw them approaching, he quickly cupped the cigarette in the palm of his hand. Then, realising that would prevent him from saluting, he dropped the cigarette to the ground and covered it quickly with the heel of his boot.

'I'm PC . . . PC Armitage, sir,' he said, looking flustered.

Woodend smiled at him. 'It sounds like you recognise me, lad. Have we met before?'

Armitage reddened. 'No, sir. But I've seen your picture in all the newspapers, sir. After that case in Blackpool, sir. The one where you made the arrest right on top of the Tower.'

'Fame at last,' Woodend said to Jane Todd, then he glanced down at the constable's boots. 'There was no need for you to go through all that rigmarole of crushin' your fag, lad. Even if you have got money to burn, you might as well enjoy it while it's burnin' . . .'

'We're . . . we're not supposed to smoke on duty, sir.'

'. . . an' if I'd been given a bloody borin' job like yours, I'd probably feel like havin' a bit of a smoke, myself.'

'Yes, sir. Thank you, sir.'

'Have forensics finished in there?' Woodend asked, jabbing his thumb in the direction of the dressing-room door.

'Yes, sir. I believe so, sir.'

'Then there's not much point in you still standin' there guardin' it, is there? Go an' grab yourself a cup of tea, then call Inspector Hebden an' say that I won't be needin' you any more.'

'Yes, sir. I'll do that, sir.'

As the constable marched away, Woodend noticed that a slight smile was playing on Jane Todd's lips.

'Have I said somethin' funny again?' he asked.

'Perhaps,' the producer's assistant replied. 'Do you want to see the dressing room?'

'Aye, I'd like to see it, but you don't have to come in with me if it'll bother you.'

'I used to be an operating theatre nurse before I realised I could do more for humanity by helping to bring it *Maddox Row*,' Jane Todd said, as an ironic smile flitted briefly across her face. 'So don't you worry, Mr Woodend, the smell of death is no stranger to me.'

Woodend stood in the doorway, and looked across the room at the dressing table. It would not have taken the killer more than a couple of seconds to cross the room and plunge the screwdriver he was carrying into Valerie Farnsworth's back. And a few seconds after that, it would've been all over – Valerie Farnsworth lying dead on the floor and the murderer making his way quickly to another part of the studio.

His gaze swept the rest of the room. There was a small desk, a couch, a clothes rack – and nothing more. The room itself would provide him with none of the answers he was looking for, but perhaps it would serve to confirm some of the suspicions he already had.

'As an ex-nurse used to blood an' gore, you don't mind bein' left alone in here, do you?' he asked Jane Todd.

'Not in the slightest.'

'Right,' Woodend said. 'I want you to wait for a minute or so, then I'd appreciate it if you'd scream at the top of your voice.'

'I beg your pardon?'

'Scream. As loud as you can. As if you were bein' murdered.'

'Oh, I see,' Jane Todd said. 'You want to see if the sound will travel.'

'That's it,' Woodend agreed.

The room next to the one which had been used by the late Valerie Farnsworth was similarly furnished with a dressing table, desk and couch, but unlike Farnsworth's room this one was occupied.

Woodend looked down at the man who was sprawled out on the couch. 'You're Jack Taylor, the Laughin' Postman!' he said, before he could stop himself. 'I'm sorry, I meant you're . . .'

'Larry Coates,' the other man replied, slurring his words slightly. 'But there's no need to apologise for the mistake, my dear man. After two years hard labour in *Maddox Row*, my own mother probably thinks I'm really Jack-bloody-Taylor. And now it looks like I'm stuck with being the

Laughing Postman till they carry me out of this place feet first.'

'I'm sorry for having disturbed you,' Woodend said. 'I didn't realise the cast would be here at this time of day.'

Coates laughed. 'When you're watching *Madro* on the telly, it may look as if we're making it up as we go along,' he said, 'but let me assure you, we're not. Our dear director, a sainted man who's really far too good for this kind of thing – or so he keeps on telling us – insists that we rehearse every line until we could say it in our sleep. And let me tell you, the way some of my fellow actors deliver their speeches, it looks as if they're doing just that.'

'You didn't happen to be in here last night, at about half past six, did you?' Woodend asked.

'Ah, from your tone I'd say you were a policeman!' Coates said. 'Either that, or one of my fellow hams who's just being *playing* a policeman and still hasn't been able to shake the role off.'

'No, I'm not acting, I'm the genuine article,' Woodend assured him. '*Were* you here last night?'

'When poor old Valerie did the Julius Caesar death scene for real? Yes, I was.' He reached on to the floor and picked up an empty glass and a half-full bottle of malt whisky. 'There's another glass somewhere on the dressing table, if you'd care to join me.'

'It's a bit early in the day for me to go on to the hard stuff, sir,' Woodend told him.

'I thought you were supposed to say, "Thank you, sir, but not while I'm on duty."'

Woodend grinned. 'I think you've seen a few too many policemen in plays an' films, sir.' He became serious again. 'You were here when Miss Farnsworth was killed, and you still didn't hear anything?'

'Not a peep. Of course, voice projection never was one of Valerie's strong points.'

'If you don't mind me sayin' so, sir, you don't seem very upset by Miss Farnsworth's death,' Woodend said.

'You're wrong there,' Coates replied. 'I'm *very* upset indeed. That's why I'm already half-pissed before the sun's even gone down. Not that I cared much for dear Valerie herself – I'd absolutely hate it if you thought that. Valerie wasn't the kind of woman to inspire affection – she'd have slit her own grandmother's throat if she'd thought that would get her moved up a couple of lines on the cast list. But she's certainly chosen an extremely inconvenient time to take her final curtain – at least from my point of view.'

Woodend walked to the dressing table, and picked up the spare glass, which was standing next to a copy of *Variety* magazine. 'Perhaps I will have a little drop of malt, if you don't mind, sir,' he said.

'I'm always delighted to corrupt a guardian of the law,' Coates said, filling the glass almost to the top.

Woodend took a sip of the whisky. It was very smooth, and probably very expensive.

'What did you mean about it bein' an inconvenient time for you, sir?' he asked.

'Oh, you don't want to hear the whole heart-rendering story of my life,' Coates said off-handedly.

'As a matter of fact, I do,' Woodend told him. 'Or as much of it as you can get through while I'm suppin' this excellent malt of yours.'

'This show was the making of all us actors who appear in it,' Coates said. 'Before we were hired by *Maddox Row*, our greatest ambition was to be promoted from "fourth spear carrier" to "third spear carrier". Which meant, as I'm sure you'll appreciate, that when we were given the chance to appear on the telly, we didn't quibble too much about our contracts.'

'I can quite see that.'

'So naturally, those contracts we were so eager to sign were heavily weighted in favour of NWTV. The way they're phrased, we pretty much have to work for them for as long as they want us to, whereas *they* can get rid of *us* any time they feel like it. Two years ago, that really didn't seem to matter much. We were all grateful for the work, even if the show were only to last for a few weeks, as we all thought it would. But times have changed. *Maddox Row* turned out to be a big success, and now we're all stars – but we're still bound by the same bloody contracts.'

'So you feel a bit insecure?'

'On the contrary. We're far too bloody *secure* – whether we want to be or not.'

'Have I missed somethin' here?' Woodend asked.

'No, you just haven't heard the whole story yet. A few weeks ago, an American television company approached me. They were going to make a series about a millionaire from Boston and his British butler. The idea was that the two of them would travel around the States, solving crimes. The Yanks had seen *Maddox Row*, and they thought I'd be just right for the part of the butler. And they'll be filming it in Hollywood! Do you realise what that means? If I played my cards right, I could make the move to being in feature films in a couple of years.'

'So you accepted it?'

'I said I'd have to talk to Bill Houseman, to see if he'd release me from my contract.'

'An' he agreed?'

'Not at first. Jack Taylor has a lot of fans. Then Bill came up with the idea of killing off one of the characters to boost the viewing figures, and it seemed the best solution all round if I was the one to get the chop.'

'But Valerie Farnsworth's death has changed all that?'

'Got it in one,' Coates said. 'Now that *Madro* has lost it's most popular character, it wants to hang on to its *second* most popular – and that, unfortunately, is me.'

There was a tap on the door.

'Come in,' Coates shouted.

The door opened, and Jane Todd stepped inside. 'I was wondering what had happened to you,' she said to Woodend, with just a hint of a rebuke in her voice.

'Sorry, lass, I got distracted.'

Jane Todd smiled. 'That's all right,' she said. 'I'm sure you had much better things to do with your time than listen to me screaming.'

'You *were* screamin', were you?'

'At the top of my lungs!'

'I didn't hear a thing.'

'I told you the sound-proofing was very good,' Larry Coates said.

'Aye, an' you weren't wrong,' Woodend agreed. He turned back to Jane Todd. 'Come with me, lass. After all that hollerin' you've been doin', you deserve a cup of tea.'

Eighteen

Ever since she'd got back from her informative tea break with the typists, Jeremy Wilcox had had Monika running around like a blue-arsed fly. First there'd been a memo to deliver to the props department. After that there'd been one for the carpenters, another for casting and a third for the lighting supervisor.

Perhaps the reason behind all the frenzied activity was that he was the kind of man who measured his own importance by the number of instructions he issued to other people, she thought. Or perhaps he was just keeping her busy as a way of ensuring that she didn't have much time to watch *him*.

Whatever his motives, it suited her. Being his messenger gave her the perfect opportunity to study the life of the whole studio. Besides, if the stories she had heard about him were true, then the shorter the time she spent with him, the better. He would have fewer opportunities to try anything on with her – and she would be less likely to find herself in a situation in which she felt obliged to break his arm.

She had just drawn level with the edge of the office block when she noticed the platinum blonde. The woman was just emerging from one of the small conference rooms, though perhaps 'emerging' was too direct – too straightforward – a word to describe what was going on.

People who 'emerged' did not first open the door just wide enough for them to be able to glance quickly up and down the central concourse. People who 'emerged' did not then step quickly out on to the concourse, closing the door behind them with the back of their stiletto-heeled shoe. No, the platinum blonde was not 'emerging' – she was 'breaking cover', like a timid animal slipping out of its lair.

116

There was nothing timid about the woman once she was clear of the conference room. She walked down the concourse like some kind of Lancashire Marilyn Monroe, her hips swinging and her buttocks involved in a life-and-death struggle beneath the seat of her tight leopardskin trousers.

She was the sort of woman who'd be a real smash down at the Whitebridge Palais de Danse on a drunken Saturday night, Paniatowski thought sourly.

And though the sergeant hated to admit it – though she personally found such sexual posturing grotesque – it had to be said that she was also being a real smash at that very moment.

Heads were turning. Men in overalls and men in smart suits stopped what they were doing to drink her in with their eyes. Even a couple of the women on the concourse were following her progress with envious expressions.

The platinum blonde's swaying progress came to a halt as she stopped to talk to a tall man in a blue suit who was obviously an acquaintance. As she chatted coquetishly, Paniatowski's thoughts shifted from the woman herself to the door she'd just come out of.

Why the caution? the sergeant wondered. Had something happened in the conference room which the blonde had no wish to be associated with?

Now was as good a time as any to find out. She crossed the concourse and was just reaching for the conference room door handle when she heard a husky voice behind her say, 'And just what do you think you're doing?'

The blonde, hands on her hips, was standing no more than a couple of feet away from her. There was no doubt that she was a strikingly attractive woman in many ways, Monika thought. Her bone structure was good, her nose was slender and her lips were full and promising. It was the eyes which spoiled the overall effect. Though they were the deepest blue, they were also cold enough to deep-freeze hot chocolate.

'I asked you what you thought you were doing,' the blonde repeated.

Monika felt her hackles start to rise. 'I could ask you the same question,' she said.

117

The other woman smirked unpleasantly. 'You may not be aware of it, but I happen to be Diana Houseman – the producer's wife,' she said, as if she were playing a trump card.

'Really,' Monika replied, refusing to hide the fact that she was not the least impressed.

'Really!' Diana Houseman repeated. 'And who might you be?'

'I *might be* Mr Wilcox's new personal assistant.'

'Are you, or aren't you?'

'I am.'

'And has Jeremy instructed you to go into that room?'

'Not in so many words,' Monika admitted.

'In fact, not at *all*.'

'You may be right,' Monika agreed.

'Then, that being the case, I suggest you go about doing what he *has* instructed you to do.'

I could slap you, Monika thought. I could slap you really hard. But aloud all she said was: 'Is there any reason why I *shouldn't* go into the conference room?'

'Do you know, one of the cafeteria staff was rude to me last week,' Diana Houseman said.

'Fascinating,' Monika replied.

'Not as rude to me as you've been – but rude enough,' Diana Houseman continued. 'I had a word with my husband, and got her sacked.'

If Diana Houseman tried to get her sacked, it would soon become obvious to everyone – from the producer down – that she didn't really work there at all, Monika realised.

She imagined outlining to Cloggin'-it Charlie the chain of events which had led to her cover being blown. Worse, she imagined what he would say in response – saw herself being at the wrong end of the famous Woodend sarcasm, which, it was well-known, could fell a rampaging rhino at twenty yards. That couldn't be allowed to happen, and if it was necessary to grovel to prevent it, then grovel was what she would have to do.

Monika took a deep breath. 'I'm *so* sorry, Mrs Houseman,' she said in a little-girl voice. 'I don't know what came over me. Really I don't.'

Diana Houseman's cold blue eyes glinted like those of a

wild animal which knows it has its prey cornered. 'Can you give me one good reason why I *shouldn't* report you to my husband?' she demanded.

I'm going to have to cry! Monika thought. The bitch isn't going to be happy until she's seen me weep!

She screwed up her eyes tightly, then forced the tears out. 'I . . . it's all been so difficult,' she sobbed. 'I've got my period, my boyfriend's left me for another girl and . . . and . . . sometimes it seems pointless to go on.'

'All right, I'll let it pass this time,' Diana Houseman said with a condescending magnanimity that made Monika want to slap her all over again. 'Now stop crying and get back to work. Jerry Wilcox will be wondering where you've got to.'

In other words, get the hell away from this door, Monika translated.

She didn't want to go. If she went now, then whatever Diana Houseman had been concealing from her in the conference room would be long gone by the time she got another chance to check on it. But given the circumstances, what choice did she have?

Aware that Diana's Houseman's eyes were following her as she walked up the corridor, she made her way back to Jeremy Wilcox's office. She wondered if Wilcox would notice that her eyes were red, and how she would explain it if he did. But the need for an explanation did not arise, because when she reached the office there was no sign at all of the director.

Nineteen

Work finished earlier at the studio on days when there was no broadcast, and the moment the canteen staff had served Woodend with tea and sticky buns, they pulled down the shutters.

The chief inspector laid his tray on the table where Jane Todd was waiting for him.

'How much was that?' the producer's assistant asked, reaching into her purse.

'Forget it, lass,' Woodend said. 'This is on me.'

Jane Todd smiled. 'Do you know what they always say in the television business?'

'No. What do they always say?'

'That's there no such thing as a free lunch. And I assume by that they mean there's no such thing as free tea and sticky buns either.'

'So you don't think I'm just showin' you a part of my naturally generous nature?'

'Of course I don't. I work for Bill Houseman, which – as you've already realised – means I know a lot of what goes on in this studio. That makes me a good source of information. But rather than coming straight out and asking me direct questions, as most of your colleagues would have done, you've decided to do it subtly – over a cup of tea and sticky buns – so I won't even realise I'm being pumped.'

Woodend shook his head admiringly. 'You're far too clever for me, lass,' he said.

'That's just what I'd have expected you to say,' Jane Todd replied. 'But both of us know it's not true – you're so sharp, Mr Woodend, that you're in danger of cutting yourself.'

'Call me Charlie,' Woodend said. 'An' what if you're right about me wantin' to pump you? Would you mind?'

'I might have done if I hadn't seen the way you treated that constable outside Valerie's dressing room.'

'Come again?' Woodend said.

'If Jeremy Wilcox had been in your place, he'd have left the poor lad a quivering wreck. And why? Because he could! Because by tearing a strip off him, he'd be demonstrating, yet again, that he's important. You could have done the same – goodness knows, the constable was expecting you to. But you didn't. You tried to put him at his ease instead. I liked that.'

'I'm not sure if that really proves anythin',' Woodend said, looking down at the table.

'But it does. It proves that you're a nice man who doesn't care about the trappings of power, and just wants to do his job as well as he can.'

'Isn't that true of nearly everybody?'

Jane Todd laughed again. 'Even *you* don't believe that,' she said.

Woodend sighed. 'Maybe you're right,' he agreed.

'And because you're not in the job just for what you can get out of it, I'm inclined to trust you more than I'd trust most people. So you tell me what it is you want to know, and as long as it doesn't hurt anybody who doesn't deserve to be hurt, I'll answer to the best of my ability. Fair enough?'

'Fair enough,' Woodend agreed. 'Accordin' to what Larry Coates told me back in his dressin' room, the contracts that the cast signed with NWTV mean that the company's got them all by the short an' curlies. Is that true?'

'It would be more accurate to say that *Bill Houseman's* got them by the short and curlies.'

'Bill Houseman? I know he's the producer, but even so he's just an employee of North West Television, like everyone else on *Maddox Row*, isn't he?'

'Yes and no. The series was Houseman's idea, and as long as things go well, the people in charge of NWTV are quite happy to let him run his own little kingdom as he sees fit.'

'An' we've already established that runnin' his little kingdom really matters to him, haven't we?'

'Indeed we have. There are a lot of people involved in this show for what they can get out of it. Jeremy Wilcox, for example, would love to have overall control of *Madro*, instead of just being the director. Jennifer Brunton, who, as you probably know, plays Madge Thornycroft, would give her eye teeth to be as popular as Val was – or as Larry *is*. But for them, it's nothing more than a step up the ladder. Jeremy would like to end up running something really artistic and prestigious – like the Royal Shakespeare Company. Jennifer sees herself as a future *Dame* Jennifer—'

'An' Larry Coates wants to be a star of the silver screen.'

'Exactly. But Bill has already reached his personal pinnacle – the top of his particular ladder. Whatever else he does after this, he'll never be anything more than the man who created *Maddox Row*. And he knows it. So he wants to hold on to that feeling of success for as long as he can.'

'At whatever the cost?'

'There are only two things which really matter in Bill Houseman's life,' Jane Todd said, side-stepping the question, '*Madro* and Diana.'

'Diana?'

'Mr Houseman's wife.'

'I don't think I've met her yet,' Woodend said.

'You can't have, or you'd certainly remember her. She's the kind of woman who leaves an impression.'

'Tell me about her.'

'She's a very striking woman, about fifteen years younger than Bill.'

'Have they been married long?'

'Less than a year. They had what you might call "a whirl-wind courtship". It took us all by surprise.'

'An' how does she feel about *Maddox Row*? Is she jealous about how much of her husband's time it takes?'

'Not at all. She likes the fact that the show makes him important – and, by extension, makes her important, too. And she likes the money it brings in. Oh God, she likes the money.'

'You're not very keen on her, are you?'

'I can't stand the bloody woman,' Jane Todd said frankly.

122

'So, tell me, who do *you* think killed Valerie Farnsworth?' Woodend asked casually.

Jane Todd stared at him for a couple of seconds, then said, 'You might start out softly, all tea and buns, but once you get down to it you're not one for beating around the bush, are you?'

'Never was,' Woodend admitted. 'An' you still haven't answered my question.'

'I have my own theories, but without any proof to back them up, I don't think I'm prepared to share them – however much I've begun to like you.'

'Give me a hint,' Woodend coaxed.

Jane Todd shook her head. 'No. I don't think I'm even prepared to go that far.'

'Don't worry, I'm not about to rush off to arrest somebody, just because you think they might be the murderer,' Woodend assured her. 'But I'd like to hear your ideas anyway. They just might give me another angle on the case.'

'Perhaps they would, but I still don't feel I could . . .'

'An' there's another thing to consider.'

'What's that?'

'This kind of crime never occurs in isolation,' Woodend said. 'It's usually no more than a single link of a chain of events. An' it's rarely the *last* link. If you don't do somethin' about the poison quickly, then it'll soon spread, an' probably damage more lives.' He paused and a grin came to his face. 'I'm mixin' my metaphors a bit there, but you get the picture.'

Jane Todd did not return his smile. Instead, her face had assumed a deathly earnest expression.

'I'll say this one thing, and then I'm saying no more on that particular matter, however much you press me,' she told him. 'Ever since Val's death, I've been constantly reminding myself that most people never come across even *one* murder during their entire lives, and the chances of them being close to two – and in the same place – are practically zero. But there's a small part of my brain that *does* worry that there could be a second one. Of course, that could just be my morbid imagination. In fact, now I think about, I'm sure that's all it is.'

'But . . . ?' Woodend said.

'But if there *is* another killing,' Jane Todd said, speaking rapidly as if she wanted to get the words out as soon as possible, 'then it wouldn't surprise me at all if the victim was Larry Coates.'

Twenty

Woodend stood just inside the main entrance to the studio, and watched the last of the staff trickle out of the building. One of them was a pretty blonde woman who did not look quite English. She was chatting energetically to her newly-made friends and, though she did glance up at him, the expression on her face showed only the natural curiosity that any office worker might feel about a high-ranking policeman.

The chief inspector waited until his sergeant was outside before allowing himself to grin. Monika would do all right for herself, he thought. She was intelligent, she was sensitive and – most importantly of all – she was gutsy. He turned his mind to Bob Rutter. Had he forced his ex-bagman's promotion through too quickly? *He* didn't think so, but he got the distinct impression that Rutter sometimes did. And that worried him because he was very fond of Bob, and sometimes he – stupidly – caught himself thinking of the lad as the son he'd never had. Or was it so stupid? As the cheeky young sod had pointed out only that morning, he was older than Rutter's mother.

His mind was too full of the case to go home quite then, he decided, and instead of heading back for Whitebridge he pointed his car in the general direction of the Pennines. Nature was in retreat, he observed, as he drove across the moors. Many of the summer birds – fair-weather friends, he supposed you could call them – had already fled the country, and even the swallows, perched in large numbers on the telephone wires, would soon be taking off for Africa. He wondered what it must be like for the young birds – scarcely out of the nest – to embark on such a journey. Were they apprehensive? Or were they thrilled to be involved in such an epic adventure?

Probably neither, he thought realistically. Probably, just like so many of the people he met, they were merely following their instincts

Had Valerie Farnsworth's killer merely been following his instincts? he pondered. Had he, as he saw it, merely struck out to defend himself? Or was there some deeper, more intricate motive behind the murder? And what exactly had Jane Todd meant when she'd said that if there were another killing, Larry Coates would most likely be the victim?

As they always did when he was thinking through a case, the hours seemed to slip by, and when Woodend consulted his dashboard clock he saw that there was no time left to slip home before his meeting with Rutter and Paniatowski in the Drum and Monkey.

It was a quarter to ten as Woodend drove down the lane which led to his cottage. He noticed, with some surprise, that there was no light on in his daughter's bedroom. Maybe Annie had finished her homework and decided to spend the rest of the evening with the family for a change, he thought.

He tried to remember when she'd stopped coming downstairs in the evening – when confining herself to her own room had become the norm. Was it while they still lived in London, or only since they'd moved up North? Perhaps the reason it was so difficult to pin it down was because he was so rarely at home in the evening himself.

He parked the car, and entered the house. The television was just warming up, and, from the sounds of it, Joan was busy preparing food. By the time he'd reached the kitchen itself, his wife was just pouring the contents of a saucepan on to a plate.

'Lancashire hot-pot do you?' she asked, looking up at him.

He didn't have much of an appetite – hadn't had much of one since the start of this bloody case – but Joan had gone to all the effort of cooking for him, so he forced himself to say, 'That sounds grand.'

'Will you be havin' it in front of the telly?' Joan asked.

'Might as well,' Woodend replied. 'Is our Annie out?'

'No. She's gone to bed.'

Woodend glanced up at the wall clock, just to check on the time. 'Bit early to be turnin' in, isn't it?'

'Well, it is a school day,' Joan said, with just the smallest hint of evasion in her voice.

'Even so, I don't remember her goin' to bed quite so early when we were in London,' Woodend said.

Joan turned away, and ran the dishcloth quickly over the top of the kitchen unit. 'Maybe she had more reason to stay up when we were livin' down in London,' she said.

Woodend frowned. 'Is she really unhappy in Whitebridge?'

Joan swung round to face him again. 'You're her father. *You* tell *me*, Charlie,' she said.

'I can't,' Woodend admitted. 'I haven't been spendin' enough time with her lately, have I?'

'Nothin' like enough. I've tried to fill in for you as best I can, but the older she gets, the harder it seems to be. Every girl needs a mother, but she needs a father as well, you know, and though she may not always show it, our Annie looks up to you.'

Woodend bowed his head guiltily. 'I'll get home earlier tomorrow night, so that we can have a really good chat,' he said.

'Yes, I think that would be a good idea,' Joan replied. 'An' not before time, if you ask me.'

Wednesday

Twenty-One

It was raining as Bob Rutter drove into the centre of Whitebridge that Wednesday morning, and though he was not as fanciful a man as his boss, it did seem to him as if his windscreen wipers, swishing back and to in front of him, were repeating Maria's message from the previous day.

'*Find a role . . . find a role . . . find a role . . .*'

But how could he do that? he asked himself. What role? His path seemed to have already been determined for him. While Charlie Woodend and Monika Paniatowski were out in the field – where the real action was – he seemed doomed to be chained to a desk in Headquarters.

He might as well have gone into accountancy, he thought – at least there he would have made some real bloody money.

There were a couple of reporters waiting for him in the police car park, but they were strictly small-fry – local stringers who hoped for any small snippet of information which might move them one small step further towards their dream of working on Fleet Street. The real journalists – the ones who mattered – would be camped outside the studio, where they could ambush the stars of *Maddox Row* and perhaps get a juicy quote for tomorrow's front page.

He brushed the reporters off with a 'no comment' and made his way into the building. His team – twelve detective constables and two sergeants – were already at their desks in DCS Ainsworth's much-vaunted 'incident room'.

This was the first murder most of the team had worked on, and the previous day there had been a buzz of excitement about the way they went about their work. Now, nearly twenty-four hours into the case, he sensed that their enthusiasm was starting to wane. Even so, they still looked up at him expectantly – as if they hoped he'd had some blinding insight in the middle of the night.

Rutter placed himself in the middle of the horseshoe of desks, and cleared his throat.

'Right, lads, this is Day Two of the investigation. Let's see if we can make a real breakthrough today,' he said.

The words sounded wrong to him – or rather they sounded wrong coming from *his* mouth. They needed to be spoken by someone like Charlie Woodend, not by a newly promoted inspector who was younger, and less experienced, than some of the men working under him.

He turned to one of his sergeants, a man in his early thirties called Cowgill. 'Want to give us a progress report, Frank?' he asked.

'The main problem is not any inconsistency in the alibis, sir – it's the complete bloody lack of them.'

Rutter nodded. 'Spell it out for us,' he said.

'The technical people – the electricians, sound crew, camera crew, floormen etc – are no problem. They either had specific jobs to do at the time of the murder, or they were takin' a break with their mates before they got to work. It's the people who have less clearly defined jobs – the actors, an' some of the management – that are a problem.'

'They don't have alibis?'

'For some of the time, yes. But each of them has a period when they *can't* account for their whereabouts.'

'It might help us if you gave us an example,' Rutter suggested.

The sergeant looked down at his notes. 'All right. Take Jeremy Wilcox, the director. We know that he talked to the scriptwriters – Drabble and Colligan – at some point, though they're all a bit vague about exactly when that point was. We know he had what witnesses have called "a heated discussion" with Bill Houseman, the producer, but again, it's difficult to pin down *exactly* when that occurred. An' even if we could, it still wouldn't help us much, because it would still leave a fair chunk of time when he *claims* he was alone in his office – an' we can't prove any different.'

'Does that make him a prime suspect, as far as you're concerned?' Rutter asked.

'It would if there weren't a couple of dozen other buggers who were in the same situation.'

It would have made life a lot easier if someone had seen the murderer heading for Val Farnsworth's dressing room with a homicidal look in his eyes and a big electrical screwdriver in his hand, Rutter thought. But life rarely worked out as neatly as that.

'We need to hone the list down to a few suspects,' he said. 'and since that can't be done on the basis of alibis, we're going to have to do it on the basis of backgrounds. I want everybody who hasn't got a watertight alibi thoroughly checked out. Go back as far as you can – as far as their schooldays, if that's possible. If one of them was caught necking with a girl behind the bike sheds when he should have been in class, I want to know about it. I want information on their careers, their friends and their love lives. If they've got so much as a parking ticket, I want a report on it. If one of them had a dog which was knocked down in the road, I should be told. No detail, however insignificant it might seem to you, should be left out. Is that clearly understood?'

The constables and the two sergeants all nodded.

'Sergeant Cowgill will assign each of you a particular suspect,' Rutter continued. 'Are there any questions?'

One of the younger detective constables raised his hand. 'What about the victim, sir?' he asked.

'It goes without saying that I want her background thoroughly checked out,' Rutter said.

The constable turned to Cowgill. 'Can I do her, Sarge?'

Several of the other constables chuckled.

'What's so funny,' Rutter asked.

'Young Pickup here's from Sladebury, sir,' Sergeant Cowgill explained, with a smile on his face.

'So?' Rutter said.

The sergeant looked surprised he even needed to ask. 'Valerie Farnsworth was originally from Sladebury herself. The only reason Pickup wants to be assigned to her is because it'll give him an excuse to nip home an' have a cup of tea with his mam.'

There were so many things he didn't know, Rutter thought, and so much he *should* know. Sometimes he felt that though the people of Whitebridge appeared to speak the same language as he did, they were, in fact, conversing in an alien tongue. He remembered the Salton case, where Woodend, a stranger to the area just as he himself was a stranger to this one, had insisted that he be assigned a young police cadet who had a detailed knowledge of the village in which the murder had taken place.

'I'll do the background work on Valerie Farnsworth myself,' he said, 'so if anybody wants to know where I am, I'll be in Sladebury. And there's no need for you to look so down in the mouth, Pickup,' he added, seeing the look of disappointment on the young constable's face, 'because you'll be coming with me. As for the rest of you, you know what you've got to do, so get on with it.'

'One question before you go, Mr Rutter,' Sergeant Cowgill said.

'Yes?'

'I understand that you want us to come up with as much background as we can, but it would help us if you could give us some guidelines. What, *specifically*, are we lookin' for?'

'I'm buggered if I know,' Rutter admitted – and this time even Woodend could not have delivered the line better.

In another part of the building, Chief Constable John Dinnage sat looking at the tea and biscuits his secretary had brought him a few minutes earlier. He should eat the biscuits, he told himself, because he hadn't been able to face breakfast, and no man should start a day's work on an empty stomach. Yet though they were his favourites – chocolate digestives – even the thought of putting one in his mouth made him feel queasy.

He massaged the left side of his chest. If only this bloody indigestion would go away, he thought.

He glanced at the stack of files which seemed to grow taller every day, no matter how many hours he put in at the office.

He hadn't realised, when he'd taken the job on, just *how* much work would be involved. Nor had he realised how few of his subordinates he would be able to use, either because he couldn't rely on them or – worse – because he didn't trust them. The rot started right near the top – with his own second-in-command, Deputy Chief Constable Henry Marlowe – but there were many others he was not entirely happy with, including his head of CID, DCS Ainsworth.

But all that would be dealt with, given time. The dead wood would be cut out, and new people brought in as replacements. He had already begun the process by grabbing Charlie Woodend when Scotland Yard no longer wanted him.

For a while, he had even contemplated moving Cloggin'-it Charlie into administration as his right-hand man, but in the end he had reluctantly come to the conclusion that Woodend would never learn to adapt to sitting behind a desk. Still, he was glad he had taken on his old colleague while he had the chance – because that meant there was at least one man working out in the field who he could have absolute confidence in.

The pain in his chest was getting worse. Dinnage rubbed it again, and wondered whether it was too soon to take another indigestion tablet. Would it do him any good, anyway? They never seemed to work on him half as well as they worked on the sufferers in the television commercials.

The tablets were at the other end of his desk, just beyond his reach. He stretched over for them, and then instinctively pulled back as a sharp pain travelled the length of his arm.

This was ridiculous, he told himself. He was not as young as he used to be, but he was certainly not yet at the stage where he should be suffering from an old man's aches and pains. He stretched out again, and the biological time bomb which had been ticking away in his chest finally exploded.

Twenty-Two

Ben Drabble and Paddy Colligan sat opposite each other at a table in the studio cafeteria. They were noted for being the first customers of the day, and that morning was no exception. What was exceptional, however, was that instead of their normal intense conversation, during which pages of script were shuffled back and forth across the table, the two writers seemed to be barely aware of each other's existence. In fact, both men seemed to be totally absorbed in their own little worlds.

Ben Drabble was thinking about his agent. The novel needed a few changes, the bloody man had blithely said the previous day.

A few changes!

And what did he mean by that? A sentence here, a paragraph there? No! The changes he wanted would necessitate a completely new plot – and possibly a new set of characters, as well!

If only his agent knew the mental anguish which had gone into writing the book. If only he could even *begin* to comprehend how, once it was finally completed, it seemed to its author to be etched in stone.

Drabble lit up a cigarette and inhaled what, in his present mood, tasted like dried camel dung.

What if his agent was right? he asked himself gloomily. What if the bloody man was only *half*-right? Wasn't it possible that Valerie Farnsworth's death, rather than being good publicity for the book, would merely expose it as flimsy and insubstantial when contrasted with a real crime?

How he wished that when he'd started writing *The Shooting Script* he'd chosen to make one of the actresses the victim, rather than the producer. But that wasn't how the idea had come to him! That wasn't how his muse had dictated the book should be written! And now that treacherous muse could well be the cause of his getting his legs broken by men working for his increasingly impatient bookmaker.

Paddy Colligan, for his part, was indulging himself in a sweeping review of his life so far. It was a far-from-optimistic exercise. Looking at it as objectively as he could, it seemed to him that while he had made a few wise decisions, there had also been a long string of foolish ones.

Despite being so poor he'd had to live off little more than bread and margarine in a rat-trap bed-sit in the worst part of Dublin, he had dedicated himself to writing his play, *Troubled Times in the Old Country,* and had eventually finished it.

A wise decision.

He had taken the play to a small theatre company, and persuaded the manager to produce it.

A *very* wise decision.

Waiting for the reviews, he had been hoping that they would hail him as the new Brendan Behan, and when they had been merely *encouraging*, he had seen it as a crushing blow.

Foolish.

He had taken the job as a scriptwriter on *Maddox Row*.

Downright bloody stupid.

And he had stuck with the job, even when it had become clear to him that as long as characters like Jack Taylor and Madge Thornycroft filled his head, he would never write another word which was really worth a damn.

Cowardly!

But it was not just his professional and artistic life he'd buggered up, he reminded himself.

With eyes wide open, he had walked into the most obvious of emotional traps, and now, though escape should have been the easiest thing in the world, he seemed unable – or unwilling – to break free.

'Mind if I join you, lads?' asked an intrusive voice from the wider world beyond the two men's own miseries.

The two scriptwriters looked up. Larry Coates, a mug of tea in his hand, was standing over them and smiling benignly.

137

The lack of an immediate response caused Coates's smile to fade a little. 'If I'm interrupting anything important, you've only got to tip me the wink and I'll go elsewhere,' he said.

'No . . . please, take a seat,' Paddy Colligan said, suddenly realising how his and Drabble's self-absorption might be interpreted as just plain rudeness. 'Sorry if we seemed out of it. We were both thinking about the script.'

'Ah, the script!' Coates said, sitting down. 'That sacred book which rules all our lives.'

He's taking the reversals in his fortunes very well, Paddy Colligan thought. Why can't I be like that?

'So what treats have you got in store for Jack Taylor, the Laughing Postman?' Coates asked, offering the two script-writers a cigarette. 'Any chance of him falling down a manhole and breaking his neck?'

Paddy Colligan shook his head regretfully. 'Jack's going to lead a charmed life, at least for the foreseeable future,' he said.

Coates sighed. 'Yes, I suppose he is.'

'You must be bitterly disappointed about not going to Hollywood,' Paddy Colligan said sympathetically.

'I *was*,' Coates said.

'But not any more?'

'It comes and goes,' Coates admitted. 'It's true that I'll probably never get such a big chance again, but while there's life there's hope. And so what if I have to stay on this show until I'm old enough to draw my pension? It's steady work, and at least it pays the mortgage.'

That's what they'll be putting on my tombstone, Paddy Colligan thought. *He did steady work and paid the mortgage.*

'Besides, there are other compensations to working on *Madro*,' Larry Coates said.

'Like what?' Paddy Colligan asked, with the sudden desperate air of a man clutching for a lifeline.

'We bring a great deal of pleasure into a lot of people's lives,' Larry Coates told him.

'Oh, that old chestnut!' Paddy Colligan said dismissively.

'The fact that it's almost a cliché doesn't make it any less true,' Larry Coates countered, with a hint of reproach in his voice. 'You only see the viewing figures, but *I* see the viewers. I've lost count of the number of times that some old dear has come up to me in a shop to say how much she enjoys the show. I wouldn't get that if I was in films, and I'd miss it – because however many times it happens, it always gives me a warm glow inside. So, by and large, I'm not *too* unhappy about staying on the show. When all's said and done, there are far *worse* places than Maddox Row, you know.'

Are there? Paddy Colligan asked himself. Are there really?

That's easy for Larry to say, Ben Drabble thought. He's stuck here now, so he's got to make the best of it. But I don't have to stay. If I'd got the guts do something about it, my book could take *me* away from all this.

Twenty-Three

The studio day was in full swing, and central concourse was as busy as any small town high street. But how many of those busy people would have noticed him turning down the alley which led to the front of the actors' dressing rooms? Woodend wondered. And of those who did notice him, how many would actually remember it later? Probably none at all!

That may well have been the murderer's calculation, too, when, two nights earlier, he made his way down the alley with a large electrical screwdriver concealed on his person. Or perhaps he didn't need to make that journey at all. Perhaps all he had to do to kill Valerie Farnsworth was step out of his dressing room and into hers!

He came to a halt at the dead woman's door. Larry Coates's dressing room was to the right of it, George Adams' to the left. He stepped to the side, raised his fist, and knocked on Adams's door.

'It's not locked,' called a voice.

Woodend turned the handle and stepped inside.

George Adams was sitting on his couch, a large cigar in his mouth. When Woodend had seen Larry Coates for the first time, he'd immediately thought of him as the Laughing Postman, but there was no such confusion in his mind about Adams and the character *he* played on the screen, because without his make-up the man bore no more than a passing resemblance to Sam Fuller, the crotchety old-age pensioner of *Maddox Row*.

Adams puffed on his cigar, and blew a smoke ring up at the ceiling. 'What do *you* want?' he demanded.

'I've had warmer welcomes in my time,' Woodend replied.

'Then they probably came from people who've got more time for rozzers than I have,' Adams said.

'Got something against the police, have you?' Woodend asked.

Adams gave him an officious smile. 'No,' he said. 'It's usually them that have got something against me.'

Woodend was starting to feel on familiar ground. 'Let me guess,' he said. 'You've been inside.'

Adams nodded. 'In my youth I was a guest at one of His Majesty's secure institutions for a couple of years.'

'What were you in for? Robbery?'

Adams looked offended. 'Of course not! Nothing so illegal! I merely hit someone who deserved it rather harder than I'd intended to. And let me tell you, by the time I came to trial I had a few bruises of my own, which your fellow so-called *police officers* had inflicted on me while I was in the cells.'

'So now you don't like bobbies,' Woodend said.

'So now I don't like bobbies,' Adams agreed.

'But you wouldn't mind answerin' a few questions, would you?'

Adams shrugged. 'I can see no objection to that – as long as it doesn't start to bore me.'

'Where were you at the time Valerie Farnsworth was murdered?'

'I certainly wasn't in her dressing room with a screwdriver in my hand, if that's what you're suggesting.'

'I'm not suggestin' anythin',' Woodend said evenly. 'All I'm doin' is askin' you a question.'

'From six o'clock until fifteen minutes before the show went on air, I was here.'

'An' you didn't hear any sound from next door?'

'You mean, did I hear Val call out something like, "No, Jennifer, put that screwdriver down"?'

'Well, did you?'

'I'm afraid not. The walls are so well insulated that I didn't hear even a peep.'

Two can play the smart-arse game, Woodend decided, looking slowly and ostentatiously around the dressing room.

'Seen enough?' Adams asked.

'I must say, it's all very egalitarian,' Woodend mused.

'Meaning?'

'In Whitebridge Police Headquarters, you can pretty much tell how important somebody is from the size of his room.'

'How fascinating,' Adams said sarcastically.

'Aye, I thought you'd be interested,' Woodend said. 'Take the chief constable's office as an example. You could throw a party in there. Whereas you'd be pushed to swing a cat in mine.'

'So?'

'It's not like that here. All the dressin' rooms are the same size, which seems to suggest that all the people who occupy them are of equal importance.'

'And so they are.'

Woodend grinned. 'Come off it, Mr Adams! You know that's crap. You're nowhere near as popular as Valerie Farnsworth was.'

Adams looked stung. 'We have a very diverse audience, and different characters appeal to different viewers,' he said defensively.

'As far as I can work out, Valerie Farnsworth appealed to all the men between the ages of thirty and sixty – an' a good proportion of the women as well,' Woodend said. 'Who watches the show to see you? A few old-age pensioners?'

'A *great many* old-age pensioners,' Adams said hotly. 'And children, too. I'm everybody's favourite granddad.'

'But you're not, are you?' Woodend asked.

'Not what?'

'Not a granddad. An' as far as I can tell, you're a long way from drawin' your pension yet.'

'I'm forty-seven.'

'So how did you get the job? Why didn't they give it to an old feller who wouldn't have needed much make-up?'

'They did – originally. And he popped his clogs a week before they were due to broadcast the first episode. That's when Bill decided it would be safer to give the role to someone younger and healthier.'

'Which is how you got your big break,' Woodend said. 'Tell me about Valerie Farnsworth.'

Adams smiled again, as if he'd realised he'd lost control of the interview for a while, but was now firmly back in the driving seat again.

'Why ask me?' he said. 'Haven't you read her obituaries in all the newspapers?'

'Yes, I have, as a matter of fact.'

'Then you already know that not only was she a great actress, but also a very warm human being with a heart as big as a mountain.'

'Was she?'

'A great actress?'

'A very warm human being.'

'Of course she was. When she wanted to be. And as long as someone was watching.'

'Is that just another way of sayin' that you didn't like her very much?'

'People who didn't like her make natural suspects as far as the police are concerned, so I'd have to say in my own self-interest that I personally worshipped the ground she walked on,' Adams replied. 'But I will tell you this – one of the two most important lessons you learn in prison is who to trust and who not to trust, and I didn't trust Valerie Farnsworth.'

'Any particular reason for that?' Woodend asked.

'If you bite the hand that feeds you, you'll bite anybody's hand.'

'An' is that what she was doin'?'

'Yes, if the rumours I've heard are true.'

'Whose hand was she supposed to be bitin'? Bill Houseman's?'

'That would be a fair assumption. His was, after all, the hand that fed her.'

'So what was she plannin' to do? Abandon him? Run off to Hollywood like Larry Coates wanted to do?'

Adams shook his head. 'No. Nothing like that. Her betrayal was of a more *personal* nature.'

'That's a bit vague, isn't it?' Woodend asked.

'Yes,' Adams agreed. 'And that's exactly how I intend to keep it.'

'Don't you want Valerie Farnsworth's killer caught?'

'The second valuable lesson you learn in prison is that if you want to survive, the best thing to do is say nothing and keep your head down. And that's what I'm doing right now – saying nothing and keeping my head down.'

Deputy Chief Constable Henry Marlowe noticed the cream-coloured ambulance, with its light flashing dementedly, the second he pulled into the Whitebridge Police Headquarters' car park. The ambulance was parked close to the back door of the station, and the driver and his mate, having unloaded their stretcher-trolley, were on the point of entering the building.

Marlowe wondered if some keen young bobby had been a little too 'enthusiastic' while questioning a suspect. And if he had, how the bloody hell would they handle it?

In the old days, it would have been easy enough to deal with a situation like that. He, personally, would first have torn a strip off the officer in question, and then blandly told the press that the suspect had fallen downstairs, and he could produce half a dozen witnesses to prove it. But the old days – sadly – seemed to be gone forever. Now that squeaky-clean John Dinnage was in charge of the force, everything had to be done by the book.

Marlowe parked his car and walked over to the crowd. 'What's going on here?' he demanded.

'It's Mr Dinnage, sir,' one of the uniformed constables said.

'What about him?'

'His secretary found him slumped over his desk a few minutes ago. They think he's had a heart attack.'

Christ, that was better news than hearing he'd won the football pools, Marlowe told himself.

But even as the thought flashed across his mind, his face assumed the troubled expression of a senior officer who has just learned that one of his valued colleagues has been struck down.

'I didn't realise you'd all had medical training,' he said, addressing the small crowd in general.

'We haven't, sir,' said the constable who'd spoken earlier.

'Then you're not much use here, are you?' Marlowe asked.

'Look, I know you must all be as shocked as I am,' he continued, lowering his voice and blunting the edge on his tone a little, 'but there's really nothing you can do, so wouldn't it be a good idea to go back to your duties?'

It was more of an order than a suggestion, and recognising it as such, the group began to disperse, leaving Marlowe in sole charge of the car park.

The DCC lit up a cigarette, and waited. It was less than two minutes later that the ambulance men emerged with their patient. The Old Man didn't look good, Marlowe thought, glancing down at the stretcher. His skin was as white as flour, his facial muscles had collapsed, leaving his features almost flat. It was possible that he would make a full recovery, but a betting man would think twice before putting any money on it.

The ambulance crew loaded the stretcher into the back of the vehicle. The driver's mate followed it, and knelt down by the sick man. The driver himself closed the doors and strode quickly round to the front of the vehicle.

As Marlowe watched the ambulance drive away, it was only the knowledge that he was being observed from every window in the station which preventing him from dancing a jig.

He jangled the change in his pocket as he thought about the grave words he would use at the press conference later in the day, and, because there was no one close enough to hear it, he permitted himself the luxury of whistling a cheerful tune.

Twenty-Four

For the first part of the drive to Sladebury, Constable Pickup seemed to be rather intimidated by the fact that he was sharing a car with an inspector, but the closer they got to the village in which both he and Valerie Farnsworth had spent their childhoods, the more voluble he became.

'The place has really grown since I was a kid,' he told Rutter. 'There was only one shop back then, but now there's three, includin' a branch of Co-op. There's a petrol station, an' all.'

'It's obviously becoming quite a little metropolis,' Rutter said, with a slight smile playing on his lips.

'You're right, there,' Pickup agreed enthusiastically. 'It's getting' so that people don't really need to go into Whitebridge at all.'

They entered the village. The houses were all built of the dressed stone which Rutter – as a man raised in the land of red brick – had found strange at first, but now was getting used to. There was a pub called the Red Lion just ahead of them, and the inspector indicated, then turned on to its car park.

'Do you fancy a drink before we get started?' he asked Pickup, as they got out of the car.

'I wouldn't say no,' the constable replied, then quickly added – as if he'd begun to suspect this might be some kind of test, 'That is, I wouldn't mind one if it's all right with you, sir.'

'I'd never have suggested it if it wasn't,' Rutter replied – and found himself wishing that he didn't always feel the urge to turn round and see who was standing behind him when anybody called him 'sir'.

Pickup seemed to assume his new boss – *being* a boss –

146

would prefer to drink in the best room rather than the public bar, and Rutter, still lacking Charlie Woodend's confidence, didn't contradict him. The landlord, a jolly-looking, red-faced man of around forty, greeted the young constable warmly and said wasn't it a terrible thing about Val Farnsworth. Pickup agreed it was, and Rutter ordered two halves of best bitter.

'Where would you like to start, sir?' Pickup asked, when the landlord had served them their drinks.

Rutter ignored the twitch in his neck muscles which told him to glance over his shoulder, and said, 'It'd probably be best to start with the immediate family.'

Pickup looked distraught. 'I'm afraid there aren't any, sir,' he confessed.

'What? None?'

'None at all. The Farnsworths were off-comers to the village. Came from Rawtenstall, or somewhere like that. There was only her an' her mam an' dad, an' both the parents are dead now.'

'But there are still people in the village who knew her, aren't there?'

'Oh yes, there's plenty of them,' Pickup replied, looking relieved. He turned towards the bar, where the landlord was polishing glasses. 'You knew Val, didn't you, Mr Gilgrass? Personally, I mean.'

'I knew her all right,' the landlord confirmed. 'Knew her *very well*, as a matter of fact. We were in the same class at school.'

'What was she like?' Rutter asked.

'Very determined,' the landlord replied, without a second's hesitation. 'She always knew exactly what she wanted, an' was always willin' to do whatever was necessary to get it.'

Rutter grinned good-naturedly – a trick he'd learned from Woodend. 'Used her feminine wiles to get her own way, did she?'

'Oh no, she wasn't like that back then,' the landlord said. 'Not at all. She was a bit of a tomboy, if the truth be told. As willin' to use her fists as any of the lads – an' better with them than most of the boys, too.'

'You must be very proud of her in the village,' Rutter said.

147

'We are. There's not many people can say they've known somebody as famous as Val Farnsworth.'

Pickup put his glass down on the counter. 'If you'll excuse me, sir, I think I'll just have to nip out the back for a minute,' he said.

The landlord watched Pickup disappear through the door which led to the toilets, then turned his back to Rutter.

'Not got the bladder for drinkin', these young lads, have they?' he asked. 'They get one half pint in them, an' they're peein' for a good fifteen minutes.'

'That's the younger generation for you,' Rutter said, choosing to overlook the fact that he was far closer to Pickup's age himself than he was to the landlord's. 'Did you see much of Val in the village?'

'Not really,' the landlord admitted. 'In fact, I can't remember the last time she was here.'

'And people didn't resent that? Didn't they feel she must have decided she was too good for Sladebury?'

'No, not at all. We understood that she must have been very busy, what with *Maddox Row* an' all the public appearances she had to put in all over the place. You'll not find one person in Sladebury who's got a bad word to say against Val Farnsworth, I can assure you of that.'

'No one? Not a single person?'

The landlord frowned. 'Well, there is *one*,' he admitted reluctantly.

'Who?'

'Funnily enough, it's young Pickup back-there's Uncle Arthur.'

'And what's Uncle Arthur got against her?'

'Well, this was years ago, I'm talkin' about now. He was engaged to a lass called Ellie Tomkins, and when she broke the engagement off, a few months before the weddin', he blamed Val for it. But nobody took much notice. To tell you the truth, everybody round here thinks he's a bit do-lally.'

Woodend made his way up the central concourse to the studio. After his slightly unpleasant encounter with George Adams, he'd had just about enough of Houseman's 'aristocracy' for one morning, he decided, and it was about time he had a word with the peasants.

The studio was full of hectic activity. Some of the sets he'd seen the day before were being taken down, and the moment the flats had been removed, new ones were being constructed in their place. Woodend watched, fascinated, as an empty space began to take the shape of the living room he'd so often watched Madge Thornycroft spread her salacious rumours from.

With a gait that would have seemed aimless to anyone who didn't know him, he wandered over to Jack Taylor's front room. The carpenters seemed to have finished their work there, and a young man with a bouffant hairstyle was fussing over the ornaments on Dot's sideboard.

'You're that policeman, aren't you?' he said.

'That's right,' Woodend agreed. 'Won't put you off if I watch you work for a few minutes, will it?'

'Not at all,' the young man replied. 'A true artist always appreciates an audience.'

The set dresser picked up a photograph which was lying on the sideboard, studied it for a moment, then moved a Toby jug a couple of inches to the left.

'Do you have to be that careful?' Woodend asked.

'Oh God, yes,' the young man said. 'If anything's even the tiniest bit out of place, we get letters. It's the same with the corner shop. If we don't have Valentine's Day cards on display there at the beginning of February, you can be sure one of our eagle-eyed viewers will complain. I've got a friend who works in prop buying, and he wakes up in a cold sweat worrying that one of the washing powder companies might have changed their packaging without him noticing.'

Woodend grinned. 'Sounds like a tough life.'

'You don't know the half of it,' the young man said earnestly. He stepped back from the sideboard, cocked his head first to one side then the other, then nodded with satisfaction. 'That should do it. Now all that's left is the blowing down – if you'll excuse the expression.'

'The what?'

'I have to spray the light switches and door handles with a fine film of dark water paint. It looks strange to the naked eye – pardon the expression again – but on camera it takes away the pristine edge and makes them seem used.'

'All is not what it seems.'

'You're telling me! In one episode we had Harry Sugden getting the daft idea of building a goldfish pond in his back yard . . .'

'Aye, I remember that.'

'Well, we got a tin bath, surrounded it with fake bricks, and filled it with water. The bricks looked fine on camera, but the water just didn't seem right. We tried different lighting and different camera angles, and it was still no good. So do you know what had to do in the end?'

'I've no idea.'

'We tipped the water away, and spread a plastic sheet across the top of the pond. And that really *did* look like water.'

Woodend suddenly realised he was enjoying himself so much that he was in danger of forgetting why he was there. 'What can you tell me about Val Farnsworth?' he asked.

'Not a lot,' the set dresser said. 'Our job's finished by the time hers starts. But if you want to talk to somebody who knew her *outside* work . . .' He searched around the studio, and his gaze fell on a short-haired woman who was dressing a set close to his. 'Can you come here a minute, Susan?' he called.

The woman stopped what she was doing, and walked over to them. She was around thirty, Woodend guessed, and perhaps a little sturdily built. Her eyes were red, and she didn't look at all happy.

'Yes?' she said tremulously, as if she would much rather be somewhere else.

'This policeman wants to know about Val Farnsworth,' the set dresser told her. 'She was a sort of a friend of yours, wasn't she?'

Tears began to well up in the woman's eyes immediately. 'She . . . I . . . can't talk about it now,' she said.

Then she turned and hurried away towards the other side of the studio.

'I never imagined she'd taken it so badly,' the set dresser

said, nonplussed. 'If I'd known she was going to break down like that, I'd never have called her over.'

'Aye, she did seem rather upset, didn't she,' Woodend agreed thoughtfully.

The woman had gone back to her own set, but instead of resuming her work she stood in one corner, head bent and shoulders heaving.

'I think I'll just go an' have a word with her – see what the trouble is,' Woodend told the dresser.

He was halfway between the two sets when he noticed that Monika Paniatowski had entered the studio, and was making a beeline for him. What the bloody hell was his sergeant playing at? he wondered.

Paniatowski came a halt just in front of him. 'Are you Chief Inspector Woodend?' she asked, deadpan.

'Aye, that's me,' Woodend agreed.

'Mr Wilcox sent me to find you,' Paniatowski explained. 'There's been a call for you from Whitebridge. Your chief constable's been taken seriously ill, and they want you back there as soon as possible.'

Twenty-Five

B ill Houseman very rarely took enough time off work in the middle of the day for a full luncheon, and as his wife sat opposite him in the Red House Restaurant, she found herself wondering why, when everyone else in the studio seemed to be in such a panic about getting the next show together in time, he had chosen to do it on that day. She wondered, too, why he had hardly said a word during the starters, though it was obvious that he had something preying on his mind.

It was after the waiter had brought them their main courses that Houseman looked up from his steak, and with an expression in his eyes which could have been pain, anger, or sadness – or a combination of all three of them – and said, 'I want you to stop coming to the studio.'

'You want *what*?' Diana asked.

'I want you to stop coming to the studio,' Houseman repeated firmly.

Diana slid a mouthful of poached salmon into her mouth, and chewed on it thoughtfully. She knew now why he'd taken her out to lunch. He'd done it so they could have this particular conversation in a place where he was almost sure that she wouldn't make a scene.

'What's brought all this on?' she asked, when she'd swallowed the salmon.

'I thought after I'd shown you just how seriously I took it the last time, you'd learned your lesson,' her husband said. 'But you haven't, have you? I can't prove it yet, but I'm sure you're up to your old tricks again.'

Diana Houseman smiled. 'My old tricks,' she said, savouring the words almost as much as she'd been savouring the salmon. 'What a quaint, old-fashioned way you have of putting it.'

'You promised me when you married me—'

'I promised you *nothing*,' his wife said cuttingly.

'I asked you if you'd stop carrying on as you had been—'

'And I said I'd try. Well, I *have* tried.'

'But not very hard.'

Diana sighed. 'Do you really think you've been giving me what I need in bed?' she asked.

'I put in long hours at the studio,' Houseman said, suddenly defensive. 'I'm exhausted by the time I get home. Soon I should be able to hand some of the day-to-day running of the show over to someone else, and then I won't—'

'You'll never hand it over,' his wife interrupted him. 'You'd never give up an ounce of control if you had any choice in the matter. And even if you did, it wouldn't make any difference. As far as you're concerned, a sex drive is what you take to get to a stag night.'

'That's very clever,' Houseman said bitterly. 'Who made it up? One of your boyfriends?'

'What did you want out of marriage?' Diana demanded. 'A dumpy little wife who'd keep your meals warm until you decided to come home, and never leave the house unless she was on your arm? Or did you want a wife who every other man looked at longingly when she walked past – a wife who all your drinking friends wished belonged to them? Because if that's what you wanted, you've got just what you paid for.'

'The price is too high,' Houseman told her. 'I didn't think it would be, but it is.'

'I'm sorry, but the deal is done and it's too late to start asking for a refund now,' his wife said indifferently.

Why did their arguments seem, inevitably, to follow this same route, Houseman wondered. Why did he always suddenly find himself in retreat?

'If you can't change, couldn't you at least try to compromise a little?' he pleaded.

'That would depend on exactly what sort of compromise you have in mind,' his wife told him.

'If you must have affairs, at least try to be discrete. Stay away from the studio, as I asked you to. And stay away from any other men I know personally, as well.'

Diana smiled again. 'Just the *men*?'

'All I'm asking is that you don't do anything to embarrass me within my own social circle – or with the people outside it who look up to me.'

Diana Houseman laughed as if her husband had said the funniest thing imaginable. 'People who look up to *you*, Squeaky?'

'I told you never – ever – to call me that!' Houseman said angrily. 'That's all behind me now.'

'Is it really?' his wife asked. 'Do you want to hear the joke that's going the rounds at NWTV?'

'This isn't the time or the place for jokes.'

'But I think you'll really like this one. What's the difference between *Squeaky, Squiggy and Softy* and *Maddox Row*?'

'I don't want to—'

'On *Maddox Row*, the characters can *just about* move without somebody's hand up their backsides.'

Houseman put his head in his hands. She should never have said that, he thought – she should never have chipped away at what he had come to regard as the very foundation stone of his being.

Diana giggled. 'They can *just about* move without somebody's hand up their backsides,' she repeated.

And Bill Houseman, who had rescripted so many lives for the fictional people of *Maddox Row*, found himself starting to rescript his own. He had been frightened of too many things for far too long. It was time to fight back. He would make a phone call to the studio as soon as he left the table – a phone call which would set in motion a campaign which would demonstrate, once and for all, that he was *Madro* and *Madro* was him. But before that, he would deal with his wife.

Houseman took his hands away from his face, and looked Diana squarely in the eyes. 'I'll divorce you,' he said.

His wife, still not understanding the transformation which had taken place in him, smiled again. 'Don't be silly, Bill,' she said. 'You know you'd never do that. You couldn't stand the humiliation of going through a divorce.'

'Do you think that would be any worse than the humiliation I'm going through now?' Houseman asked. 'At least if we were divorced, there might be the possibility of seeing some light at the end of the tunnel.'

Now – finally – Diana began to pick up some of the danger signals. Perhaps she had pushed him too far, she thought. Perhaps she had led him such a dance that it really *would* be less painful for him to divorce her than to go on as they were.

'If you divorce me, I'll make sure I take you for every penny you've got,' she threatened.

Houseman laughed – and to her horror she realised that it was with genuine amusement.

'Do you really think that any judge in the land, after what he'd heard *in open court* about the way you've behaved, would hand all my hard-earned money over to you?' he asked. 'You'd be lucky if he let you leave with the coat on your back.'

Oh God, he's right! Diana's brain screamed, as it was flooded with realisation and panic. There isn't a judge in the country who'd give me a penny!

She looked down at her hand, and realised that it had started to tremble. 'You're . . . you're bluffing about a divorce, aren't you?' she said, and this time she was the one who was almost pleading.

'Maybe I *was* bluffing at the start,' Houseman admitted. 'But, do you know, I'm really not any more.'

'We could work things out if we really tried,' Diana said.

'Oh, there'll be jokes and finger-pointing behind my back for a few weeks after the case, but then it will all die down again,' Houseman said, as if she'd never spoken. 'And then I'll be free – free to find myself another gorgeous blonde if I want to, one who *does* know how to behave herself.'

'Don't you think you're being a little hasty?'

'No, I don't,' Houseman said, his voice growing more and more triumphant. 'You were right – you'll never change. The best thing I could do would be to cut my losses.'

'But what will become of me?'

Houseman positively beamed. He was no longer the cuckolded husband. He was Errol Flynn. He was Clark Gable. Tall, confident and masculine.

'What will become of you?' he asked. 'I don't really know. And frankly, my dear, I don't *give* a damn!'

Twenty-Six

False modesty had never been one of Monika Paniatowski's failings, and she was well aware she could sometimes change the atmosphere of a room just by walking into it. Normally, however, the atmosphere she created was one of interest – and perhaps of speculation. This time, as she entered the scriptwriters' office, it was as if she'd brought a chill Arctic wind with her – a wind which had instantly frozen Ben Drabble and Paddy Colligan to their desks.

For a few moments the icemen were perfectly still, then Drabble, thawing a little under Monika's questioning gaze, managed to say,

'It's . . . it's Miss Peignton, isn't it?'

'That's right,' Monika agreed.

'And . . . er . . . how can we help you, Miss Peignton?'

'Mr Wilcox would like to see copies of the draft scripts right away, please,' Monika told him.

The two writers exchanged uneasy glances.

'To tell you the truth, we've hit a few snags we didn't expect, and there's not much to show him yet,' Ben Drabble said awkwardly.

'Yes, we've still not got beyond a very rough outline,' Paddy Colligan chimed in, with very little conviction.

'Mr Wilcox expected that,' Monika said. 'He told me to ask for *whatever* you'd got.'

The muscles in Ben Drabble's left cheek twitched as he remembered the phone call he'd had from the Red House Restaurant not ten minutes earlier. 'Honestly, we don't really have anything *at all*,' he said apologetically.

The office door swung open so violently that it crashed noisily against the wall, and turning, Monika saw Diana Houseman framed in the doorway.

The platinum blonde seemed to have lost all of the self-assurance she'd displayed the last time they'd met, the sergeant thought. Mrs Houseman's hair was dishevelled, her cheeks were unnaturally red. But it was her eyes which were really telling – they were as wide and troubled as those of a frightened rabbit caught unexpectedly in the beam of a car's headlamps.

'I . . . I thought you'd be alone,' Diana Houseman gasped.

Who was she talking to? Monika wondered. Drabble? Or Colligan? Both of them looked shocked, but more by the sudden nature of her instrusion than the fact that she was there at all.

'I need . . . I need to talk to you,' Diana Houseman continued, still looking in the general direction of both men, so it was impossible to say which one she was addressing. 'It's very important.'

'We're always here to help in any way we can, Mrs Houseman,' Ben Drabble said awkwardly. He looked pointedly at Monika. 'If you'd excuse us, Miss Peignton . . . ?'

'But what about the script?' Monika asked, more to see how he would react than anything else.

'I've told you, we've nothing to show to Jeremy Wilcox at the moment,' Ben Drabble said irritably.

'He won't like that,' Monika replied.

Ben Drabble snapped the pencil he was holding in his hands. 'I don't care whether he likes it or not,' he said. 'If Jeremy Wilcox has got any complaints, tell him to take them up with the producer. Now, if you wouldn't mind leaving us . . .'

Yes, but leaving who, exactly? Monika wondered as she backed out of the room and stepped into the corridor. Did Drabble mean all three of them? Or was he just talking about himself and Diana Houseman?

How many people had he and Constable Pickup spoken to in Sladebury? Rutter asked himself as he drove back to Whitebridge.

Fifteen? More than that?

And what had they learned from all those interviews? Absolutely bugger all of any use!

157

Val Farnsworth had been a smashing kid, the villagers had all agreed – a bit wild sometimes, but there'd been no real harm in her – and they were tremendously proud of what she'd achieved.

But there was one person in the village who didn't share everyone else's admiration of Val, Rutter reminded himself, remembering what the landlord of the Red Lion had *almost* said. So perhaps it was still possible to squeeze one small pearl of information out of the day after all.

He turned to the constable who was sitting in the passenger seat beside him. 'Tell me about your Uncle Arthur,' he said.

Pickup jumped, as if he'd been given an unexpected electric shock. 'What was that, sir?'

'Your Uncle Arthur. Tell me why he doesn't like Val Farnsworth.'

'How did you . . . who told you—?'

'That doesn't really matter,' Rutter interrupted. 'I am right, aren't I? He doesn't like her? Because of what happened with Ellie Tomkins?'

'Well, yes, in a manner of—'

'So tell me what happened.'

The young constable had turned as red as a beetroot. 'It all happened a long time ago, sir,' he said awkwardly, 'back when I was nowt but a nipper.'

'So you don't really know?'

'I know all right. What I wasn't told, I've managed to piece together myself, but even so . . .'

'What?'

'Well, it isn't something you like to talk about, is it?'

'How will I know that until I've heard what you've got to say?'

'Well, it's like this,' Pickup said reluctantly. 'My Uncle Arthur an' Ellie Tomkins had been walkin' out together for over three years, and they were just six months off getting wed. Then Ellie broke off the engagement, and went to Manchester to live with Val.'

'And your uncle blames Val?'

'That's right, sir.'

'Isn't that a bit harsh?' Rutter asked. 'There could have been any number of reasons why Ellie decided not to go through with the marriage, and if Val Farnsworth was kind enough to offer her a roof over her head . . .'

Pickup sighed. 'You don't understand, sir.'

'Don't I?'

'No. You're like all the people in Sladebury. They thought Val was just being kind, an' all – but she bloody wasn't. Ellie didn't just go to live in Val's house, you see. She went to really *live* with her . . . if you see what I mean.'

'Yes,' Rutter said pensively. 'Yes, I think I do.'

'They said *what*?' Jeremy Wilcox demanded.

'They said that they really didn't have any new bits of script to show you,' Monika answered levelly.

'Not even for Friday night's show?'

'Apparently not.'

Wilcox had been sitting in his swivel chair, but now he got up and began to pace the room. 'They're like the Freemasons,' he said angrily.

'Who are?'

'The people who've worked on *Madro* right from the beginning. No, I take that back – they're *worse* than the Masons. At least the funny-handshake brigade are usually willing to let you join them if you've got the right qualifications and think you have something to contribute. But not this lot! Oh no! If you weren't here at the birth of the show, you're nothing – and you never *can be* anything, no matter how good you are.'

'If you'd tell me what you'd like me to be getting on with, Mr Wilcox . . .' Monika said, with all the uncertainty she imagined a real assistant would feel in this situation.

Then she saw that she might as well not have bothered with the ham acting, because he wasn't even listening.

The director's pace had quickened, so that now he was covering the length of his office in three angry strides, then swinging round to repeat the action in the opposite direction. And though he was still talking, it was fairly obvious that he wasn't talking to *her*.

'They never wanted me on the show in the first place,' he said angrily. 'Especially Bill Bloody Houseman! He's always been the worst of the lot. He wanted a poodle, not a director – somebody who'd be happy to sit at his feet and wait to be told what to do. And now they've all got together and think that they can freeze me out. Well, they're wrong – oh *so* wrong. I'm sticking with this show until *I'm* ready to go. And if anyone tries to get in my way, they're going to be very, very sorry.'

Twenty-Seven

Woodend was late for the meeting in the Drum and Monkey. He hadn't planned to be, but he was, and as a result Rutter and Paniatowski found themselves alone together in the bar. For the first couple of minutes they both tried to maintain a friendly façade by making safe – almost sterile – comments on topics that even *they* could not possibly disagree over, but that soon became a strain, too, and they lapsed into awkward silence.

It was a relief to them both when the chief inspector finally walked into the bar a good twenty minutes after he'd intended to.

'Sorry about that,' he said, as he sat down. 'I tried to get away earlier, but it's not always easy to walk out on the Brass.'

'You were discussing what should happen now the chief's in hospital, were you?' Rutter asked.

'Aye,' Woodend agreed. 'For all them buggers have muttered about how useless John Dinnage was in the past, they're runnin' round like headless chickens at the thought that he might not be there any longer.'

'How does it look?' Paniatowski asked.

'Not good,' Woodend said heavily. 'Even if he does pull through this time, I doubt he'll ever be fit enough to take the drivin' seat again.' He sighed. 'I'll miss John. He's been a bloody good bobby. An' I don't even want to think about what useless prat they'll probably put in to replace him.' He reached into his pocket and pulled out his Capstan Full Strengths. 'But enough of that,' he said. 'Let's get on with the job we've come here to do, shall we?'

For the next half an hour, Woodend and Paniatowski did

161

most of the talking. Rutter, for his part, was quite content to keep his bombshell to himself for a while – if not exactly holding it back, then at least waiting until he could explode it with maximum effect.

It was as Paniatowski was outlining that afternoon's incident in the scriptwriters' office that Woodend held his hand up for silence. He closed his eyes for a few seconds, then opened them again and said, 'I don't like the picture I'm startin' to build up. I don't like it at all.'

'What's wrong with it?' Paniatowski asked.

'It's all a bit too neat. A bit too much like paintin' by numbers.' The chief inspector shrugged. 'But then even if it *is* obvious, there's still no reason why it can't be the truth, is there?'

'What's obvious?' Paniatowski said. 'Do you think you know who killed Valerie Farnsworth?'

'Aye. An' I think I know *why*.'

Rutter grinned at the look of exasperation which had appeared on Paniatowski's face. He might have looked like that once, too, but he had been working for Cloggin'-it Charlie for long enough now to accept that the oblique statements and long pauses were vintage Woodend, and that the easiest thing to do was to let him move at his own pace.

'It's not a motive that would make *me* want to kill,' the chief inspector continued, 'but then I'm not him, am I?'

Rutter wondered idly how long Paniatowski could hold out. He had counted to eight when she finally said, 'So what *is* the motive?'

'It's very simple,' Woodend told her. 'Valerie Farnsworth was killed as a way of ensurin' the continued success of *Maddox Row*.'

'Go on,' Paniatowski said.

'After a long run as an unprecedented success, the show was starting to lose some of its audience. So what could the producer, the man who reaps most of the rewards for success – an' takes most of the blame for failure – do about it? Well, killin' off one of the leadin' characters has worked for other shows, an' so Bill Houseman started playin' around with the idea of doin' just that on *Maddox Row*. But *Madro* isn't like any of the shows that have gone before it – it's trail blazin' an' unique – so there were no guarantees that the same old solutions would work this time. On the other hand, if instead of just killin' off a character, you actually killed off the actress who's playin' her—'

'But why does it have to be Houseman?' Paniatowski interrupted. 'Why couldn't it have been someone else who'd lose out if *Maddox Row* went down the drain?'

'Because it matters a lot more to him than it does to anybody else,' Woodend said. 'When you've been involved with as many murders as I have, you find you start askin' yourself what it'd take to make *you* kill. Well, I think I've come up with an answer for myself – the only reason I'd murder anybody would be to protect my daughter.'

'*Just* your daughter?' Paniatowski asked. 'Not your wife as well?'

'Joan an' me have been together for a long time, an' if anythin' ever happened to her, it would be the end of me,' Woodend said seriously. 'But I still don't think I could force myself to kill for her. Annie's different. I know I've not always been the ideal father . . .' He paused. 'No, let's be honest, I've *never* been the ideal father, I've not even come close to it. But I do bear part of the responsibility for bringin' Annie into the world, an' that gives me a duty to look after her. She might be all grown-up now, an' not even want my help any more, but that doesn't matter. However she sees herself, to me she's still my baby. An' *Maddox Row* is Houseman's!'

'But even if you're right, why choose the most popular character in the whole programme?' Paniatowski asked. 'He'd been planning to kill off Larry Coates's character – why not kill off Coates himself?'

It was the moment to drop the bombshell, Rutter decided. 'I think I might have an answer to that,' he said, smiling.

'Go on, lad,' Woodend said.

'Monika thinks that Diana Houseman is – for want of a better phrase – a loose woman,' Rutter said.

Paniatowski frowned. 'From what I've seen today, I'd say she's having it off with *somebody* at the studio – and I've got a good idea who,' she admitted.

'I think you're only seeing one side of the picture,' Rutter said.

'So why don't you show us the other side,' Paniatowski countered.

Rutter turned to Woodend. 'When you were talking to George Adams this morning, he accused Valerie Farnsworth of biting the hand that fed her – Bill Houseman's hand – didn't he?'

'That's right, he did,' Woodend agreed.

'And when you pressed him, he said it was a personal matter rather than a professional one.'

'True.'

'So what you have to ask yourself is how Valerie Farnsworth hurt Houseman in a personal way.'

'Why don't you just tell us – since you've obviously already worked it out?' Paniatowski said sourly.

'I learned something very interesting about Valerie Farnsworth this afternoon,' Rutter said. 'She was a lesbian.'

'Oh well, if she was a lesbian, she got no more than she deserved,' Monika Paniatowski said. 'There's no point in us wasting any more of our time investigating a *lesbian* murder, is there?'

'Shut up, Monika,' Woodend said. 'I think Bob may be on to something here.'

'Perhaps Diana Houseman *is* having an affair with a man at the studio, as the sergeant seems to think,' Rutter said, 'but perhaps she was also having an affair with a *woman.*'

'With Valerie Farnsworth?'

'Exactly. Now it's possible that Houseman doesn't know she's having an affair with this man. But it's equally possible that he does, and has forced himself to come to terms with it. He wouldn't be the first man to play it that way.'

'No,' Woodend agreed. 'He wouldn't.'

'But to find out your wife has been betraying you with another *woman* . . . well, that's an entirely different matter. I can't think of any man I know who'd be willing to accept that.'

'So you're saying that any man who discovered his wife was

164

having an affair with a lesbian would kill her?' Paniatowski asked.

'No, of course not,' Rutter said dismissively. 'But given that he was planning to murder *someone*, anyway, wouldn't that discovery automatically make her the prime candidate? Wouldn't it be the perfect way of killing two birds with one stone – of protecting his programme *and* getting revenge on Val Farnsworth for the way she's humiliated him?'

'Yes,' Paniatowski said grudgingly. 'Yes, it does make sense. But even if you're both right about Houseman, it won't be easy to prove it.'

'Won't be easy!' Woodend repeated. 'Given the chaos in the studio on the night of the murder, and the fact that we've got over two dozen people without watertight alibis, it could be nearly bloody impossible.'

Woodend knew that something was wrong the moment he turned the corner and saw his wife standing in front of their cottage door.

Joan never waited on the doorstep for him! When she heard his car approaching, she automatically switched on the kettle and the television, then started cooking the meal. That was what she always did. That was what she'd done every working day of her entire married life!

He brought the car to a halt at the far side of the house, and as he put on the handbrake, he noticed that his hands were shaking. He didn't even have time to get out of the vehicle before Joan was by his side.

'What's the matter, love?' he asked fearfully.

'Annie . . .'

'What's happened to her?'

'She . . . she told me she was goin' over Rosemary's house after school, an' that Rosemary's dad would bring her home.'

'Then what are you worryin' about?'

'I went up to her room about half an hour ago, to see if she had any washin' she needed doin'. The first thing I noticed was that her suitcase wasn't on top of her wardrobe, and then I saw this lyin' on her bed.' She thrust a piece of paper into Woodend's hand. 'Read it! Read it, Charlie.'

'Dear Mam and Dad,' Woodend read,

I know this letter will come as a shock to you, and for a long time I've put off writing it, but now I don't feel as if I have any choice. I've tried to like Lancashire, but I just can't. I miss London and I miss my friends. So I've gone back.

The words clawed their way around Woodend's brain like a ferret trying to bite its way out of a sack.

Gone back! Gone back! Gone back!

The letter continued:

You don't need to worry about me. I won't do anything foolish, and I'll keep out of trouble. I promise I'll give you a ring as soon as I'm settled somewhere. In the meantime, please don't try to find me.

Love
Annie

'We have to do somethin', Charlie!' Joan sobbed. 'We have to find her an' bring her back.'

'That's just what she asked us not to do,' Woodend replied, as he felt the world he thought that he knew crumbling around him.

'She's only a kid!' Joan protested.

'She'll be sixteen in a couple of weeks. That means that legally she can live away from home if she wants to, as long as she doesn't break the law.'

'Bugger the law!' said Joan, who rarely swore. 'I want my daughter back again.'

'An' so do I. But there's ways an' ways to go about it.'

'Forget that you're a bloody bobby for once, can't you?!'

'I am forgettin' it,' Woodend said. 'I'm tryin' to put myself in Annie's place. If I went down to London tomorrow, I could probably find her. An' I could probably talk her into comin' back home. But it wouldn't last. She'd be off again in a fortnight – and this time she'd make sure she vanished without trace.'

'So what do *you* suggest we do?'

'Wait until she calls us—'

'An' what if she doesn't?'

'She's promised she will. An' you know our Annie – she always keeps her promises.'

'So she'll call. What happens then?'

'Then I *will* go down to London an' talk to her. Or you can go, if you'd prefer it.'

'No, it'd be better if you went,' Joan said. 'She's always paid more attention to what you say – though God knows why, because you're hardly ever here to say *anythin'*.'

Woodend could count on the fingers of one hand the number of times his wife had criticised him during their married life – and he could not recall her ever saying anything which had hurt him more. Yet he recognised the justice behind the remark. He hadn't been there often enough. Even when he'd planned to be, his work had usually got in the way.

'We'll ring all her friends,' he said. 'We'll tell them that if they see her, they're to pass on the message that we miss her, an' that there's always a place for her back home whenever she feels she needs one.'

'An' we'll ask them to call us, an' tell us where she is,' Joan said.

'No, we won't,' Woodend told her. 'That would be the worst thing we could possibly do. It would make her feel hunted. It would make her go to ground.' He put his arm around his wife's shoulder, and felt a tension there which was new to him. 'This is the best way, love. I promise you it's the best way.'

'The best way would have been if she'd never felt the need to run away at all!' Joan said bitterly.

An American Interlude

Though it was already the chilly dead of night in England, it was still a pleasantly sunny mid-afternoon in California, and the Plymouth Fury which roared down the canyon pretty much had the road to itself.

The man behind the wheel of the Fury had been christened Walter Schmidt, but for the previous twenty years the only name he had gone by had been Preston Vance. He was drunk, and he was angry. And he was driving much too fast.

He pulled hard on the wheel of the Fury to negotiate a sharp bend. He loved this car. It had a 6276cc engine and tailfins the size of small cities. It was not the most expensive automobile on the market, but the very fact that he could afford to buy pricier, yet had chosen not to, was a statement in itself.

Could have afforded, he corrected himself. Not 'could afford', but 'could *have*'!

He took another swig from the Jack Daniels bottle which he had wedged between his body and the door, and he felt his foot, as if it had a mind of its own, press down harder on the gas pedal. And why shouldn't it press down harder? He had been born to drive fast cars, sleep with fast women, earn his money fast and spend it in the same way.

It had been a mistake to go to the brunch. A big mistake. Everybody there had been polite – friendly even – but he had caught the occasional condescending stare, and he was sure that the moment he'd left, his hosts would be among the first to start the back-biting.

Well, screw them!

He had drunk their booze. He had sniffed up their lines of coke. He had vomited into their swimming pool.

So let them talk about him, if they wanted to. Let them talk about him until they'd talked so much that their own existences paled into nothingness, and his misfortunes became the centre of their lives.

It didn't matter a damn, because underneath it all he was still the big star he'd always been.

For a second he found his vision was starting to blur, but he wiped the back of his hand across his eyes and they began working properly again.

How much had he drunk in the last couple of hours, he wondered as the needle on the speedometer passed the sixty mark. A whole bottle of whiskey? More than that? It didn't matter. Nothing mattered when you lived in a town without pity – a town where everyone loved a winner for just as long as he was winning, then rubbed their hands with glee when he fell off his perch.

He took another slug of whiskey, and decided that what he really needed now was a cigarette. He patted the pockets of his tuxedo, but the pack was not there.

'Where are my goddam smokes?' he shouted into the rushing wind.

Had they known – those people back there at the brunch – that the tuxedo was rented? Well, screw them if they did, and screw them if they didn't.

He still needed a smoke – worse than ever now. He glanced down at the floor, and saw the pack lying there, next to the brake pedal.

He must have dropped it, his befuddled mind told him. He must have dropped it, and that was why it was on the floor.

He bent down to pick the pack up. It was more of a stretch than he'd thought it would be. He gasped with the effort, then felt his fingers wrap around the Luckies. He straightened up again, and saw that something strange had happened. The road, which should have directly in front of his hood, had somehow managed to sneak away to the side when he wasn't looking.

He'd have to do something to correct that, he thought.

He was still thinking it when his Plymouth smashed into the tree at over seventy miles an hour.

172

Thursday

Twenty-Eight

W oodend had tossed and turned for most of the night, and it was not until shortly before dawn that he had finally dropped into a troubled sleep.

He'd woken less than two hours later, with the hope that the nightmare in which Annie had left home would quickly dissipate itself from his befuddled mind. It had taken him only a few seconds to realise that it was no dream at all – that Annie really had gone – yet a vague kind of hope continued to cling to him as he went mechanically through his morning routines.

Annie saw what she was doing as glamorous, he told himself as he shaved, but it wouldn't take her long to realise that it wasn't, and she would be back on the evening train.

Annie was punishing him, he decided as he sipped lethargically at his tea and drew on his first Capstan Full Strength of the morning, but it would only be a short punishment, because she was too kind-hearted to make him suffer for any real length of time.

Annie . . .

Annie had *gone*, he finally accepted, as he knotted his tweed tie in front of the mirror. She'd hadn't done it because of some romantic idea of adventure, or because she wanted to get back at her father. That wasn't his Annie at all. She'd left simply because she was too unhappy where she was to stay there any longer.

When it was time for him to set out for the studio, Joan handed him his jacket and brushed the lint off his shoulders, as she always had done – but she did not look him in the eye.

He couldn't say that he blamed her!

Whatever else his faults, Jeremy Wilcox was by no means a

stupid man. But even had he been a complete imbecile, he could still have worked out, within the first two minutes of the regular Thursday meeting, that something he was sure he would find personally unpleasant was afoot. How could he fail to work it out, when he had the tangible evidence – a perfectly typed script – right there in his hands?

Wilcox laid the script on the table and looked in turn at the other three men in the room. Drabble and Colligan seemed so uncomfortable that they were practically huddled together, he decided, but Bill Houseman – sitting in splendid isolation at the head of the table – was positively glowing with self-assurance.

The director cleared his throat. 'Now here's a strange thing,' he said, forcing himself to keep his voice level and even. 'Yesterday, when I sent my assistant for the script, you said you had nothing at all to show me. Yet less than a day later, you're in a position to present me with a complete episode. How is that possible?'

'We worked through most of the night,' Ben Drabble said, avoiding eye contact.

'And here's another strange thing,' Wilcox continued. 'I haven't had time to study the script properly yet – how could I, when it's only just been handed to me? – but there seem to be all kinds of changes in it that we haven't even discussed.'

'There simply wasn't the time to talk to everybody about it, Jeremy,' Ben Drabble said.

Wilcox's control cracked, and he slammed his hand down hard on the table. 'Didn't have time to talk to *everybody*!' he repeated. 'Well, for your information, I'm not just part of this "everybody" you're talking so glibly about. I'm the *director*. I'm what makes the whole bloody thing work!'

'Is that right?' Bill Houseman asked. 'You're the one who makes the whole thing work, are you?'

'Of course I am,' Jeremy Wilcox said hotly. 'You'd have to be blind not to see that.'

'Then isn't it odd that though you've only been here for six months, the show's been a huge success for over *two years*?' Houseman mused.

176

'That depends what you mean by successful,' Wilcox countered. 'Which of the episodes we have in the archives do you think will survive the test of time? Which of them will the future historians of television hold up as examples of truly groundbreaking work? The ones I've directed in the last six months – or the ones my predecessor cobbled together before that?'

'If I were you, I'd worry more about the audience you've been getting recently than I would about what future generations will think,' Houseman said.

'Are you saying that's my fault?' Wilcox all but screamed. 'Are you blaming *me* for the drop in viewing figures?'

'No,' Houseman replied, sounding almost reasonable. 'In fact, I'm more than happy to have you take all the credit for the *successes* of the show and none of the blame for its *failures*.'

'We all know that it's not as simple as you two are trying to make it sound,' Ben Drabble said. 'There could be dozens of reasons why the viewing figures have been falling.'

Houseman shot Drabble an angry look. I was under the impression that when you agreed not to show Wilcox the script, you realised which side your bread was buttered on, he thought. But you don't, do you? You're still trying to play both ends against the middle – and that won't work any longer.

'There are people who I'm obliged to take lectures from – but you're not one of them,' he told Ben Drabble. 'You're nothing but one of the writers. And writers are two a penny.'

'I was only saying that—' Drabble began.

'I'm not interested in what you were "only saying",' Houseman told him. 'I'm heartily sick of working with ingrates. I created *Maddox Row*. Me – and nobody else! If it wasn't for my efforts, you two scribblers would be drawing the dole every Friday, and talking incessantly over your halves of bitter about the great English novel which you secretly knew you were never going to write. And as for Jeremy . . . well, I expect he'd be back to directing commercials for washing powder.'

'There was more real drama in my commercials than there ever was in *Madro* before I arrived,' Jeremy Wilcox said.

177

'Your big problem, Bill, is that you wouldn't recognise good television if it hit you in the face.'

'I think we all might feel a lot better after a short break,' said Ben Drabble, who, in the past, had borrowed money from both the producer *and* the director to pay off his gambling debts.

'I've been far too liberal up to now,' Bill Houseman said, ignoring Drabble's interruption. 'Well, that's all about to change. There are people working here today who'll be finding themselves out on the street by the end of the week.'

Oh God, let one of them be me, Paddy Colligan prayed silently. Force me to do what I haven't got the guts to do for myself – force me back into the work I *should* be doing. Yet even as the idea crossed his mind, he felt his stomach turn to water at the thought of being poor again.

'You can't threaten me, you know,' Wilcox told Houseman.

The producer smiled. 'People in a strong position – as I am – don't need to make *threats*,' he said.

And the looks on the faces of the three men showed that they knew he was right. He *didn't* need to make threats. Now that *Madro* was riding high again, he had the power to do whatever he liked.

A loud bell, suddenly screaming out its warning from the corridor, made them all jump.

'That was the fire alarm going off,' Paddy Colligan said, unnecessarily.

'It wouldn't be the first time that some idiot's accidentally set it off,' Houseman said indifferently. 'The safety officer will stop it in a minute or two.'

But the bell continued to ring insistently, and through the office window they could see a stream of people making their way down the corridor in a manner which suggested that while they knew the whole thing was only a drill, it was still a welcome break from routine.

'Should we leave ourselves?' Ben Drabble said.

'You might as well,' Bill Houseman told him. 'I've said everything that I wanted to say.'

'Well, I certainly haven't!' Jeremy Wilcox retorted.

'That may possibly be true,' Houseman replied. 'But you've said all I'm prepared to *listen* to.'

178

The bell droned on. The flow of people past the office window was starting to decrease.

Ben Drabble rose uncertainly to his feet. 'Well, I suppose we'd better go, like we've been instructed to,' he said.

'Yes, get out,' Bill Houseman said. 'Get out the lot of you.'

Jeremy Wilcox stood up so violently that his chair fell over behind him. 'I'm going now,' he said, 'but you've not heard the last of this.'

Houseman smiled again. 'Did you catch that?' he asked Paddy Colligan. 'It's quite a good line – in a clichéd sort of way. Maybe you could use it in one of the scripts. It would sound just right coming from the mouth of an old harridan like Madge Thornycroft.'

For a moment, it seemed as if Jeremy Wilcox would lash out at Houseman across the table. Then the director flicked his hair back haughtily, and stormed out of the door. After a second's hesitation, Ben Drabble followed him.

Paddy Colligan had stood up, too, but instead of joining the others, he looked down at Bill Houseman. The producer appeared to be studying the revised script in front of him – though how he could concentrate with all that racket going on was a mystery to the Irishman.

'Are you coming, too, Mr Houseman?' Colligan asked.

The producer looked up. 'What was that?'

'The fire bell's still ringing. I was wondering if you were planning to leave, like everybody else.'

Houseman shook his head. 'A good captain does not abandon his ship,' he said, 'and I am a *very* good captain.'

'If it turns out to be a real fire—'

'Then I will probably be burnt to death – which, I should imagine, would do nothing but delight several people who are already living in trepidation of the axe falling on their unworthy necks.'

'You shouldn't talk that like,' Paddy Colligan said quietly.

'I'll talk how I damn well please,' Houseman told him. 'Now why don't you take yourself off, like a good little script-writer? And drop the blind on your way out. Now I've got the building to myself, I might finally be able to get on with some real work.'

Twenty-Nine

It was a long time since he'd been involved in a case which he so much wanted to see the back of, Woodend thought, as he drove through the village towards the old mill which had once provided it with a livelihood.

He really wanted it over! Done with! Wrapped up!

And he wanted the man who had taken another human being's life simply for the sake of his own ego to be safely behind bars, so that he himself could have a few days clear to try and sort out his own life.

He caught his first sight of the mill from some distance away, but it was not until he turned a bend in the road that he got a clear view of the car park and saw that it was full of people.

Something out of the ordinary had happened, he realised, something which had meant the mill had had to be evacuated – and he felt a sudden chill of misgiving run down his spine.

You're worryin' unnecessarily, he reassured himself. It's nothin' but a fire drill. What else could it be?

In a way, it was a stroke of luck. With all those people around, it might just be possible to slip into the building without being noticed by the gentlemen – and one very unscrupulous lady – of the press.

It was as he parked that he saw the man in the grey suit standing in front of the main entrance to the studio. The suit was so severe that it could almost have been a uniform, and that fact – combined with the megaphone that he held in his hand – was enough to identify him as the security officer.

The man raised the megaphone to his mouth. 'Can I have your attention, please!' he called.

The mechanically distorted voice travelled across the car

park, and the small knots of people who had been chatting to one another turned to face him.

'The entire building has been thoroughly checked out, and it is now safe to enter it again,' the security officer said. 'Please return to your posts in an orderly fashion. Thank you for your co-operation.'

The moment the announcement was finished some of the people began walking back towards the building, but there were others who preferred to linger a little, while they finished their cigarettes or their conversations.

Woodend looked around for Bill Houseman, but there was no sign of the producer anywhere. If he was going to avoid being spotted by the reporters, he had better make his move now, the chief inspector thought, joining the stream of traffic flowing back into the studio.

As Woodend walked past the Actors' Garden, he glanced beyond it to the dressing room where Valerie Farnsworth had met her lonely, terrifying death. He would get Bill Houseman for that, he promised himself – whatever it took.

But as he had told Paniatowski and Rutter the previous evening, it would not be easy. Houseman was nobody's fool. Without any witnesses to place him at the scene of the crime, he probably thought he was going to get away with it, and as long as he was confident of that, he would not put a foot wrong. So the trick would be to undermine that confidence – to suggest that he might have left behind one telling clue which would betray him. He would fight off the instinct to check he had completely covered his tracks at first, but in the end he would surrender to it. And when he did that – when they caught him in a suspicious circumstance he could not explain away – they would have him.

Woodend passed the scenery workshop and the technical store, and drew level with Houseman's office. The blind was down, but since it was only thirty-six hours to the next show, it was probable that the producer was inside. Perhaps he had been inside all through the fire drill. Perhaps that was why the chief inspector had not seen him in the car park.

Woodend knocked on the door. There was no answer, but the door was not properly closed, and his knock made it swing

181

open just wide enough for him to see part of the office – and to wish that he hadn't!

He pushed the door open. Houseman was slumped over his desk. His arms were stretched out in front of him, so that the tips of his fingers drooped over the far edge. His head was resting between his in-tray and his out-tray.

John Dinnage had been found in a similar position. But it was not a heart attack which had reduced Houseman to this state, it was a large carving knife – buried in his back almost up to the hilt.

Woodend closed the door behind him, stepped forward, and placed his index finger against Bill Houseman's neck. There was no pulse. Bill Houseman, his main suspect in the murder of Valerie Farnsworth, was indisputably as dead as a dodo himself.

Woodend stepped back and let his gaze sweep the room, as if hoping to find the killer crouching in a corner. But apart from himself and the corpse, the office was empty.

He walked over to the door, opened it just wide enough to step outside, and looked at the stream of people making their way back to their posts. Any one of them could have used the confusion of the fire alarm to slip into Houseman's office and stick the knife in his back. Any bloody one of them!

The chief inspector took his packet of Capstan Full Strengths out of his pocket, and lit one up.

How was DCS Ainsworth going to react to the news of a second killing, especially when the officer in charge of investigating the first had been, if not in the building, then at least in the area?

How was the press – the pack of hungry jackals outside – going to report it the next day?

'Shit!' Woodend said aloud – and realised that was exactly what he was in.

Thirty

L ike most of the windows in the studio, the one in the safety officer's room had a view of the central concourse and, looking through it, Woodend could see Bob Rutter's team organising the staff of *Maddox Row* into lines outside the conference rooms. It was probably almost an exact replay of the scene on Monday night, after Val Farnsworth's body had been discovered, he thought gloomily.

He turned to face the people in the room. One of them was the safety officer himself, the other a spotty-faced youth who looked as if he were about to soil his trousers.

'Let's start at the beginnin', shall we?' Woodend suggested to the safety officer. 'What was the first thing you did when you heard the fire bell ringin'?'

'I checked on the panel on the wall over there, to see where it had been set off,' the other man replied, pointing with his finger. 'The flashing light told me it was in one of the rehearsal rooms, so I went straight there. That's where I found young Brian.'

The spotty youth jumped at the sound of his own name.

'Why did you set the alarm off?' Woodend asked.

'B . . . Buildin' maintenance sent me there to sweep up,' the youth stammered. 'There was, like, this big old tea chest in the corner of the room. I think it belongs to the props department. There was smoke comin' out of it.'

'They use it for their rubbish,' the safety officer said. 'I told them it isn't safe, but they never listen. My guess is that some idiot dropped an unextinguished cigarette end in there.'

'So you saw the smoke, an' you set off the alarm?' Woodend said to the boy.

'That . . . that's right.'

'There was no need for it,' the safety officer said. 'He could probably have stamped it out with this shoe. And if that had failed, there was a fire extinguisher on the wall.'

'Why *didn't* you use the extinguisher?' Woodend asked Brian.

'I p . . . panicked,' the boy admitted.

'You're sure that's what it was?' Woodend demanded.

'W . . . what do you mean?'

'You're sure someone didn't pay you to set off the alarm?'

'No! I . . . I just saw the smoke, an' then I broke the glass.'

'All right,' Woodend said wearily. 'You can go.'

Brian did not need telling twice. He took a quick gulp of air and fled from the room.

'Do you believe him?' Woodend asked, when the boy had slammed the door behind him.

'Yes, I do,' the fire officer said. 'It was a stupid way to behave, but then half these kids haven't got the sense they were born with.'

'I believe him, too,' Woodend said. 'What happened after you'd located the source of the lad's panic?'

'I gave it a quick squirt with the extinguisher, just to make sure it was properly out.'

'So at that point you knew there was no real danger?'

'That's right.'

'Then why didn't you simply abandon the evacuation?'

'A lot of people were already outside in the car park by then. Besides, we've been told it's dangerous to issue counter-instructions once an evacuation's actually in progress. And our procedures specifically state that, whatever the reason the alarm's been set off, we still have to check every room to make sure it's safe before we can allow anybody back in the building.'

'An' that's what you did?'

'That's what I did – starting with the studio and working my way towards the main door.'

'So you checked Mr Houseman's office?'

The safety officer looked sheepish. 'I called out to ask if anybody was in there, but there was no reply,' he confessed.

184

'No, there wouldn't have been,' Woodend said dryly. 'Dead people are *often* unnaturally quiet. So while you were doin' your checkin', did you see anybody else around?'

The safety officer looked down at the floor. 'No.'

'You're absolutely sure of that?'

'Look, try and see it from my point of view,' the safety officer said. 'As soon as your investigation's over, you'll be gone. But I have to keep on working here – and it won't make my job any easier if I've got anybody into trouble.'

'So you'd rather shield a murderer than make your own life a little uncomfortable, would you?'

The safety officer shook his head. 'Of course I wouldn't. But the people I found had anything but murder on their minds.'

'Tell me about them anyway.'

The safety officer sighed. 'There was this couple,' he conceded. 'Well, they're not really a couple as such, if the truth be told. As a matter of fact, they're both married to other people.'

'What about them?'

'I found them in the props store. Her knickers were round her ankles, and he was just pulling his trousers up.'

'I noticed Mrs Houseman, the producer's wife, in the car park,' Woodend said. 'She didn't happen to be the woman you're talkin' about, did she?'

'No. It wasn't her. The woman I'm talking about works in make-up, and the man who was with her is from props.'

'But you weren't really surprised when I suggested it *might* have been Mrs Houseman, were you?' Woodend asked.

'Well, you know . . .' the safety officer said embarrassedly.

'No, I don't know,' Woodend told him. 'Are you saying that it's common knowledge that Diana Houseman has been having an affair?'

'*An* affair!' the safety officer repeated.

'You're telling me she's had more than one?'

'I'm not going to give you any names, because I've no proof one way or the other, but if the rumours are to be believed, nobody in trousers was really safe from her.'

Woodend nodded. 'Let's get back to the buildin' check

that you did,' he said. 'Apart from this couple grabbin' the chance for a spot of nookie in the cupboard, did you see anybody else?'

'Nobody. But that doesn't really prove a thing. If somebody didn't want me to see them, there are dozens of places in this studio where they could hide until I went off to check somewhere else. The only reason I found that couple I told you about was because they were more intent on what they were doing to each other than they were on what was happening around them.'

Despite his general feeling of despondency, Woodend grinned. 'What instructions were the staff told to follow once they were outside?'

'Their *instructions* were for them to form up in their assigned groups,' the safety officer said. 'All the kitchen staff should have been in one group, all the props people in another, and so on. That way, we can do a head count to make sure nobody's gone missing.'

'But I take it that didn't happen.'

'The big trouble with this kind of thing is that nobody ever takes it seriously,' the safety officer complained. 'They hear the bell ring, and their automatic assumption is that it's nothing more than a drill. So they leave the building like they're supposed to, but once they're outside, all procedure goes by the board. It never occurs to them that this time it *could* be the real thing, you see. It never enters their heads that the people responsible for their safety need to know if there's anybody left inside.'

'In other words, instead of doin' what they're supposed to do, they do pretty much what they feel like?'

'That's about the long and short of it,' the safety officer admitted sadly. 'Oh, I've no doubt that some of them assembled at the correct points, but the majority probably didn't. You know what people are like. They drift off to their cars to listen to the racing on the wireless. They go and chat with their mates from other departments. It wouldn't surprise me if some of them didn't slip off to the nearest pub for a quick one.' He sighed heavily. 'It's not easy, under any circumstances, to get the general public to co-operate with safety procedures in the proper disciplined manner, but with this lot from the entertainment industry—'

'You think you've got problems?' Woodend interrupted. 'You should try conductin' a double murder investigation among this lot from the entertainment industry.'

Thirty-One

The ragged queues outside the studio's conference rooms were shorter than they had been earlier, but there was still a fair number of people waiting to have their statements taken down.

Woodend, standing in front of the safety officer's room, wondered how long it would take Bob Rutter's team to complete their work. Probably no more than an hour or two, he decided. Not that he was entertaining any great hopes that the statements would actually lead anywhere. He'd seen the confusion in the car park for himself, and was well aware of just how easy it would have been for the killer to slip back into the building for a couple of minutes without anybody else noticing.

'We need to have a word, Woodend!' said a self-important-sounding voice to his left.

The chief inspector turned towards the man who'd addressed him. 'Do we, sir?' he asked. 'An' exactly what word might that be? I can think of several that might fit the bill.'

'You know what I mean,' Wilcox said, flushing slightly. 'We should have a talk. Right now!'

'Aye,' Woodend agreed. 'I rather think we should.'

'The best place for it would be my office,' Wilcox told him, and without waiting to see whether or not that was acceptable, the director turned on his heel and strode back to his lair.

Woodend followed. When he entered the office, the first thing he saw was Monika Paniatowski, sitting in the corner and trying to look as shocked as a civilian who'd just heard about a murder would.

Wilcox noticed her, too. 'Get lost for about half an hour, Monika with a K,' he said, off-handedly.

Paniatowski was just about to rise from her seat when Woodend shook his head.

'Stay where you are, Monika,' the chief inspector said. 'You might come in useful.'

'Since when have you assumed the authority to order my girl around?' Wilcox demanded furiously.

'She's not *anybody's* girl, Mr Wilcox,' Woodend told him. 'But she is *my* sergeant.'

'Do you mean to say . . . do you actually have the nerve to tell me . . . that you've planted one of your police spies in my office?' Wilcox asked, outraged.

'We much prefer the term "undercover officers",' Woodend said mildly. 'But yes, in general terms, that's what she is.'

'I shall complain!' Wilcox said.

'Who to? Your bosses or mine?'

'To both of them. I'm sure Lord Throgmorton will be as angry as I am when he learns that—'

'Horry Throgmorton's known about it all along,' Woodend interrupted. 'It was my idea, but he seemed to think it was quite a good one.'

The information seemed to knock the wind out of Wilcox's sails. 'I see,' he said, slightly shakily. 'Well, in that case, I have no objection to Monika – to your *sergeant*, I should say – staying.'

'That's very kind of you, I'm sure,' Woodend said dryly. 'Now what was it you wanted to see me about?'

'I'd like to know how long all your PC Plods will be here, getting underfoot and generally buggering things up.'

'Or to put it another way, you want to know how long my officers will be here investigating two separate cases of murder,' Woodend said. 'An' the short answer to that is that I've absolutely no idea.'

Wilcox sighed theatrically. 'Look, I'm trying to be reasonable about this,' he said.

'Reasonable?' Woodend repeated incredulously. 'Is that how you see yourself? As bein' reasonable?'

'What else would you call it?' the producer countered. 'The next episode of *Madro* goes out tomorrow night, as you're well aware. We've already had to cope with the radical change in the script necessitated by Val's death. Now I'll have to take over Bill's duties as well as my own – and having all *my* people tied up answering *your* people's questions isn't helping me at all.'

'You don't seem too daunted by the prospect of runnin' the whole show yourself,' Woodend commented.

'Why should I be? If I didn't have confidence that I could do the job well, I'd never have taken it on. But that's not what I got you in here to talk about. What I want to know is whether you can at least tell me how long it will be before I have all my staff back?'

'Aren't you even the tiniest bit curious?' Woodend wondered.

'Curious? About what?'

'About whether it'll be the Russians or the Yanks who put a man on the moon first!' Woodend said. 'Or could I have meant curious about who killed Valerie Farnsworth and Bill Houseman?'

'Well, of course I'm curious about that,' Wilcox said exasperatedly. 'Anxious, too. But I have to put first things first. It won't help Bill and Val if I allow *Madro* to fall to pieces, now will it? In a way, going on with the show will be a sort of tribute to them.'

'So you're doin' it for purely unselfish reasons, are you?'

'No! Frankly, I'm doing it for myself as well. In a couple of years' time, my memories of Val and Bill will have started to fade, but if I mess up this opportunity I've been given, I'll wake up every morning for the rest of my life bitterly regretting it.'

'So you're curious, but not *too* curious,' Woodend said. 'You mentioned a moment ago that you were anxious, too. Is that because you think you might be next on the killer's list?'

Wilcox looked genuinely shocked. 'Of course not! That's a preposterous suggestion.'

'So what *are* you anxious about?'

'That you might arrest one of the key members of the cast – and leave me with a huge hole in the script just before we go on air.'

190

'You really *don't* care about the murders, do you?' Wood-end asked.

'Let me ask *you* a question, Chief Inspector,' Wilcox replied. 'When you're working on a case like this, does anything apart from finding your killer really matter to you?'

'No, but . . .' Woodend said uncomfortably.

'But nothing!' Wilcox said. 'We're both professionals. We give our jobs our all. And because our jobs are so different, so is our view of the world. You see your policemen as instruments of even-handed justice – I see them as nothing more than an obstacle standing in the way of the creative process.'

'You were with Bill Houseman when the fire alarm went off, weren't you?' Woodend asked, changing tack.

'Yes, I was.'

'Where were you when he was killed? Out in the car park with all the other people?'

'All those details are in the statement I gave up so much of my valuable time to dictate to one of your officers.'

'I'm sure they are,' Woodend agreed. 'But I've never been much of one for studyin' paperwork. When a man answers one of my questions, I like to be lookin' him in the eye at the time.'

'I was here,' Wilcox said, resignedly. 'In this very office.'

'So you ignored the fire alarm, just like Mr Houseman?'

'As, I'm sure, did several other members of the senior staff. We're operating on a very tight schedule, as I've been at pains to point out to you.'

'All right, let me ask you another question,' Woodend said. 'You're worried that I might arrest one of the more important members of your cast for the murders. Why?'

'Because, as I've already explained, it would leave a big hole in the—'

'No, you misunderstand me. What I meant is, why do you assume that it's one of the actors who will turn out to be the murderer?'

Houseman shrugged. 'I haven't really thought about it, but I suppose it's because I can't see why anyone else in this building would want to kill Bill and Valerie. What interest would a carpenter or a make-up girl have in murdering them?'

'You mean that leadin' characters are usually killed by other leadin' characters, not by somebody with a walk-on part?'

'Yes, I suppose that's what I do mean,' Wilcox agreed.

Aye, Woodend thought, Bill Houseman might be dead but, as in the case of Shakespeare's kings, some of his spirit lived on in his successor.

'I'll do my best to get my lads out of the way as soon as possible,' Woodend promised, 'but I'd like somethin' in return.'

'What?'

'If you come across any information which will help my investigation, you'll pass it on to me – even if it does land one of your leadin' actors in lumber.'

Wilcox nodded. 'You can rely on me to do my duty,' he said ambiguously.

Jane Todd was standing alone on the concourse. She smiled uncertainly as she saw Woodend and Paniatowski emerge from Wilcox's office.

'You look lost,' Woodend said.

'I am, in a way,' Jane replied. 'I've given one of your nice young men my statement, so I'm free to return to work. The only problem is that, with Mr Houseman dead, I don't have a boss to work for anymore. I suppose if I could get back into the office I could find something to do, but it's been sealed off. I can't even get a cup of tea, because the cafeteria has been sealed off too, so that your men can dust for fingerprints – or whatever else it is they do. So here I am, wandering lonely as a cloud.'

'An' hopin' to get a chance to talk to me,' Woodend said.

Jane's smile changed from uncertain to mildly amused. 'Am I really that obvious?' she asked.

'Only to a trained observer,' Woodend told her, with a slight grin.

Paniatowski coughed discreetly. 'Do you still need me?' she asked.

'No, I don't,' Woodend replied. 'So, to borrow a phrase from the charmin' Jeremy Wilcox, why don't you get lost for half an hour, lass.'

'Will do,' Paniatowski said, turning towards the studio and walking away.

'Shall we stroll down towards the Actors' Garden?' Woodend suggested to Jane Todd.

'If you like.'

They set off at a leisurely pace. 'So what's on your mind, lass?' Woodend asked.

'I feel such a fool for telling you that if there was another murder – and I never thought there actually *would be* one – the most likely victim was Larry Coates. Well, I couldn't have been wronger, could I?'

'Perhaps not,' Woodend agreed, 'but what interests me is why you came up with Coates's name in the first place.'

'I thought he was in the way.'

'That's why most people are murdered – because they're in the way,' Woodend agreed. 'How does Larry Coates fall into that particular category?'

'Back at the beginning, when nobody expected the show to run for more than six weeks, there weren't any such things as stars,' Jane said. 'The writers were just feeling their way as they went along, so one week it would be Queenie Dobson from the corner shop who had the biggest part, and the next it would be Madge Thornycroft, the Row's gossip, who got most screen time.'

'Aye, I remember those early days.'

'But gradually stars *did* start to emerge, either because they had particularly good lines or because they somehow managed to strike a chord with the viewers. And the biggest star of them all was Val Farnsworth. At first she was as surprised as anybody, but it didn't take her long to start coming over the *prima donna*.'

'An' you think the other actors resented it?'

'Well, they were bound to, weren't they? They must have looked at her and thought: That could have been me! I could have been the one who rose out of the ranks.'

'An' if she was dead, I could *still* get my chance?'

'Exactly. After all, the only real competition she had was Larry, and Larry was going to leave the show. So once Val was dead, the field was open again. Except that things didn't turn out quite that way, did they? With Val gone, the show needed Larry, so he was told he had to stay on whether he wanted to or not.'

'An' this murderer – whoever he or she is – was in as bad a position as he or she had been before Val Farnsworth died?'

'Exactly. But if Larry were to die, too . . . You see how my mind was working?'

'Yes, I do. What happened to change it?'

'Bill Houseman's murder, of course.'

'An' why was that?'

'Well, because Bill couldn't possibly have been killed by one of the cast.'

'Jeremy Wilcox would disagree with you on that.'

'I'm not surprised,' Jane Todd said. 'He's bound to tell you he thinks it's one of the cast, because—'

She came to an abrupt halt and clamped her hand over her mouth.

'Because of what?' Woodend asked.

'Because . . . er . . . he has his opinion, and I have mine.'

'That isn't what you *were* goin' to say, is it?'

'Perhaps not. But it's what I *did* say.'

'All right, we'll leave that aside for a minute,' Woodend said. 'Do you want to tell me why you think none of the cast would have killed Houseman?'

'Because he was the devil they all knew, and whatever else they might have thought about him, they could at least take comfort from the fact that he'd chosen them to be part of his team. Jeremy Wilcox is quite another matter. He's only been on the show for six months, and he probably wants to find ways to make his own mark.'

'An' that might include bringin' new actors in? People who would be beholden to him for their big break, rather than to Bill Houseman.'

Jane Todd smiled. 'Now you're starting to think like someone in this industry,' she said.

'Which means that, as far as the cast of *Maddox Row* is concerned, Bill Houseman's death is the worst thing that could have happened?'

'Absolutely.'

194

'So who did have a motive for killin' Houseman?'

Jane Todd looked away from him. 'I have no idea,' she said.

Woodend chuckled. 'Oh, come now, lass. I'd have to be really dense not to see the direction you've been tryin' your best to point me in for the last five minutes.'

Thirty-Two

If Elizabeth Driver had been waiting in ambush for him when he, Rutter and Paniatowski walked into the Red Lion that lunchtime, Woodend had already determined that he would find a reason – *any* reason – to have her arrested and locked away for a couple of hours. But there was no sign of the journalist with the dyed jet-black hair, and they made their way to a corner table unmolested.

Rutter was the first to taste his drink. He took one sip from his half of best bitter, then pulled a face and laid his glass back on the table.

'Somethin' wrong with your ale?' Woodend asked.

'Probably not,' Rutter answered. 'Anything would taste sour at the moment. Do you know, taking down those statements this morning was like watching a programme you've already seen. You go through the motions of listening, but all the time you know exactly what's going to be said next.'

'Meanin' what?' Woodend asked.

'Meaning that this lot of statements will read exactly like the ones that were taken after Valerie Farnsworth's murder. Everybody was so busy attending to their own concerns during the evacuation that they've only got a vague idea – at best – of what anyone else was doing.'

'Look at it this way,' Monika Paniatowski said, trying to sound positive. 'The killer's not just exposed himself once – he's done it twice. And that's given him two opportunities to make mistakes. All we have to do is find out what those mistakes were.'

'So that's how you see it, is it?' Woodend asked. 'Two murders an' one murderer?'

Paniatowski frowned. 'Isn't it how *you* see it?'

'No, it bloody well isn't. I don't think we're lookin' for one murderer – I think we're lookin' for two. Or rather, since one of them's already dead, we're lookin' for the second one.'

'You still think Bill Houseman killed Valerie Farnsworth?'

'Why wouldn't I? We put a pretty strong case for him bein' the killer last night, an' nothin's happened since to change our minds.'

'True,' Bob Rutter agreed. 'But if Houseman really did kill Valerie Farnsworth, we'll never be able to prove it now.'

'Tell me somethin' I *don't* know,' Woodend said gloomily.

'So where does that leave us?' Rutter asked.

'Given the depressin' fact that we can't prove Houseman committed the first crime, probably the best we can hope for is to find out who killed *him*, an' hope that the brass back in Whitebridge – an' the press, which is probably howlin' for our blood by now – will be satisfied with that. So what have we got to go on, as regards Houseman's killer?'

'It's a fair assumption that he's a desperate man,' Paniatowski ventured.

'Is it?' Woodend asked. 'Why?'

'Well, he must have been, to take the chances that he did.'

'He took practically no chances at all. He could have murdered Houseman on his way out of the buildin', or slipped back in again durin' all confusion. Whichever it was, it will only have taken a couple of minutes. An' he could have been fairly sure that nobody was likely to miss him. No, I don't think we can say he was desperate – but he was certainly opportunistic.'

'In what way?' Rutter asked.

'He couldn't have been planning to kill Houseman at the moment he did, because he had no way of knowin' that the fire alarm would go off. But when *it* did go off, he saw his opportunity, and he grasped it with both hands.'

'Do you have a suspect in mind?' Paniatowski asked.

'Well, there's Jeremy Wilcox, for starters,' Woodend said. 'He wanted Houseman's job so bad that it hurt, an' for a while – when the viewin' figures were startin' to slump – he probably thought he'd get it. Then Valerie Farnsworth was murdered, an' suddenly Houseman was lookin' very secure again. It must have been very frustratin' for him.'

'Isn't he just *too* obvious a suspect?' Paniatowski asked.

Woodend grinned. 'I admit Wilcox isn't the one the *Madro* scriptwriters would have chosen as the murderer. If they'd been writin' this particular case for television, they'd probably have picked on somebody much less likely – like one of them three lasses from the typin' pool that you were talkin' to in the canteen on Tuesday.'

Paniatowski smiled back at him. 'But why should one of them have done it? What motive could a typist possibly have had?'

'Exactly!' Woodend agreed. 'That's the whole point – she would have *no* apparent motive. But the smart-arse bobby who was investigatin' the case would eventually have found out that she wasn't what she seemed. It would turn out that Bill Houseman was her father, an' that he'd abandoned her mother to a life of abject poverty. The mother had said nothin' about it until she was on her deathbed, then she'd revealed the whole story to the girl. So the girl had got a job on *Madro*, and when she saw her chance, she took her revenge.'

'But why would she go through all that rigmarole?' Paniatowski asked, falling in with the game. 'If she'd wanted to kill him, why pretend to be a typist at all? Why run the risk of bringing herself within the scope of the investigation? Wouldn't her easiest course have been just to wait for him in a dark alley one night?'

'Of course it would,' Woodend agreed. 'But then you wouldn't have a programme, would you? You see what I'm sayin', lass? This isn't a story we're involved in. This is real life – an' the fact that a suspect is bloody obvious is no guarantee at all that he's innocent.'

'So we're targeting Wilcox as our likeliest suspect, are we?' Rutter asked.

'He's certainly up there with the contenders,' Woodend said.

'But you have others in mind as well?'

'People *do* kill for power,' Woodend told him. 'But more often they kill for either money or sex. An' we've got a couple of candidates who fall into both those categories.'

*   *   *

The Glades Golf Club was midway between Whitebridge and Preston. Its members were on the whole reasonably affluent – without being obscenely wealthy – and most of them habitually attended their local Anglican Church nearly every Sunday and often twice at Easter. The club did not encourage any members of Whitebridge's growing Asian community to join, because the current membership felt that Pakistanis and Indians would simply not have felt comfortable in such surroundings. And since it was a well-known fact that Jews didn't really like golf either, there was no real point in inviting any of them to apply for admission.

The Glades had many amenities, not the least of which was a well-stocked bar in the clubhouse, and it was reassuring to know that if you decided to drop in for a drink, you were only likely to meet men you would wish to meet. And it was in the bar that Detective Chief Superintendent Ainsworth ran into Deputy Chief Constable Henry Marlowe – apparently by chance – that lunchtime.

'How's the Chief?' Ainsworth asked, trying to look concerned.

'He's as well as can be expected – for a man who died half an hour ago,' Marlowe replied.

Ainsworth bowed his head. 'He'll be sadly missed,' he said.

'Yes, he will,' Marlowe agreed. 'But not – if we're honest about it – by either of us.'

It was perhaps wisest to get off the subject of John Dinnage, Ainsworth decided. 'So you're in charge now, are you, sir?' he asked.

'Yes – temporarily, at least,' Marlowe agreed.

But *permanently*, if you have any say in the matter, Ainsworth thought. 'You can rely on me to give you all the support I can, sir,' he said.

Marlowe took a sip of his gin and tonic. 'The best way you can help me is to see I don't have any additional problems landing on my desk. How's this investigation over at NWTV going, by the way?'

'I've instructed Charlie Woodend to brief me on the whole matter tomorrow morning.'

Marlowe raised an eyebrow. 'So you're keeping Woodend on the case, are you?'

'Mr Dinnage gave specific instructions that—'

'Mr Dinnage will be far too busy in that big interview room in the sky to worry about what we're doing down here. If you choose to keep Woodend on the case, then that must be entirely your own decision.'

'But if you'd care to give some guidance . . .'

'Unlike John Dinnage, I'm not the kind of man who goes breathing down my subordinates' necks.'

Ainsworth's hands had started to sweat. He did not like the direction this conversation was taking at all.

'On the whole, I think that taking Woodend off the case would be a mistake,' he said, watching Marlowe carefully for any reaction. 'It wouldn't look at all good in the papers.'

'Wouldn't it? Not even after a second murder in only three days?'

'*Especially* after a second murder in three days,' Ainsworth said. 'If I pulled him out now, it would look as if he should never have been assigned to the case in the first place.'

'So you're keeping him on for the good of the force?'

'Exactly, sir.'

Marlowe's eyebrow quivered again, almost like a butterfly in flight. 'And there's no personal motive behind your decision?'

'None at all, sir.'

'Shall I tell you what I think, Dick?' Marlowe asked.

'If you'd like to, sir.'

'I think you've done some very careful calculations, and decided this may well be a case we won't get a result on, *whoever's* in charge of it.'

'It's far too early to make any kind of judge—'

'We've both got where we are today by making judgements before anybody else realised they even needed to be made,' Marlowe said dismissively. 'So where was I? Oh yes. You've decided it's unlikely you're going to get a result, which, in a widely publicised case like this one, means that someone is going to have to take a fall. Now if you replace Woodend, the person who takes that fall could be you. Whereas if you keep him, you could make the argument that the decision was John Dinnage's, and it was far too late in the game to reverse it. So Dinnage's reputation takes a battering – but he's dead, so that doesn't matter. And Charlie Woodend gets a serious black mark on his record – but you've been trying to get rid of him ever since he was first foisted on you, so that's something of a bonus.'

'I assure you, sir—' Ainsworth protested.

'It could all go disastrously wrong, of course. So wrong that even I end up taking some flak – and I wouldn't like to be in your shoes if that happened.' A sudden, unexpected smile appeared on Marlowe's lips. 'On balance, though,' he continued, 'I think you'll probably get away with it.'

Thirty-Three

When Paddy Colligan looked through his office window and saw Woodend and the blonde woman that the office grapevine had now identified as his sergeant, the Irishman prayed that they were not about to pay a visit to him, even though, from the way they were slowing down, it was obvious they were going to do just that.

So this was it, the Irishman thought. This was the moment he had been dreading ever since he had first seen the big man in the hairy sports jacket and noted how deep and penetrating his eyes were.

The knock on the door was firm and authoritative – as he'd expected it to be – and made him jump – as he'd been hoping it wouldn't.

'Come in,' he said, hoping that, even at this point, they might still look at him in surprise and say they'd made a mistake and come to the wrong office.

The door opened. Woodend and Paniatowski entered the room.

'If you don't mind, Mr Colligan, we'd like to ask you a few questions,' the chief inspector said.

No mistake, then. No bloody mistake at all.

'I don't think I can tell you any more than I've already put in my statement,' Paddy Colligan said, trying to sound matter-of-fact, rather than defiant.

'Oh, I don't know about that. You'd be amazed what you can drag up from the recesses of your mind when you make the effort,' Woodend said easily. 'Do you mind if we sit down?'

'No, no, of course not,' Colligan replied, wishing that his mouth didn't feel quite so dry.

The two detectives sat down in the chairs in front of his

desk. Almost in touching distance, Colligan thought. Almost in grabbing-you-and-beating-the-crap-out-of-you-until-you-tell-them-what-they-want-to-know distance.

'Paddy Colligan,' Woodend said reflectively. 'That would be *Patrick*, would it?'

'That's right,' Colligan agreed.

'I read a play by a Patrick Colligan once. I think it was called *Troubled Times in the Old Country*.'

'That was mine,' Colligan said, surprised.

'Hmm,' Woodend said. 'Read a lot of Dickens, do you?'

'How in God's name did you know that?!' Paddy Colligan exclaimed.

'Just a guess. There's the same broad sweep of characters in your play as there is in Dickens, the same willingness to face gritty reality.' Woodend smiled. 'An' under all the harshness and honesty, there's a bit of the same romantic soul hidin', as well.'

I never expected this, Colligan thought. I expected trickiness and belligerence, but I never expected *this*. He scares me even more than I thought he would.

'What did you think of the play?' he said. Cursing himself for asking. Cursing himself for really *wanting to know* the answer.

'I think it showed a great deal of promise, but that it wasn't quite there yet,' Woodend said. 'I think you should write some more – refine your craft a little.'

'You're quite right, of course,' Paddy Colligan admitted.

'So tell me, what you did you do after the fire alarm went off?' Woodend said, abruptly changing the subject.

'Ben, Jeremy Wilcox and I were in Bill Houseman's office for the regular Thursday morning meeting. When we heard the alarm, we went outside.'

'Together?'

'No. Jeremy and Ben left first. I asked Bill Houseman if he was coming, and he told me he wasn't. So then I left.'

'An' did you look him in the eye when you asked him if he was comin'?' Woodend said. 'Did you *ever* look him in the eye when you were talkin' to him?'

'I don't know what you mean.'

'Oh, I think you do – though my sergeant disagrees with me,' Woodend said. 'But we'll leave that for the moment. After you left Houseman's office, did you go straight to the car park?'

'Yes.'

'An' what did you do once you were there? Did you go an' find your writing partner?'

'No.'

'Don't you think that's a bit odd? You were under a great deal of pressure, because there had to be a lot of script changes after Valerie Farnsworth's death. I would have thought you'd have grabbed every opportunity to spend as much time with Ben Drabble as you possibly could.'

'I had a lot on my mind. I needed time to be alone to think things through.'

'A lot on your mind,' Woodend repeated. 'Were you worried about work? Or was it more in the nature of a personal matter you were concerned about?'

'It was work,' Colligan said, unconvincingly.

'So you didn't talk to anybody?'

'Not that I remember.'

'Why wouldn't you give me the script when I asked for it yesterday?' Paniatowski asked, speaking for the first time.

'Bill Houseman told me not to.'

'An' why would he do that?' Woodend asked.

'He didn't say.'

'But what do you *think*?'

'I think he was trying to keep Jeremy Wilcox off-balance – to make him feel isolated.'

'For what reason?'

'To knock the fight out of him. So that when Houseman gave him the push, he'd go without too much trouble.'

'An' you went along with that?'

'I didn't have much choice, did I? Bill Houseman was the boss.'

'What's your relationship with Mrs Houseman?' Woodend asked.

'Mrs Houseman? What do you mean?'

'Somebody in this office has been havin' an affair with her.

Paniatowski here thinks it's Ben Drabble, but I think she's wrong. He's certainly obsessed by somethin' – but I don't believe it's a woman.'

'Ben's a compulsive gambler,' Paddy Colligan admitted. 'And as far as I'm concerned, Mrs Houseman is just the boss's wife.'

Woodend sighed. 'A man who was honest enough to write *Troubled Times* shouldn't have denied his true feelings like that. Or aren't you that man any more? Has working on *Maddox Row* drained all the honesty an' integrity out of you, Mr Colligan?'

Paddy Colligan looked down at his desk. 'I always felt that when I fell in love, it would be with someone who was really worthwhile as a person,' he said. 'I never expected her to be beautiful – I rather thought she wouldn't be – but I knew she'd have a deep core of decency and honesty – that virtue would run through her as naturally as blood.'

'Like Biddy, in *Great Expectations*?' Woodend suggested.

'*Exactly* like Biddy,' Colligan agreed enthusiastically. 'And then I met Diana,' he continued, his voice dropping. 'She's an out-and-out materialist. She likes money and all the things it can buy – she even married for it. She's vain. She can be spiteful. Yet there's a kernel of something else buried deep inside her – the seed of a Biddy which only needs watering and taking care of to blossom to its full glory.'

'In other words, you're in love with her.'

'With all my heart.'

'Did Bill Houseman know about the pair of you?'

'He may have guessed that she was having an affair with *someone* at the studio, but I don't imagine for a second that he thought it was me. Why would it have been me? I'm a nothing. I could never have kept her in the same style as he could. No, if he suspected anyone specifically, it would be someone like George Adams. A man with a bit of glamour about him. A man who could soon be earning even more than Bill was himself.'

'We've talked about you, now what about her? How does she feel about you?'

'I think that she loves me as much as I love her.'

'Do you, indeed?' Woodend asked sceptically. 'I would have thought you'd be just a little bit unsure about that – given her track record.'

'She's had other affairs – I won't deny that.'

'Quite a lot of them, from what I've heard.'

'That's all in the past – before the real Diana had begun to break through the hard shell that life has made her coat herself in. With me, she's becoming a different person.'

'If you say so.'

'I believe she truly loves me for much the same reason as I believe that Bill Houseman would never have suspected me – because I don't really count for anything. Because if she were really the person that everyone else thinks she is, she'd have nothing to do with me.'

'So sex doesn't come into it at all?' Paniatowski asked disbelievingly.

'We sleep together, if that's what you're asking. But I don't fool myself that I'm any great lover,' Colligan said. 'If it were merely sexual satisfaction she was after, she could do far better than me.'

'She was here this morning, when the fire alarm went off, wasn't she?' Woodend asked.

'Yes, she was here.'

'Why?'

'She's often here. She used to be an actress – this is her world.'

'An' did you see her in car park?'

'For a moment or two.'

'Did you speak?'

'No. Whenever we meet in public, we're always afraid that we'll give ourselves away by a look or a gesture. So we've decided it's safer to virtually ignore each other – just in case Houseman is watching.'

'But Houseman wasn't watchin' on this particular occasion, was he?' Woodend asked.

'No, he wasn't.'

'An' the reason for that was that he was lyin' across his desk with a kitchen knife stickin' in him. So there was no real need for caution at all, was there?'

'What are you suggesting?' Colligan demanded.

'What were your long-term plans?' Woodend asked, ignoring the question. 'Did you intend to carry on with your little affair behind Houseman's back for ever?'

'Of course not. That would have been intolerable.'

'So what *were* you goin' to do?'

'I wanted Diana to leave him, and move in with me.'

'An' did you expect to keep your job on *Maddox Row* once that had happened?'

'No. Bill Houseman would have fired me – and who could have blamed him?'

'So as soon as you ran off together, there'd be no more pay cheques from NWTV. Does Diana Houseman have any money of her own?'

'Not that I know of.'

'What would you have lived on?'

'We'd have got by.'

'But Diana Houseman isn't used to just *gettin' by*, is she? She married Bill so she wouldn't *have to* just get by.'

'People change,' Paddy Colligan said defensively.

'But it's rarer than you think,' Woodend countered. 'You asked me earlier what I was suggestin' when I said there was no need for you an' Diana to be careful in the car park this mornin'. Well, I'm not sure that I've got grounds enough to suggest anythin'. But I have got an idea for a film script.'

A slight and weary smile came to Paddy Colligan's face. 'Everybody thinks they've got a film script or a novel somewhere inside them,' he said. 'And they think that all they have to do is open the floodgates, and it will automatically gush out. Writing isn't like that. Lots of people could get their hands on good wood, but only a few of them – like Hepplewhite – could fashion beautiful cabinets out of it. And just having an idea isn't nearly enough to be able to fashion a worthwhile story.'

'Let me tell you my idea anyway,' Woodend said. 'A young man writes a play, an' knows he should write another. But he doesn't. Instead he gets a job which pays well, but doesn't really satisfy him. An' the tragedy of it is that the longer he does the job, the less confident he becomes that he'll ever be able to write another play. So what does he do? He looks around for another purpose in his life, an' he finds a beautiful, but mercenary, woman who he thinks he can transform into somethin' better. In other words, the woman herself becomes his work in progress. But the catch is that she's addicted to money, an' until the transformation's completed, she still needs her fix. Now the young writer doesn't have any money. An' neither does she. But if she were a widow instead of a wife, she'd be rollin' in it – so all they have to do is make sure that she *becomes* a widow. Is that plausible?'

'It's very plausible,' Colligan admitted. 'But it's not how it happened.'

'You mean you had nothin' to do with Bill Houseman's death?'

'I mean *neither* of us had anything to do with his death.'

'In your place, most people would be pointin' the finger of suspicion at somebody else, in order to divert attention from themselves,' Woodend said.

'I'm not most people,' Colligan answered.

'No, you're not, are you?' Woodend agreed. 'Well, like I said, I might have enough to make up a story, but I certainly don't have enough to make an arrest, so we'll be off now.'

'Just like that?' Paddy Colligan asked, astonished.

'Just like that,' Woodend agreed. 'An' as they say in the entertainment world, "Don't ring us" – because if we come up with anythin' more, we'll most certainly be ringin' you.'

Thirty-Four

There were only the two of them in the small conference room, but the ashtray was spilling over with cigarette butts and the atmosphere was almost as thick with smoke as it was with tension.

'Where is the bloody woman?' Woodend asked irritably. 'Has she gone into hidin', or what?'

'It's a big studio,' Paniatowski pointed out. 'Even if she's not trying to make herself scarce, it could be a while yet before Inspector Rutter's team find her.'

Woodend took a deep drag on his Capstan Full Strength, and felt the acrid smoke rake against the walls of his lungs. 'The problem is, everybody in this case is either an actor or has been so close to actors that some of the bullshit has rubbed off,' he said.

Paniatowski nodded sympathetically, but said nothing.

'I can normally tell when most people are lyin',' the chief inspector continued. 'But these buggers make a livin' out of lyin'. Was Paddy Colligan tellin' us the truth back there?'

'I don't know,' Paniatowski confessed.

'An' neither do I. How the hell am I supposed to get these people to give themselves away when they spend their whole time thinkin' on their feet?'

There was a knock on the door, and a constable entered the room, followed by the dead producer's wife.

Diana Houseman was wearing a thick red lipstick which emphasised her sensuous lips, and a purple mascara which made her eyes look even larger than they actually were. The hem of her dress fell well below the knee, but the split up the side of the skirt virtually ensured that when she sat down she would display a considerable amount of leg. She

209

overdid things, Woodend thought – maybe that came from her theatrical background – but there was no question that she was an astonishingly attractive woman.

'Mrs Houseman, sir,' the constable announced, unnecessarily.

'Thanks, lad, you can go now,' Woodend said. He waited until the constable had backed out of the room, then turned to the widow. 'Would you like to take a seat, Mrs Houseman?'

Diana Houseman stayed close to the door. 'I resent being here,' she said in her husky voice. 'You should be showing me some consideration. My husband's just been murdered, in case you've forgotten.'

'I haven't forgotten,' Woodend told her. 'It's precisely *because* your husband's been murdered that you are here.'

'And isn't it a bit late in the day for you to start playing the role of the grieving widow?' Paniatowski asked nastily.

Diana Houseman shot her a look of pure venom. 'I liked you better when you were pretending to be Jeremy's downtrodden assistant.'

'Yes, you would have,' Paniatowski agreed. 'I was a bit easier to intimidate then, wasn't I?'

'Sit down, Mrs Houseman,' Woodend said. 'Sit down, and I promise you we'll get it all over with as quickly an' as painlessly as possible.'

The producer's widow hesitated for a split second more, then, swaying her hips, walked over to the table and took a seat.

'Thank you,' Woodend said. 'Now I'm afraid I'm goin' to have to ask you some rather personal questions.'

'And if I refuse to answer them?'

'Why should you, when you might be helpin' to bring your husband's killer to justice?'

Diana Houseman turned his words over in her mind for a moment. 'Ask your questions,' she said, 'but I'm making no promises about giving you the answers you want.'

'Let's start with somethin' easy,' Woodend suggested. 'Could you tell me anythin' about your husband's state of mind in the period leadin' up to his death?'

'That's not an easy question at all. In fact, it's almost impossible to give you an answer.'

'An' why's that?'

'Because Bill was incapable of sustaining one state of mind for any length of time. He was a very driven man. He had considerable energy, and most of it was devoted to his work. Minor irritations, which would probably hardly bother you at all, could seem like major tragedies to him. On the other hand, minor triumphs could buoy him up to incredible heights. And since he experienced several minor irritations and several minor triumphs in the course of one working day, his state of mind was very difficult to pin down.'

He'd heard more ringing endorsements of a loved one's life and work – and deeper outpourings of grief at their departure – Woodend told himself. He didn't think about his own death very much, but he hoped that when his time *did* come around, Joan would be able to find it in herself to give him a better send-off than Diana Houseman was prepared to give Bill.

But perhaps she wouldn't. Perhaps, after what had happened with Annie, Joan would be as glad as Diana Houseman had been to see the back of her husband. And who was to say she'd be wrong? Who was to say that he deserved any better?

'Sir!' Paniatowski said sharply.

Woodend pulled himself back from the brink of his own misery, and turned his attention to Diana Houseman again.

'Did your husband have any enemies?' he asked.

The widow smiled – almost pityingly. 'You don't have much experience of the world of entertainment, do you, Chief Inspector?' she asked.

'No, I don't.'

'I thought not. If you had known a little more, you'd have asked if he had any *friends*.'

'An' did he?'

'He had *allies*.'

'I'm only a simple bobby, so I'm afraid you're goin' to have to explain in words of one syllable just how those two things are different.'

'Friends are people who you're nice to because you *like* them,' Diana Houseman replied. 'Allies are people you're nice to because you *need* each other, which means that, as situations change – and they can change very quickly in television – allies can quickly become enemies, and enemies allies.'

'But that's just business, isn't it?' Woodend asked.

'There's no such thing as *just* business, if this is the business you're in. People like my husband don't live *in* television, they live *for* it.'

'So you're suggestin' that he was killed for what you might call "professional" reasons?'

'Of course,' Diana Houseman replied, as it had never occurred to her to consider any other possibility.

'Why were you in the studio this mornin'?'

'Because staying in the house bores me. There are some woman who can play the role of being the little home-maker, but I'm simply not one of them.'

'Where were you when the alarm went off?'

'Talking to one of the girls in the make-up department.'

'Why?'

'She was giving me some professional tips.'

'We can check on that, you know,' Woodend warned.

'I'm sure it's already down in black and white – in the statement she gave to one of your officers.'

'You left the buildin' immediately?'

'Yes, I did.'

'Who did you talk to while you were standin' in the car park, waitin' for the all clear?'

'I carried on my conversation with the girl from make-up for a while, then I went for a stroll in the direction of the village.'

'You're sure you didn't nip back into the buildin', take a knife from the cafeteria, an' plunge it into your husband's back?'

'I lived with Bill. If I'd wanted to kill him, I'd have had ample opportunity to have done it somewhere there was no chance of me being observed.'

'True,' Woodend agreed. 'But if you'd killed him at home, you'd have been the obvious suspect, whereas doin' it here, there are scores of other people to choose from.'

'Then I suggest you talk to some of them,' Diana Houseman

212

said, 'because while I'm not entirely devastated by the thought of being a moderately prosperous widow who can do as she chooses from now on, I had nothing at all to do with Bill's death.'

She was a cold, hard bitch, there was no doubt about that, Woodend thought. But how calculating was she? How much was her callousness simply her nature, and how much of it was simply designed to make him think that anyone who was so candid couldn't possibly have deeper secrets that she was attempting to hide from him?

'Tell me about your relationship with Valerie Farnsworth.'

'My relationship with her? Well, I certainly knew Val.'

'In the biblical sense?' Paniatowski asked.

Instead of taking offence, Diana Houseman merely looked amused. 'Are you asking me if I slept with her?' she asked.

'That's right,' Woodend agreed.

'No, I didn't. Valerie, like most of the *men* I meet, would probably have liked me to sleep with her. She may even have dropped hints about it once or twice. But, I never went to bed with her, because, unlike Val, I'm no lesbian.'

'So where did George Adams get the idea that was exactly what you'd done?' Woodend asked.

Diana Houseman shrugged indifferently. 'He probably got it from my husband. Or from someone else who Bill had blubbered out his self-pitying worries to.'

'An' where would *your husband* have got the idea from?'

'From me.'

'But you just said you hadn't—'

'I told *him* I'd slept with her, but that doesn't mean I really did.'

'Most people lie about *havin'* committed adultery, not about *not* havin' committed it,' Woodend pointed out.

'I'm not most people. I was angry with Bill. I wanted to say something which would hurt him, and I knew that that would.'

'An' how did he react?'

'He asked me to give her up.'

'An' you agreed?'

'Since there was nothing to give up – and since the lie had already served its purpose – yes, I did.'

'And I'll bet he bought you a nice present for being such a good little girl,' Paniatowski said.

It was the first barb which had come anywhere near to hitting its target, and Diana Houseman flinched a little.

'He was *always* buying me presents,' she said, sounding just a little uncomfortable.

Aye, I bet he was. An' I wouldn't put it past you to have told that particular lie *in order* to get the present, Woodend thought.

He wondered if Diana Houseman realised that by telling the lie she had sealed Valerie Farnsworth's fate – and if she did, whether she cared! He hoped that she was the one who had stuck the knife into Bill Houseman's back, and that he could lock her away for a long, long time.

'Tell us about you an' Paddy Colligan,' he said.

The producer's wife smiled again. 'Now there's someone who I *have* slept with.'

'Good in bed, is he?' Paniatowski asked sneeringly.

The smile disappeared, and Diana Houseman looked Paniatowski straight in the eyes. 'You may not believe this, but I really do love him,' she said.

'An' you were goin' to leave your husband, an' move in with him?' Woodend asked.

'Who told you that?'

'Paddy Colligan himself.'

'People believe what they want to believe, whatever you try to tell them,' Diana Houseman said calmly.

'Then you *weren't* goin' to leave your husband?'

'The situation Paddy and I found ourselves in was far from ideal – but it was certainly better to live apart, as we were, than to live together in penury.'

'Weren't you takin' a big chance, carryin' on like you were?'

'Not really. Bill had forgiven me for my other affairs – both the real and the imagined ones. He would have forgiven me for this one, too.'

She was lying, Woodend thought. No, that was not quite it. What she was doing was trying to make the whole situation seem a lot more straightforward than it actually was.

'He might have forgiven you for the affair, but he wouldn't have forgiven *Colligan*,' Woodend said. 'Paddy would have been out of a job, and Bill would have seen to it that he never worked for NWTV again. So what would Paddy have done then? He'd have had to move away from the area to find new work – probably down to London – and you'd hardly ever have seen him.'

Diana Houseman smiled again. 'For that to happen, Bill would have had to catch us at it, wouldn't he?'

'People who are havin' a bit on the side never think they're goin' to get caught – but they usually do,' Woodend pointed out.

'That's because they don't take precautions.'

'An' you did?'

'Oh yes.'

'Are you goin' to tell us what they were?'

Diana Houseman considered it. 'No, I don't think I am,' she said finally.

'Even if it will clear you of the suspicion that you played a part in your husband's death?'

'I did not kill Bill, and nothing I tell you about my precautions will help to either prove or disprove that.'

'So why won't you tell us?' Paniatowski demanded.

Diana Houseman looked a little uncomfortable again. 'Because I'm . . . because I'm a little embarrassed by it.'

'I find it very hard to believe that you could be embarrassed by anything,' Paniatowski said cuttingly.

'I don't give a toss *what* you believe,' Diana Houseman told her. She turned her attention back to Woodend. 'Is there anything else you want to ask me, or can I go now?'

'You can go,' Woodend said. 'But don't leave town without lettin' us know where you're goin'.'

'Leave town?' Diana Houseman repeated. 'Why should I want to do that?'

Thirty-Five

As Woodend drove towards the village which he had lived in just long enough to start thinking of it as his home, he found his mind contemplating the long and tortuous series of events – many of them occurring even before he was born – which had led to his present dilemma.

He pictured the long-dead cotton magnate, dressed in top hat and frock coat, selecting the site for the mill which would add to his already considerable fortune. If only the bugger had chosen a plot of land just a little closer to Manchester . . .

He thought of the boundary commissioners, a large-scale map of the area spread out on the table in front of them, deciding just where to draw the line between the city and the county. Would it have hurt them to have inked it in a hundredth of an inch further south?

He imagined the meeting at which the Big Wheels at NWTV had decided to go ahead with the purchase of the mill. Wouldn't there have been a few dissenting voices, men who had felt it might be wiser to locate the new studio closer to the rest of the organisation? And if there had been, why, for God's sake, had they not won the day?

But it was pointless to speculate on what might have been. The mill owner had chosen that spot, the boundary commissioners had drawn that line, NWTV had decided to buy the studio – and instead of the double murder being Manchester Police's headache, it was his.

And a real bugger of a headache it was – a champion among migraines. John Dinnage would have understood the complexities of the case, but Dinnage was dead, and a much lesser man had stepped into his shoes. If it would protect his own back, Henry Marlowe would be more than willing to see other men's heads roll, and there was no question about whose would be first on the block.

Not that his would be the only one, Woodend thought miserably. The stink of failure would cling to Bob Rutter and Monika Paniatowski, too, and though the axe would not fall on their necks as quickly as it fell on his own, their careers were as doomed as his.

Bob and Monika were good, loyal bobbies – and they deserved better than that. Yet though he accepted that he was the only who could save them from their fate, he did not even know how to begin. He was never going to prove that Bill Houseman had killed Valerie Farnsworth, and though he had at least three plausible suspects for the murder of Houseman himself, they had only to keep their nerve to escape scot free.

He was surprised to discover that he had reached the centre of the village, and that the post-office store was just ahead of him.

Might as well buy an evening paper while I'm here, he thought, signalling and pulling up in front of the shop.

He'd grown accustomed to receiving a cheery greeting from Ted Bryce, the postmaster, but that early evening he was out of luck. Far from being pleased to see him, Bryce looked as if he'd be much happier if the chief inspector took his custom elsewhere.

'Somethin' the matter, Ted?' Woodend asked, concerned. 'Not had bad news, I hope.'

Guilt replaced embarrassment on the postmaster's face. 'No . . . er . . . nothin' like that,' he said awkwardly. 'It's . . . it's been a long day, that's all.'

'Most of them are,' Woodend agreed. 'Has the evenin' paper come in yet?'

Bryce nodded. 'It has,' he admitted reluctantly. 'You don't want one, do you?'

'Actually, I do,' the chief inspector replied. 'That's why I asked if they'd come in.'

The postmaster reached for a paper from the stack, but as he handed it over his eyes were fixed on a point somewhere on the other side of the shop.

So that's why it feels like the Antarctic in here, is it? Woodend thought. Because there's somethin' about me in the paper!

He stepped out of the shop and unfolded the newspaper. He saw the headline right away – it would have been very hard to miss it!

SECOND DEATH AT NWTV
THE RESULT OF POLICE BUNGLE?
By our special correspondent Elizabeth Driver

One of the signs of a good police force is that it arrives on the scene shortly after a crime has been committed. In the case of the murders at NWTV's *Maddox Row* studios, however, the Mid-Lancs Police were *already* on the scene – investigating the death of popular actress Valerie Farnsworth – when a second murder, that of producer Bill Houseman, took place.

'I'm completely baffled,' Chief Inspector Woodend, the officer in charge of the case, admitted to me in an exclusive interview this afternoon. 'The killer appears to be fiendishly clever, and has left no clue behind him whatsoever.'

'Bollocks!' Woodend swore.

There was more – several columns more – but he saw no reason why he should waste his time reading it and, aware that he was being watched from inside the shop, he stuffed the paper into the litter-bin.

Well, you had to give the lass credit for one thing, he thought – she'd promised to make him look like a buffoon, and anyone reading the article would have no doubt that he was. If DCS Ainsworth and his pal Acting Chief Constable Henry Marlowe needed any more ammunition to fire at him, Elizabeth Driver had certainly provided them with it.

As he got into his car again, he was tempted to turn around and head back to the studio. But what would have been the point of that? The show did not go out until the following evening. Aside from the NWTV security men and the few uniformed bobbies he'd left behind to keep an eye on things, there would be nobody there. And even if there had been, he was not sure that he had anything to ask them which had not already been asked.

It had been dark for some time. Woodend stood alone, on the edge of the moors of his childhood – looking up at the stars and listening to the wind moaning softly in distance. Then, almost before he realised what was happening, he found himself replaying in his head the conversation that he and Joan had had about Annie's disappearance.

Slowly and painfully, he analysed what Joan had said, then pulled apart his own comments to see if they still made sense. When the process was finally over, he was exhausted but convinced that he'd handled the situation correctly. The worst thing they could possibly do would be to drag Annie back against her will, he told himself. Doing that would lose them the part of her they still had left.

'I made the right decision!' he shouted into the darkness.

Right decision? Right decision?

The whisper he heard was no echo – there was nothing in front of him for his voice to echo against – so he knew it must be coming from inside his head.

Would he have handled Annie's disappearance in *exactly* this way if he hadn't been up to his neck in a murder investigation which threatened to rob him of everything he had worked for all these years? he agonised.

Wasn't there something in him – just as there was something in the people most involved in *Maddox Row* – that would do its best to deceive himself and deceive others, because the truth was an inconvenience and a diversion?

And because, whatever else happened, the show must go on?

219

Friday

Thirty-Six

The rain should have been pouring down in buckets, Woodend thought as he drove along the snaking road which ran across the tops of the moors. There should have been thunder and lightning, and a wind which shrieked like a soul lost in hell. That kind of weather would have matched his mood perfectly. And what had he got instead? A sunny morning which gave the indications of turning into a perfect autumn day. It seemed as if even nature was against him!

He turned to Paniatowski, who was sitting silently in the passenger seat beside him.

'Say somethin' to cheer me up, Monika,' he told her.

'I wish I could, but nothing really springs to mind,' Paniatowski confessed. 'Shall I tell you what's in the papers?'

'Oh aye, you do that,' Woodend said sourly. 'Readin' about what a bungler I'm supposed to be would really perk me up.'

'There's other things in the news,' Paniatowski pointed out. 'Shall I go to the sports page and see how the Rovers are doing?'

'Don't bother with that, either,' Woodend said dismissively. 'If it weren't for the fact that even at the best of times you have to be half-pissed to sit through one of their matches, the way they've been playin' this season would turn any man to drink.'

Paniatowski rifled through the paper. 'Here's something interesting,' she said. 'Preston Vance is dead.'

'Oh aye? Shot straight through the heart with a Comanche warrior's arrow, was he?'

Paniatowski chuckled. 'No, it was a car accident, apparently. Do you want me to read it out to you?'

'Aye, you might as well.'

'Hollywood film star Preston Vance died on Wednesday at the age of forty-eight, Orange County officials confirmed last night,' Paniatowski read. 'Mr Vance died as a result of a road accident in which his was the only car involved. Preliminary findings suggest that he had been drinking, and had possibly taken illegal drugs.'

'He should have stuck to ridin' horses,' Woodend commented. 'What else does it say?'

'Vance made his name in the 1940s and the early 1950s as the strong, silent hero in numerous western films including *Ambush at Dry Gulch.*'

'Aye, it was a cracker, that one,' Woodend said. 'I especially liked the bit where he knocks the crap out of six fellers in a saloon brawl an' hardly even ruffles the partin' in his hair.'

'His career had taken something of a dive in recent years,' Paniatowski continued, 'and he was forced to accept roles in low-budget B films such as *Gunfight at Cross Creek.* Recently, however, he had being hoping to make a comeback as a television star. Plans have been under way for some time for him to appear in a series of dramas in which he would play a gentleman amateur detective, and friends feel that it was the television network's decision not to go ahead with the series which caused him to begin drinking heavily and, ultimately, led to his death. The series, which was to have been called *Arbuthnot and I*—'

Woodend slammed on the brakes so violently that the sergeant was jerked forward in her seat. The Humber skidded slightly, then came to a halt at the side of the road.

'What's wrong, sir?' Paniatowski asked.

'Arbuthnot!' Woodend said. 'Arbuthnot! That's not a Yank name, is it, Monika?'

'No, I think it's Scottish originally,' Paniatowski said. She scanned the remainder of the article. 'That's right, it is. The "I" in the title of the series was going to be Preston Vance himself, and Arbuthnot was going to be the name of his Scottish—'

'Of his Scottish butler,' Woodend interrupted.

'How did you know that?' Paniatowski asked. 'Have you read some other article about it?'

'No. It's as much news to me as it is to you.'

'Then I don't see how you could have even guessed that—'

But Woodend was no longer listening to her. He had covered his face with his big hands and was thinking so hard that she could almost hear the wheels turning round in his head.

For a full five minutes neither of them said anything, then Woodend lowered his hands again and looked into his sergeant's eyes.

'I've had it all wrong,' he told Paniatowski. 'I've had it all wrong right from the start.'

Thirty-Seven

Woodend and Paniatowski had already been sitting in the small conference room for fifteen minutes when a uniformed constable led Diana Houseman in. The producer's widow was wearing a slinky black dress which revealed a considerable amount of cleavage, and would not have looked at all out of place at a cocktail party.

Paniatowski supposed that the dress was her idea of being in mourning. Woodend, his mind racing at top speed, did not even notice it.

'I strongly object to being dragged from my home in this totally unreasonable manner,' Diana Houseman said, sitting down.

'I don't really give a bugger *what* you object to,' Woodend told her.

'I beg your pardon!' Diana Houseman said, outraged.

'Have you lost your hearin' – as well as your morals?' Woodend demanded.

Diana Houseman stood up. 'I have no intention of staying here to listen to your insults,' she gasped.

'Sit down again, or I'll have you locked up,' Woodend said. 'An' that's not a threat – it's a promise.'

Diana Houseman hesitated for a moment, then reluctantly sank back into her seat. 'What's this all about?' she asked.

'It's about you bein' indirectly responsible for two murders,' Woodend replied.

'But that's absurd. I would never—'

'I didn't say you planned them. I know you didn't. But you *did* start the ball rollin'. An' now you're goin' to help us clear the whole bloody matter up, whether you want to or not.'

226

For once, Diana Houseman looked cowed. 'I'm more than willing to do anything I can to—' she began.

'Here's the new rules,' Woodend interrupted her. 'I ask you a straight question, an' you give me a straight answer. If you don't do that, I'll find a way to make sure you serve time behind bars, even if it's only a couple of years. Have I made myself clear?'

'Yes,' Diana Houseman said quietly. 'You've made yourself perfectly clear.'

'Right, now we've established that, we can get down to business,' Woodend said. 'Yesterday you told me an' my sergeant here that you'd taken precautions to ensure that your husband didn't find out about you an' Paddy Colligan. Is that correct?'

'Yes.'

'But you weren't prepared to tell us what those precautions were.'

'Why should I? It's really none of your business.'

Woodend shook his head. 'You still don't get it, do you?' he asked. 'You still can't see how one thing led to another?'

'I'm not a detective,' Diana Houseman said sullenly.

'No, you're not,' Woodend agreed. 'There's other words I could think of to describe you, but I won't use them now, because they'd make even my hard-bitten sergeant blush. So instead I'll just tell you what these so-called precautions of yours were, and you can tell me whether I'm right or wrong. Let's go back to the beginnin', which is weeks or maybe even months before Valerie Farnsworth was killed. You'd already started seein' Paddy Colligan, an' you knew your husband would suspect you of havin' an affair sooner or later. But that really didn't matter, because you also knew you could sweet-talk him into forgivin' you. What *did* matter was that he shouldn't find out your lover was Paddy. Correct?'

'More or less.'

'But you also knew you'd have to give your husband a name – because if he was goin' to forgive *you*, he had to have *somebody else* to blame.' Woodend paused to light up a Capstan Full Strength. 'Now this is the bit that really turns my stomach,' he continued. 'You couldn't just pick a name at random, because when your husband challenged your supposed lover, he'd obviously deny it – an' there was always a chance that Bill would believe him. So what did you do?'

'You tell me,' Diana Houseman hissed.

'All right, I will. The best way to make sure that your husband believed that the man you pointed the finger at was guilty was to fix it so that he really *was*.' Woodend paused for a moment. 'You didn't discuss this idea of yours with Paddy Colligan, did you?'

'Of course I didn't.'

'I thought not. He's a romantic soul. He'd never have agreed to anythin' so hard-boiled an' callous. But you had no such scruples, an' so you started a *second* affair – with the man you'd decided to set up to take the fall when that became necessary.'

'I did it for Paddy,' Diana Houseman said weakly.

'You did it for yourself – so you could carry on havin' your cake an' eatin' it as well.'

'And now I suppose you want me to tell you who this second lover of mine was?'

Woodend shook his head. 'That won't be necessary. I took a while gettin' there, but in the end I worked it out for myself.'

Ben Drabble and Paddy Colligan were knocking a few of the rough edges out of the following Monday's script when the door opened and Woodend entered their office in a purposeful manner.

'Can I help you?' Ben Drabble asked.

'It's your mate I want a word with, not you,' Woodend told him. 'I noticed that now my lads have finished workin' on it, the cafeteria's open for business again, so your best plan would be to go an' grab yourself a quick cup of tea.'

Drabble looked first at his partner, then back at Woodend. 'I'm not thirsty,' he said.

'Don't you think he'll work a lot better after he's had a brew?' Woodend asked Paddy Colligan.

'Go and get yourself a drink, Ben,' the Irishman said.

Drabble hesitated for a second, then stood up and left the room.

Woodend slid his big frame on to the chair the writer had just vacated. 'How do you feel about justice, Mr Colligan?' he asked.

'I beg your pardon?'

'From readin' that play of yours, I'd guess that you were brought up a Catholic. Are you still a believer?'

Paddy Colligan nodded slowly. 'I suppose I must be. I wouldn't feel so guilty about my own sins if I wasn't.'

'It's interestin' that you should mention sin,' Woodend said. 'As I understand it, your lot think that a sin can never be forgiven as long as it's kept hidden. Have I got that right?'

'Where's all this leading?'

'I know who killed Valerie Farnsworth an' Bill Houseman,' Woodend told him. 'My only problem is that all my evidence is circumstantial. What I really need now is a confession. An' I thought you could write it for me.'

'You want me to confess to the murders!' Paddy Colligan demanded, outraged. 'Well, I won't do it! My hands may not be entirely clean, but there's certainly no blood on them.'

'Did I say I wanted you to confess to the murders?' Woodend asked mildly.

'You said you wanted me to write a confession!'

'So I did,' Woodend agreed. 'But I never said it was *your* confession you'd be writin', did I?'

Jeremy Wilcox looked down at the sheets of paper which had dropped on his desk in front of him, and then back up at Woodend.

'What's all this?' he asked.

'Read it,' Woodend told him.

'I haven't got the time to—'

'It's only three pages. Bloody read it!' Woodend said commandingly.

After the first few lines Wilcox looked troubled, and by the time he had reached the bottom of the third page, his eyes were wide with astonishment.

'You see what it means, don't you?' Woodend asked.

229

'I understand the words, if that's what you mean, but I find it completely incredible that—'

'It's all true,' Woodend said firmly.

'Does that mean that you're going to . . . that you're going to . . . ?'

'Make an arrest?' Woodend supplied. 'Yes, as soon as this little scene's been played out, that's exactly what I'm goin' to do. But I'll need your help.'

'You're asking me to sabotage my own show!' Wilcox protested. 'I refuse! I absolutely refuse!'

'Do this one thing for me, an' I'll be out of your hair forever,' Woodend promised him. 'Don't do it, an' I'll have my lads create so much disruption that it'll be impossible for you to broadcast a show tonight, or any time in the next month for that matter. So what's it to be? It's your choice.'

'You call that a choice?' Wilcox asked.

'It's more of a choice than Val Farnsworth an' Bill Houseman were ever given,' Woodend pointed out.

Thirty-Eight

'What's all this?' George Adams asked, as Paddy Colligan dumped a sheaf of papers in front of him, then walked around the table and dropped a similar pile in front of the rest of the cast members who had been summoned to Rehearsal Room Two.

'It's next Monday's script,' Jeremy Wilcox said from the doorway.

'We've already been given it,' Jennifer Brunton said.

'Not this one, you haven't, Jennifer. It's a new version. We've made a few changes, and I want to see how they work out,' Wilcox told her. 'The scene is the bar of the Tinker's Bucket. You've all just come back from Liz Bowyer's funeral and—'

'Then why are there so few of us?' Jennifer Brunton asked. 'The pub would be absolutely packed on an occasion like that.'

'More people will drift in as the scene progresses and—' Jeremy Wilcox stopped, suddenly, as if something had just occurred to him. 'Let's get one thing clear,' he continued in a much louder voice. 'I'm the producer of this show now, which means that what I say goes. And if I tell you the script calls for you to dance naked with a chimpanzee, you don't argue, you ask whether I want you to do the waltz or foxtrot! Got that?'

The actors moved their heads slightly in what may – or may not – have been grudging nods of acceptance.

'Right, let's have a read-though,' Wilcox said. 'And just to make my job a little easier, could you try to do it without fluffing any of your lines or stopping to ask stupid questions?'

Jennifer Brunton looked down at her script. 'Liz could be

a bit of a devil sometimes, but I'm really goin' to miss havin' her around,' she read.

'Yes, so I am,' Larry Coates read. 'She was a bit too free with her favours at times, but at least she wasn't calculatin' about it, like some women are.' He looked up from his script. '"A bit too free with favours"?' he repeated. 'Would Jack Taylor really say that?'

Jeremy Wilcox sighed. 'Am I talking to myself here? I said I wanted it reading through without interruptions.'

'Still, it's a bit close to the bone,' Larry Coates said dubiously.

'It's an idea – that's all. We're playing around with a few *ideas*.'

'That's all very well for you to say,' Larry Coates replied, 'but any character who besmirches the memory of Liz Bowyer isn't going to be very popular with the viewers, now is he?'

'That's the only bit about Liz, and if you really don't like it, we can cut it later on,' Wilcox assured him. 'Let's just get through the rest of the scene, shall we?'

'Yes, at least she wasn't calculatin' about it, like some women are,' Coates read from the script in his Jack Taylor voice. 'Not like a woman I knew in my last job.' He looked up again. 'What's all this about my last job? I thought I'd always been a postman.'

'So you have, but not always in the same post office,' Jeremy Wilcox said exasperatedly. 'Read on, and you'll see how it all fits together.'

'She was the head postmaster's wife, this other woman,' Coates read. 'We had an affair. What I didn't know was that she was already havin' another affair with one of the clerks in the back office.'

'An' didn't she give him up when she started goin' out with you?' Jennifer Brunton read, her bemusement evident in her voice.

Larry Coates frowned, as if he was starting to suspect something was seriously wrong, but could not be entirely certain what.

'No, she didn't give him up,' he read, 'because he was the one she was really interested in.'

'So why did she have the affair with you?' Jennifer Brunton asked, now so confused she was almost starting to sound panicked.

'She did it because she wanted someone to accuse, if her husband started to think she was playin' around,' Larry Coates answered.

'This will never bloody work, Jeremy!' George Adams protested. 'It doesn't sound like *Maddox Row* at all. And Larry's right. There's no reason at all why you should ask his character to commit professional suicide.'

'If you don't like the direction I'm taking the show in, I'm sure I can always find some other starving actor to play a loveable old-age pensioner,' Jeremy Wilcox said nastily. 'And that goes for the rest of you, as well. Can we *please* proceed, Larry?'

Coates's face had turned grey. 'The chief postmaster said he was goin' to fire me for havin' an affair with his wife,' he read, 'but it was a good job an' I didn't want to leave it. That's when I . . . when I decided to kill him.'

'This is ridiculous,' George Adams protested. 'This is brain-buggering insane.'

The door clicked softly open, and Woodend stepped into the room. 'I was listenin' outside,' he explained, 'but I thought I'd come inside to see the really interestin' bit in the flesh. I believe you still hold the centre stage, Mr Coates.'

Larry Coates looked up at him. 'I don't want to read any more,' he said.

'You're surely not goin' to back out now, are you?' Woodend coaxed. 'This is your big scene. Don't you want to see how it ends? Wouldn't you like to know if it really works as a piece of theatre? Or would you rather somebody else read the lines for you? I can do it, if you like.'

'You'd only make a hash of it,' Coates said contemptuously. He looked down at the script again. 'The only problem was that even if I killed the head postmaster, I couldn't be sure I'd keep my job, because the other bosses had all agreed with him that it would make the post office more popular if they sacked one of us,' he read in his Jack Taylor voice. 'So before I murdered him, I had to make sure I was indispensable. That's why I decided to kill the most popular postwoman in the office first – so they'd have to give me her job.'

'This . . . this isn't about the Laughing Postman at all, is it?' George Adams gasped.

'No, it isn't,' Woodend agreed. 'Shall you an' me go an' have a private chat, Mr Coates?'

Woodend and Larry Coates sat facing one another across the table in the conference room.

'This theory of yours is all supposition, you know,' Coates said. 'You can't actually prove a thing.'

'Maybe not at the moment,' Woodend agreed, 'but once we know where to start looking, it's remarkable what we can find. I've got a team goin' through your dressin' room at this very moment. They don't need to find much – a speck of Valerie Farnsworth's make-up stained with her blood; a thread from the clothes she was wearin' when she died. It'll only take a little thing to make the case against you cast-iron. But why wait for that? If you co-operate now, it'll go in your favour at the trial, an' that – combined with the fact that you'd never have killed anybody at all if you hadn't been caught up in the web of lies that bitch Diana Houseman had woven – is bound to work in your favour. Besides, you're an actor – a man of spirit. If you've got to go down, then at least go down with some panache.'

'Is it true that the only reason Diana slept with me was to cover up her affair with Paddy Colligan?' Coates asked.

'Perfectly true.'

Coates laughed. 'And there was me thinking I was totally irresistible.' He paused for a second. 'How did you get on to me?'

Woodend forced himself to suppress a sigh of relief. 'My good luck an' your bad,' he said. 'If Preston Vance hadn't died when he did, I'd never have found out that the good job you were supposed to be goin' to after you'd left *Maddox Row* had fallen through. An' that would have meant that I'd never have realised how important it was for you to stay on the show.'

'You spend your whole working life performing in draughty

provincial theatres in front of audiences who wouldn't recognise good acting if it hit them in the face,' Coates said sadly. 'And finally you make it. Finally you're a star. Then some bastard says he's going to take it all away from you.'

'How often did you sleep with Diana Houseman?' Woodend asked.

'Three or four times. No more.'

'But Bill Houseman didn't believe that?'

'No, he didn't.'

'Of course not. Whatever Diana told you she'd said to her husband, she'd done her best to convince him that you'd had a long, passionate affair – that all the time she'd been spendin' with Paddy Colligan, she'd actually been spendin' with you. What I don't understand is why he didn't just sack you. Why both pretend that you were goin' off to a new job in California which no longer existed?'

'It was a way of saving both our faces,' Coates said. 'I didn't have to admit I was being kicked out on to the street – and he didn't have to admit that the reason he was getting rid of me was because I'd slept with his wife.'

'I lied to you earlier, you know,' Woodend said. 'The judge an' jury might show you a bit of sympathy for killin' Bill Houseman, but they're never goin' to forgive you for killin' Valerie Farnsworth.'

'For killing *Liz Bowyer*, you mean, don't you?' Larry Coates said.

'Aye, maybe I do mean that,' Woodend agreed.

'You underestimate my powers as an actor,' Coates told him. 'The judge and jury are an audience like any other, and by the time the trial is over, I'll have them eating out of my hand.'

Thirty-Nine

The first hint the pack of reporters had that something significant was about to happen was the black police car pulling up right in front of the studio's front door. The second, even clearer, came when the doors themselves burst open and half a dozen uniformed constables emerged in a tight phalanx – but not tight enough to hide the fact that in the middle of them was a man with a jacket completely covering his head.

The police urged the journalists to stay back, the hacks interpreted that as an invitation to surge forward. Flash bulbs were popping, questions were being hurled. The constable at the front of the phalanx opened the back door of the car, and two others guided the man with the jacket over his head towards the opening.

'Duck down a bit lower, Mr Coates,' one of the constables said, louder than he'd probably intended.

'What was that?' asked the journalist in the crush next to Elizabeth Driver.

'I think he said, "Duck down a bit lower, Mr *Adams*,"' Elizabeth Driver lied. 'Isn't there somebody in the show called Adams?'

'Don't think so,' the other journalist replied. 'Anyway, you probably misheard. Could have been Allen or Atherton.'

The man with jacket over his head was now firmly ensconced on the back seat of the car, and the constable who he was handcuffed to slid in beside him. Another constable slammed the door closed, and the driver eased the vehicle slowly forward, trying his best to avoid staining any of his tyres with journalists' blood. Then the car was clear of the pack, and heading out away from the studio.

'I'd think twice before I bandied names about,' the journalist next to Elizabeth Driver said. 'Like I said, you could have misheard, and you'd look a complete bloody fool if you got it wrong.'

And having offered a seasoned reporter's advice to the young novice, he rushed off to file the exclusive story that George Adams had been arrested for the double murder.

Elizabeth Driver stayed where she was, considering her position. It was a pity she'd written such a critical article about Woodend just hours before he'd made the arrest, she thought. Perhaps now was the time to eat humble pie – to admit to the chief inspector that she'd been wrong, and promise to be a good little girl in the future.

But even as these considerations were running through her mind, a large headline was elbowing them out of the way. 'THE DEVIL'S OWN LUCK?' she composed. 'In what appears to be more by chance than ability, Chief Inspector Woodend of the Central Lancashire Police today arrested Laurence Coates for the double murder at NWTV's studios . . .' Yes, something along those lines would do very nicely indeed.

Ben Drabble and Paddy Colligan sat at their desks, scoring out large chunks of that evening's scripts with red pencils.

'How much do you reckon we're going to have to rewrite?' Paddy asked.

'My best guess is around seven minutes,' Drabble replied miserably.

Seven minutes! Paddy repeated to himself. Seven whole bloody minutes! And they didn't have long to do it, because the cast would need to learn their new lines – or at least have some idea of what they were – long before the seven-thirty broadcast. Nor did the crisis end there. By the time Monday's episode of *Maddox Row* went out, they would have to have come up with some reasonable explanation for the disappearance of Jack Taylor, the Laughing Postman. It was going to be a bugger of a job which would keep them working round the clock.

His mind turned to Diana Houseman. He wondered if he still loved her. Or if he ever really had? Because how could you love a woman you didn't understand at all? And how could he pretend that he *had* ever understood her, when even now he found it hard to believe that she would go to bed with another man in order to hide the fact that she was sleeping with him?

He would give her up, he decided. He would give her up – and he would give his job up. He would go back to Dublin, and the only words he wrote from now on would be ones that mattered – ones that had something significant to say about the human condition.

But in order to be truly creative, didn't a writer actually *need* the kind of creature comforts his current wages brought him?

And how would he *ever* be truly inspired again, when all the time he was squandering his emotional reserves on thoughts of Diana Houseman's warm body lying beside his?

He suddenly realised that he didn't mind the extra work the murders had brought – almost wished there was more of it – because as long as he was wrapped up in the fictional life of *Madro*, he could keep himself free of the twists and complications which made up his own *real* life.

Sitting next to him, his partner, Ben Drabble was doing some serious thinking, too. The publicity which had come from the second murder – the murder of a *producer*, like the one in his plot – would almost certainly guarantee success for his book. But he was starting to wonder whether a novel was the right way to go, or if he could squeeze more out of the idea by turning it into a screenplay. The project would be a new departure for him, and he was not quite sure he was up to the job – but perhaps, if he approached it in the right way – he could persuade Paddy to work on it with him.

Jeremy Wilcox sat at his desk, trying to convince himself that he was furious. After all, didn't he have a *right* to be in a rage? That bastard Charlie Woodend had bullied him into going through the charade with the special script Colligan had written, and, as a result, he had lost one of his principle actors just a few hours before they were due to go on air.

And yet there were compensations, if he really looked for them. Despite all that had happened, he would still produce a smooth, professional show by seven thirty, and the people who made all the decisions back in head office would realise how much they needed him. Then there was the warm glow he felt when he looked back on the script reading which had led to Larry Coates's arrest. Halfway through, Coates had realised what was happening, but he had gone on to read the rest of it. And why? Because his director had led him through it – cajoling and coaxing, yet being firm when necessary.

'Nobody else could have directed that denouement quite like me,' Wilcox told himself self-satisfiedly. 'Nobody!'

Acting Chief Constable Marlowe and DCS Ainsworth stood at the bar in the Glades Golf Club, glasses of the club's finest malt whisky in their hands.

'It's a good result for us, sir, isn't it?' Ainsworth said.

'A very good result,' Marlowe agreed. 'Couldn't have been better, in fact. Not only do we have a murderer behind bars, but he turns out to be a nationally known actor. Think how much more publicity mileage we can milk out of that than if he'd been some obscure studio electrician assistant with a grudge.' He paused. 'Of course, you do realise that while it will undoubtedly help both of us, it will also help Charlie Woodend. There's no way we can possibly prevent him from coming out of all this with at least some share of the credit.'

'I'd already worked that out,' Ainsworth told him.

'So it looks as if your prospects of getting rid of Cloggin'-it Charlie have been somewhat dimmed.'

'It's only a temporary set-back,' Ainsworth said easily. 'I know Woodend, and before the printer's ink's even dried on the story, he'll be putting his size nine foot into it somewhere else. And next time, I'll have the bastard.'

Woodend, Rutter and Paniatowski sat in the studio cafeteria, drinking lukewarm tea and thinking their own thoughts.

'We'll give the reporters outside another half-hour to clear off, an' then we'll head for the nearest pub an' have the almighty piss-up you both so richly deserve,' Woodend said.

'I'm not sure I've earned it this time,' Rutter said, perhaps a little despondently.

Woodend raised his eyebrows in mock amazement. 'Don't

start goin' all modest on me, lad,' he said. 'I'm not sure I could cope with it.'

'I really thought I'd contributed something to the investigation when I found that Valerie Farnsworth was a lesbian,' Rutter told him.

'An' so you did.'

'No, I didn't. All it did was shore up your erroneous suspicion that Bill Houseman was the murderer, a suspicion you'd probably soon have discarded if I hadn't—'

He stopped suddenly. He had been talking to Woodend just as he would have done at the end of a case in the old days, when he was Woodend's bagman and neither of them had even heard of Monika Paniatowski. Now he had remembered that Paniatowski was there, and was beginning to think that he'd spoken too freely.

A few seconds awkward silence followed, then Paniatowski said, 'That's a bit of a simplistic view – if you don't mind me saying so, Inspector.'

'And if I *do* mind you saying so?' Rutter replied.

'Then I'll just have to make myself even more unpopular with you than I am already,' Paniatowski said calmly.

'Tell us how he was bein' simplistic,' Woodend said quietly.

'He was forgetting – just for the moment, I'm sure – that an investigation is the sum of its parts, and it needs all those parts for it to roll forward, even if a few of them are thrown out on the way.'

'Go on, lass,' Woodend said.

'The fact that Valerie Farnsworth was a lesbian is a case in point. If we hadn't known that when we first confronted Diana Houseman, we wouldn't have been able to unnerve her as much as we did. And if she hadn't been unnerved, she'd never have let slip the fact that she'd taken precautions to make sure her husband didn't find out about her secret lover.'

'I think you may be right,' Rutter said, brightening considerably.

'With respect, sir, I know I'm right,' Paniatowski replied.

Rutter glanced down at his watch, then stood up. 'Before I go to the pub, I'd just better check that my lads are mopping up properly.'

My lads! Woodend, thought, hiding a smile.

He waited until Rutter was well away from the table, then turned to Paniatowski. 'That was nice thing you just said to Inspector Rutter,' he told her.

'It was true,' Paniatowski replied defensively. 'I wouldn't have said it if it wasn't.'

Woodend shook his head. 'You two really should try to get on a bit better,' he said.

'I know we should,' Paniatowski agreed, without holding out much hope that the age of miracles was in any danger of imminent arrival.

They sat in silence for a while, then Paniatowski said, 'Do you know what my favourite part is in all those "B" picture detective stories?'

'No. What is it?'

'It's when the hapless assistant turns to his boss, and says, "There's just one thing I don't understand, Inspector."'

Woodend grinned. 'Is that right?'

'Of course, it would never happen in real life.'

'Of course not.'

'There's one thing that's been puzzling me about the case,' Paniatowski said.

Woodend's grin broadened. 'An' what's that?'

'I can see how that newspaper article about Preston Vance's death would have led you to suspect that Larry Coates killed Bill Houseman, but what I *don't* see is how it could also have made you immediately drop your theory that Houseman had killed Valerie Farnsworth.'

'I was assumin' that once Houseman had decided to kill one of the cast for the good of the show, he selected Val Farnsworth because she'd had an affair with his wife.'

'Because he *thought* she'd had an affair with his wife,' Paniatowski corrected him.

'Same difference,' Woodend said. 'It's what he believed which was important.'

'True.'

'But when you read me that article, I realised that he believed that while his wife had had no more than a fling with Val, she was actually *in love with* Larry.'

'How did you work that?' Paniatowski asked.

Woodend grinned again. 'You tell me.'

Paniatowski frowned, then clicked her fingers. 'He didn't fire Val, because that would have been bad for the other love of his life – *Maddox Row!*' she said. 'But the same was true in the case of Larry Coates, yet he still gave him the boot.'

'Because?'

'Because it hurt him more – because he felt that what she'd had with Larry was much more than a fling.'

'So if he'd been going to kill anybody, it would have been Larry, not Val.'

'And once you realised that the brass candlestick had been made in deepest Romania by a left-handed man, it was obvious that the simple groom was not a groom at all, but the son of the ruined count who had come to take revenge on Lord Ponsonby for seducing his sister,' Paniatowski said.

'Exactly,' Woodend agreed. 'Now you're finally startin' to think like a real detective.'

Epilogue

The leaves of the horse chestnut trees were already edged with rust, and the conkers which they had borne had burst from their spiky green armour and now lay brown and unprotected on the fading grass. Bees buzzed busily from one wild Michaelmas daisy to another, and grey squirrels made brief and nervous forays along the ground before retreating once more to the safety of the trees.

Woodend studied the girl who was sitting on the bench at the top of Parliament Hill, looking down – without much apparent interest – at the bathing ponds below. It had only been a few days since he'd last seen her, but she seemed much smaller and much more vulnerable than he remembered. He stuck his hands deep into his pockets – as if he thought that would give him courage – and began to walk towards her.

She saw him coming, and while she showed no sign of welcoming him, she at least made no effort to leave.

He came to a stop in front of her. 'Fancy runnin' into you,' he said.

'How did you know I'd be here? Did Jill tell you?'

Woodend shook his head. 'No. I *did* call at her house, but while her mam admitted you were stoppin' there, she swore she didn't know where you'd gone today.'

'So why come looking for me on Hampstead Heath?'

'Just a hunch. I used to bring you here as a kid, an' you always seemed to enjoy it.'

'Always!' Annie repeated. 'You make it sound as if it was a regular thing.'

'Wasn't it?'

'You had no time for "regular things". You must have brought me here five or six times. Seven at the most.'

Woodend sighed. 'You're right,' he agreed. 'Seven at the most. Listen Annie, I know you said in your note that I shouldn't try to find you, but I assume that's only because you were worried that if I did, I might try to take you back. Well, that's not why I'm here.'

'So why are you here?' his daughter asked.

'To talk. To put a proposal to you.'

'What kind of proposal?'

'I know you miss your friends, so if you can persuade Jill's mam to put you up on a regular basis while you finish your schoolin', we'll pay for your board and lodgin's.'

'A few days ago, I would have jumped at the chance,' Annie said.

'But not now?'

'No. You can't turn back the clock, however much you might want to. I've only been away for a few months, but already my old friends seem to have new lives. Besides, staying on at school is not what I want to do anymore.'

'So what do you want to do?'

'I'd like to go to nursing college.'

'I see.'

'Is there anything wrong with that?' Annie demanded.

'I . . . No. Nurses do a wonderful job. Your gran was a nurse durin' the Great War.'

'But . . . ?'

'But I suppose I'd always thought you'd go to university, so I could swank about you in front of Bob Rutter,' Woodend said, trying to make a joke of it.

'That's *your* dream for me,' Annie said, refusing to share in the humour. 'Does it have to be mine as well?'

'Nay, lass, we're all entitled to make up our own dreams,' Woodend admitted. 'But if you're goin' to study to be a nurse, does it have to be in London? Or could it be in Lancaster or Manchester, where me an' your mam get a chance to see you now an' again?'

'I wouldn't mind studying in Manchester.'

'An' would you mind comin' home – I mean, back to Whitebridge – while we make the arrangements?'

Annie smiled. 'No, I wouldn't mind that, either.'

She stood up, and Woodend put his arm round her shoulder. Together, father and daughter began to walk down the hill.

'I told you not to come, and you came anyway,' Annie said, 'but if you *were* going to do that, why didn't you do it *sooner*?'

'I . . . er . . .' Woodend said uncomfortably.

'You were up to your neck in a case?' Annie suggested.

'It wasn't easy to get away right then,' Woodend said in his own defence. 'Reputations were at stake. Perhaps lives as well.'

'I've never known you be on a case it *was* easy to get away from,' his daughter told him.

Woodend came to a halt and looked his daughter in the eyes. 'I'd die for you, Annie,' he said. 'I'd give up my life for you without a second's thought.'

Annie met his gaze with her own. 'I know you would, Dad,' she said, perhaps a little sadly. 'But give up on a murder investigation right in the middle of it? Well, that's quite a different matter altogether.'